ALPHA'S TEMPTATION: A BILLIONAIRE WEREWOLF ROMANCE

ALPHA BAD BOYS BOOK 1

RENEE ROSE

LEE SAVINO

Published in the United States of America

Renee Rose Romance and Silverwood Press

Editor:

Kate Richards, Wizards in Publishing

ACKNOWLEDGMENTS

Thank you to Aubrey Cara and Katherine Deane for their beta reads! Thank you to Margarita for the contract that made our author partnership legal.

CG: Catgirl was here.

King1: I see you.

CG: Nice code.

King1: You're going down. No pity for the kitty.

CG: Oooh, talk tough to me, baby.

— Conversation between hacker and Jackson King, CEO and founder of SeCure, 2009

1

Kylie

Holy irony, Batman.

As a teen, I hacked into a company and waved a virtual victory flag in the founder and CEO's face. Nine years later, I'm interviewing for a job there. And not just any job—one in infosec. Information systems security, that is. If I get the job, I'll be defending the company against hackers. Like Catgirl—my old DefCon identity.

So here I sit, in the opulent lobby of SeCure's international headquarters, wondering if they'll somehow recognize me and send me out in handcuffs.

A group of employees stroll past me, laughing and talking. They look relaxed and happy, like they're headed into a resort, not their nine-to-five grind.

Damn, I want this job.

I changed my outfit approximately ninety-seven times this morning—and I usually don't care what I wear. But this is the interview of a lifetime, and I've obsessed over getting every detail right. In the end, I chose a sleek black suit, the kind with a fitted jacket and short, tight skirt. I opted for no hose, going bare-legged, but stuffed my feet in a pair of sexy heels. Underneath the suit jacket went my favorite Batgirl shirt. It fits tight around my breasts, and the hot pink glittery bat nestles perfectly between the lapels of my jacket.

The outfit screams "young and hip" IT genius, while the suit flips a nod to the conservative corporate thing. I debated over heels or Chucks, but, in the end, the heels won out. Which is too bad, because when Stu, my contact, comes down for me, I'll have to stand up in them. And walk.

If my teenage hacker self saw me now, she would laugh in my face and call me a sellout. But even she shared my obsession with SeCure's billionaire founder/owner, Jackson King. An obsession that's morphed into admiration with a heavy dose of sexual attraction.

Okay, it's a crush. But Jackson is totally crush worthy. Billionaire philanthropist, he's endlessly impressive. Not to mention smoking hot. Especially for a geek.

And the one moment we shared—the moment when I made it past all his security measures and found myself face-to-face with him—well, cursor to cursor—is branded in my memory as the hottest encounter of my youth. I didn't steal anything from him. I simply wanted to see if I could get in—crack the genius code. I backed out after he found me, and never risked going back.

Now, I might have another shot at cyber sparring with King, and the thought thrills me.

Especially since, this time, my actions wouldn't be illegal.

"Ms. McDaniel?"

I shoot to my feet, hand already extended, ready to shake. I only wobble a little on the heels. "Hi." Damn, I sound breathless. I force my shoulders down and smile as I grip the offered palm.

"Hi, I'm Stu Daniel, infosec manager here at SeCure." He looks like a proper nerd, glasses, collared shirt, slacks. Thirty or so. His eyes flick to the pink bat in the middle of my boobs and then away. Maybe the T-shirt was a mistake.

I keep pumping his hand, probably for too long. I read five business books to prep for today, but can't remember what *Interviewing For Dummies* said about the proper length of time to shake a hand. "Nice to meet you."

Fortunately, Stu is just as awkward as I am. His eyes keep detouring downward. Not like he's trying to perv, but like he's too shy to maintain eye contact. "If you'll follow me, we'll head to the sixth floor for the interview."

In addition to unbreakable cyber security, SeCure's physical fortress is also well-protected. When I walked in across the gleaming marble floors and checked in at main reception desk, they told me to wait in the lobby for an "escort" to my interview.

I trail after my escort. "Beautiful building you have here."

Okay, that was lame. I suck at small talk. Like, really suck. Maybe I shouldn't have spent the last eight years hiding from all social interaction. IT geeks shouldn't have to interview like normal people. They should just have to take a test or hack something. But, presumably, SeCure already knows about my code-cracking abilities, or so the head-hunter said. I nearly choked on my coffee when she called me up out of the blue. I thought it was a prank by one of my old online compatriots—the Clean Clan. But, no, it was legit.

Besides, the chances of anyone from my old life finding me now are nil. At least, I hope so.

Stu leads me to the elevator bank and hits the up arrow. The doors of one elevator swing open to reveal a man in an elegant suit, his head bent over his phone. Tall and broad-shouldered, he takes up more than his fair share of the elevator. Without looking up, he moves to the side to make room for us.

Stu lets me step on first, and I push down panic. It's a small elevator, but not too small. I can handle it. If I get the job, I'll find out where the stairwells are.

I focus on the bright buttons and hope it's a fast ride.

Before my escort can board, someone calls his name.

"One sec," Stu says as a young woman bustles over, followed by two other people. "Stu, the Galileo server shut down this morning..."

Great. Just what I need—extra time in an elevator. I swallow, ignoring the prickling on my skin. A panic attack will not make a good impression.

Stu takes his foot out of the door as the young woman opens her laptop to show him something.

The door snicks closed, and the elevator ascends. Just like that, I've lost my escort. So much for tight security.

I punch the number six button. I know where I'm going. The sooner I'm off this tiny box of death, the better.

We're halfway up when the lights flicker. Once, twice, then off.

"What the..." I trail off to focus on breathing. I have about a ten second window before full on freak out.

The suit next to me mutters something. The light from his phone casts an eerie blue light on the walls.

The elevator car grinds to a stop.

Oh no. Here it comes. My heart slams in my chest; my lungs grab for breath.

Stop, I tell my panic. *It's nothing. The elevator will start up again in a second. You're not stuck here.*

My body doesn't believe me. My stomach clutches, skin grows clammy. Everything goes dark. Either my vision has dimmed or the guy has just put his phone to his ear. I sway on my feet.

The big guy curses. "No reception in here."

My heel twists under me, and I grab the rail, breath coming in quick gasps.

"Hey." The guy has a voice to match his giant size, deep and resonant. I'd find it sexy under different circumstances. "Are you freaking out?" Slight disdain in his tone.

Not my fault, buddy. "Yeah." I barely get the word out on a pant. My death grip on the handrail tightens.

Stay on your feet. Don't faint—not now. Not here.

"I don't like small spaces." *Understatement of the year.*

Did the elevator just move? Or is my body reeling out of control? Old panic grips me. *I'll die in here. I'm never going to get out.*

Two large hands push me back against the elevator wall, pinning me with pressure on my sternum. "Wh-what are you doing?" I gasp.

"Triggering your calm reflex." He sounds calm, as if he shoves hyperventilating girls up against a wall on a daily basis. "Is it working?"

"Yeah. Having a strange guy grope me always calms me down." I swore I'd hide my sarcasm until I landed the job, but here it comes, spewing out. Being seconds away from passing out will do that to a girl.

"I'm not groping you," he says.

"That's what all the guys say," I mumble.

His short chuckle cuts off as soon as it starts. Almost like he didn't mean to let it out.

Who is this guy?

My heart rate slows, but my head still spins. I've never had a man stand so close to me before. Not to mention touch me. A few inches over, and he'd be cupping my breasts.

Now, there's a thought. Sensations I haven't felt before outside the privacy of my bedroom thrill through me.

"Not that I mind you groping me," I babble. "I just think you should buy me dinner first—"

His hands leave my sternum so fast, I lurch forward. Before I can fall, he catches my shoulders and flips me around. He locks his arms around me from behind, applying pressure to my breastbone again.

"How's this?" He sounds amused. "Better? I don't want my good deed to get me written up on charges of sexual harassment."

God, his voice. His lips are right next to my ear. He's not trying to seduce me, but, man oh man, just the words "sexual harassment" light my body up.

"Sorry." My voice strangles a bit. "I didn't mean to accuse you. What I meant was...thank you."

For a moment, he doesn't move, and I breathe into his firm hands, surrounding me, protecting me, keeping me safe. And all I can think is...*damn.* I thought a panic attack would be bad. Now I'm stuck in an elevator, wrapped in a total stranger's arms. So. Very. Turned. On. It's like my pussy is disconnected from my body. The rest of me is running around wringing my hands with worry, but my hooha thinks being manhandled by a stranger in a dark elevator is a good reason to get all excited.

"You should sit down."

Apparently, I have no choice, because he lowers me to the ground with steady, inexorable pressure. Once there, he eases me against the wall, his firm, yet gentle hands maneuvering me like a doll. Sharp words dance on the tip of my tongue—*I'm a grown ass woman, not Barbie*—but sitting feels good. Despite his blunt caveman act, he's taking care of me. I almost miss his hands on my sternum.

"Where'd you learn that?" I ask to distract myself from the fact I'm trapped in a tight rectangle of space with a guy who has no qualms about running his hands all over me. I am totally qualm-less about it, too, though I wish I could remember what he looks like. All I have is a vague impression of a rugged jaw and air of impatience. I was too focused on psyching myself up to ride the elevator to check him out.

"Years and years of terrifying women in dark places."

Ah. A kindred spirit in dry wit. I like him even more. "Thanks," I say after a moment.

He sits down next to me, his suit jacket brushing mine. "You're still freaking out."

"Yeah, but it's better. Talking would help. Can we talk?"

"Okay." He adopts a German accent to sound like Freud, "Ven did you first notice zee problem?"

~.~

Jackson

The beautiful human female's laugh comes so hard, she almost chokes on it. She continues to giggle for a moment—somewhat hysterically. Little bubbles of laughter keep rising to the surface every time she tries to speak. Finally, she chokes out, "I meant talk to distract me—about something else."

I never joke—especially at work—but the leggy brunette in a short, tight skirt puts my body on alert in an all-too pleasurable way. It's better now that I'm not touching her. When I did, the electricity between us set my skin on fire. The itch and burn of the change came upon me as fast as it does a pubescent teen just learning how to shift. I nearly shoved her legs apart, pulled that miniscule skirt up around her waist, and claimed her right there.

Actually, my wolf senses went haywire the moment she stepped onto the elevator. It was all I could do to keep quiet and study her. Her scent intoxicates me—like some exotic flower begging to be plucked, except decidedly human. None of it makes sense. There's no reason I should be attracted to her, apart from the fact she's gorgeous. I've never been attracted to a human before—hell, I've hardly ever been attracted to a she-wolf, even at the full moon.

To make it worse, she became aroused when I touched her—the scent of her nectar fills the confined space. For the first time in my life, my fangs sharpened, slick with serum, ready to sink into her flesh and forever mark her as mine.

But that is insane. I can't mark a human—she wouldn't survive it. This human—beautiful though she may be—can't be my mate.

I look her over, at a distinct advantage because I can see in the dark and she can't. She's stunning in every way—long, shapely legs, an ass that fills her short skirt, and Batgirl tits. That is, she has a hot pink bat on the front of her shirt, right over a pair of perky tits. And something about that bat just throws me over the edge. Spunky little superhero, begging to be bested.

Guess that makes me the villain.

"What's your name?" she asks.

I hesitate. "J.T."

"I'm Kylie. I'm here for an interview, so I was nerved up to begin with."

I don't do friendly. I discourage my employees from engaging with me except to give me information in its most distilled format. But, for some reason, I don't mind her feeble attempt at conversation. Which doesn't mean I'll bother answering.

I'm too busy convincing my wolf not to jump her.

She tries again. "What department are you in?"

I'm not going to admit I'm the CEO. "Marketing." I infuse the word with the disgust *marketing* inspires in me. It's true that the majority of my time is now spent on marketing or management, when I'd much prefer programming and never interacting face-to-face with another soul.

She laughs, a husky, sweet sound. Despite the fact she can't see me, she peers up in my direction with a look of fascination on her face. Her hair, a thick shiny chestnut, hangs in loose waves over her shoulders. It's too dark to tell the color of her eyes, but her full lips are glossed, and the way they part now makes me want to claim that lush mouth.

"One of those guys, huh? That is sad."

I smile—a rare occurrence for me. She's already made me laugh, something I haven't done in twenty years.

"What position are you interviewing for?"

"infosec."

Hot and nerdy. Interesting. She must have mad skills to rate an interview. My company is the best in the world for information security. "You have much experience in the field?"

"Some." She sounds noncommittal in that way that makes me think she actually knows her stuff.

The power has been out for a long time—at least ten minutes. I fish my phone from my pocket and try to dial my secretary again but still can't get a signal.

"How long do you think we'll be stuck in here?" Her voice wavers on the word *stuck.*

Fates, I've never had the urge to pick up a woman's hand before. My shirt collar's too tight. I wish to hell I hadn't worn a suit and tie. Of course, I wish that every day, but rarely have a choice, even though it's *my* damn company. Once we reached a certain level, I had to conform to the dress code of corporate America when I had outside meetings—even in Tucson, which is notoriously relaxed in its dress code.

My little programmer, however, nailed the outfit—just the right mix of hipster with the bat tits and bare legs, and corporate with the suit and heels. I don't know when I started thinking of her as *my* little anything, but I have. The second she walked on the elevator and I inhaled her scent, my wolf screamed *mine.*

"I mean, do you think it will be hours? It won't be hours, right?" She's losing her breath again. It's all I can do not to pull her onto my lap and hold her until all that trembling stops.

"Don't make me grope you again." Okay, I definitely shouldn't say that, even if she said it first. The remark has its intended effect, though.

She snorts, which changes up her breathing pattern and helps her chill out.

"So you're nervous about the interview?" I ask. Chitchat isn't part of my repertoire, but it seems I'd do anything to calm her down. Or maybe I just want to hear her voice again. "You don't seem nervous."

"Besides the whole panic attack thing you're doing a manly job distracting me from?"

My wolf preens at the compliment.

"I'll let you in on a secret," she says, and the muscles of

my groin seize almost painfully at the purr in her voice. She's seducing me, and she doesn't even know she's doing it.

Maybe talking is a bad idea.

"Okay," I respond.

"I've never worked a real job before. I mean, I have a job now, but it's all telecommuting. I've never been in an office like this."

"Think you can take it?"

"You know, five years ago I would've barfed at the thought. But, actually, SeCure is the one and only company I would put a suit and heels on for."

And every male in the building thanks God she did. "Why is that?"

"SeCure represents the pinnacle of infosec. I mean, Jackson King is a genius. I've been following him since I was ten years old."

I try to stop my wolf from strutting. "You sure you want to leave the pajamas at home and come into an office every day?"

"Yeah. It'd be good to have a reason to leave the house. Programming can be lonely. I mean, I do my best work alone but, it might be nice to be around people like me. Maybe find my tribe. Feel normal, you know?"

I don't know. I haven't had a tribe since I abandoned my birth pack with my fur soaked with my stepfather's blood.

A company full of humans is a poor substitute.

"If you're interviewing here for infosec, you must be talented," I say to distract myself from bad memories.

"I have been coding since I was young," she says dismissively, which again makes me think she's downplaying her talent. "Being a teen geek girl definitely disqualified me from normal."

"Normal is overrated. You just need to find your pack."

"Pack?"

"I meant tribe."

"No, I like pack. That makes me a lone wolf." There's a smile in her voice, and I bite back a sharp remark. Being a lone wolf isn't as cool as it sounds. Even if it is all I deserve.

"So..." She has the tone of someone who's been waiting to ask something.

"Have you ever met Jackson King?"

I hide a smile, even though she can't see it. "Mmm. A few times, yeah."

"What's he like?"

I shrug in the darkness. "Hard to say."

"Hard to say because he doesn't reveal much?"

I keep my mouth shut.

"That's what I've heard. So is he the awkward kind of geek or the creepy kind?"

I wasn't aware of the various categories of geek. I don't consider myself a geek, but, then, as a shifter, I don't consider myself in any human category.

"I'm guessing the creepy kind," she goes on. "Because no one that hot should be so anti-social. I mean, he must have some serious flaws. According to rumor, the man never dates. They say he has no social life whatsoever. Never goes out. Total recluse. He must be damaged. Or else gay. I bet he's the type who keeps his boyfriend tied up in a closet for whipping when he comes home at night."

Again, my face almost cracks into a smile. *I'll show you whipping, little Batgirl.* "Sounds like you know a lot about him."

"Oh...I, uh...I guess I'm interested in him. He's kind of a celebrity to fellow geeks. I mean his original coding was pure genius, especially for the time."

This time, I do grin. Her assessment of me, apart from

the gay whipping boy part, makes my pulse pick up speed. Another anomaly. I don't care for attention, and she's right —I don't give up personal information. I have too big a secret to hide. But her interest in me has my wolf pirouetting.

Mine.

"So, what kind of geek are you?" I ask.

"Apparently the kind who blathers like an idiot to strange men when she's confined in elevators. But I'm sure you already picked that up. Sorry—I normally have a better-than-average filter. It's a good thing we can't see each other because I've thoroughly embarrassed myself this morning."

It's getting harder and harder to keep from kissing her senseless. I've never been so happy to sit and listen to a human babble. My wolf doesn't even mind being confined for over ten minutes. Usually, it'd be growling to break free and attack the threat. Which could be deadly.

My wolf seems more interested in protecting this lovely, feisty human. It took me a moment to recognize it, but now that I do, my pulse picks up and I have to force myself not to put my arm around her. Pull her close. Especially when she leans into me.

"Maybe you could agree not to look at me when the lights come back on so we can meet later under normal circumstances."

I don't answer.

"Hopefully, I won't do this blathering thing during my interview and screw it up."

"You really want this job?"

"Yeah. I do. It's weird because eight years ago I would've laughed in your face if you'd told me I'd want to work for SeCure, but I guess I've changed. To me, Jackson King and the company he built represent the ultimate in infosec coding, and I want to be a part of that."

The lights flicker on, and the elevator lurches into motion. *Damn.*

"Oh, thank God," she breathes, scrambling to her feet.

I follow her to stand.

When she turns to look up at me, the smile freezes on her face.

Surprise.

She blanches and stumbles back.

The light illuminates her beauty. Flawless skin. Full lips. Big eyes. High cheekbones. And, yeah...the tits and legs looked as good now as they did in the dark. She's a ten all around. And she's figured out who I am, which gives me the upper hand.

"Well, now you're quiet."

"J.T.," she mutters, sounding bitter. She glares as if I'd been the one smack-talking about her rather than vice versa. "What's the "T" stand for?"

"Thomas." My mother gave me a decidedly human name.

The elevator stops on the sixth floor, and the doors open. She doesn't move.

I hold it with my hand and gesture for her to get off. "I believe this is your floor."

Her mouth opens then snaps closed. She squares her shoulders and marches past me, two bright-pink spots on her cheeks. *Adorable.*

Even though I'm late for at least twenty meetings, I follow her off. Not because my body can't be parted from hers. Certainly not because I have to know more about her. Just to torment her a bit more with my presence, now that she knows who I am.

"Ms. McDaniel, there you are," Stu says. He's waiting in front of the elevators--must've taken the stairs. Luis, SeCure's chief security officer, stands with him.

"We're getting maintenance up here right away, Mr. King." Luis signals one of his men, who takes his place at the elevator to stop anyone from boarding. "We'll have it fixed in no time, sir. And I see you escorted Ms. McDaniel. "

Stu glances guiltily at me. "I didn't mean to leave her unattended like that. I took the stairs up to make sure I was here when she got off." He makes it sound like he deserves a medal for his heroics.

I don't answer.

"I've got her from here. I'm sorry to have disturbed you."

"I'm going to sit in on her interview," I say, surprising even myself.

Both Stu and Kylie's heads whip around, and they gape at me. Kylie flushes further and blinks her big brown eyes. In the light, they are a warm chocolate-brown with a starburst of gold in the middle. *Incredible.*

The alpha in me doesn't mind her discomfort. I'm used to making people squirm. But my wolf isn't happy about the tinge of anger in her scent. An apology is on my lips—another first. Jackson King doesn't apologize. I don't owe her one, either. If I had my way, I'd pull her into the nearest conference room, spank her ass for the whipping boy comment, and spend the next three hours teaching her pleasure at the tip of my tongue. I'd go down on her until her screams of pleasure told everyone in the building that's she's mine. That would take care of her annoyance, and her nervousness. Or is it arousal?

"Oh, it's just a routine interview—no need to take up your time," Stu says.

I'll be damned if I let Stu—or any other male—get her alone.

Luis clears his throat, warning Stu he's on the verge of pissing me off.

I narrow my eyes at Stu. "I decide how to spend my time. Shall we go into the conference room, or are we interviewing her here in the hallway?"

Stu scowls as if I busted up his frat party.

~.~

Kylie

Holy awkward, Batman. So much for acing the interview. I didn't think it could go more wrong, but being caught in a tug of war between Stu and Jackson is another precious moment in this craptastic day. I can't believe I just had a meltdown in front of *Jackson King*. And gushed like a schoolgirl about what type of nerd he was and whether he was gay, and *oh God did I really insinuate that he whips his sexual partners?* What the fuck is wrong with me? Not even *Interviewing for Dummies* can save me now.

Of course, he let me think he wasn't the CEO. Kind of a dick move, really. I should be glaring at him, but no, I'm still flustered from him touching me. Too bad getting felt up by Jackson King isn't one of the perks of the job.

Damn, I really, really want this. Groping aside, SeCure is the pinnacle of cybersecurity. As a teen, it was the ultimate hack. After almost ten years of hiding, it feels like coming home. Like I've trained my whole life to stand here, and now that I've gone legit, I can step into my rightful place.

The fact that I'd be working under Jackson King has nothing to do with it. Well, maybe a teensy, tiny bit. My body would certainly like to be under him—right now. Lordy, I have to get through the interview without imagining his hands on me...

The death stare between Stu and Jackson has gone on long enough.

"Where's the conference room?" I chirp. I take several deep gulps of breath and follow Stu into a large conference room. I can do this. I've handled much more difficult things —major heists at the age of twelve, losing my mom and dad, being trapped in an air duct for ten hours... This is nothing. It's only an interview.

I sit down, and the three men position themselves across from me. The chairs are big and plushy but barely accommodate Jackson's muscular frame. He swivels a little, eyes on me. The man can intimidate even sitting down.

I allow myself a tiny frown in his direction. He lied to me. And now he's making me interview with him, as if this day could get any more awkward.

He meets my glower with raised eyebrows.

Why, oh, why did I say all those things in the elevator? It was like I'd swallowed truth serum.

Maybe that is one of Jackson's superpowers: making people tell him every thought that pops into their heads. I've never been so real with anyone in my life. I've told a million lies, but a little bit of comfort after a panic attack, and all my training fell away. My dad would lecture me—if he was still alive.

Stu shuffles some papers and shoves one toward Mr. King. "Here's her resume," he says. "You can see her qualifications are quite impressive."

Stu definitely overstated my resume. Sure, I'd graduated summa cum laude with an IS degree from Georgetown—after convincing them to let me take all my classes online—

but my work experience was writing code for the gaming company where I currently work. At least, the only work experience that was legal. There's plenty of stuff I can't mention. The result: I don't look that impressive on paper.

"Her professors all gave her rave recommendations," he goes on, seeming a little flustered.

Not half as flustered as I am, though. It doesn't help that Jackson King gazes at me like he knows my life secrets. Now that's a terrifying thought.

"Do you want to start?" Luis asks King.

King leans back in the chair and crosses his long, elegant legs. Damn. I've always drooled over his pictures online, but he's even more handsome in person. Photos didn't do him justice—not even the spread in *Time Magazine* when he was named "Man of the Year" for solving the world's credit card fraud problems. Nothing about him says "geek" at all, actually. With thick dark hair, kept on the long, shaggy side, a square jaw, and jade-green eyes, he looks rugged. He also holds an air of danger, his power barely contained by his expensive suit.

He looks back at me, his face an inscrutable mask. "What do you know about infosec, Kylie?"

I lace my fingers together on the table. No sense being nervous. I blew any chance I had of winning this job when I called him a deviant sociopath in the elevator. He probably just wants payback, and making me sit through the most awkward interview in the history of the world is his preferred form of torture.

Fuck this. I'm not getting the job. Why stay and suffer?

I push my chair back and rise. "You know, I don't think this is a good idea."

Stu shoots to his feet, looking angry. "Why not? Wait just a minute."

"I'm sorry to have wasted your time."

Stu steps between me and the door, like he's not going to let me go. His job must be on the line if he can't fill this position. *Not my problem, buddy.* What's he gonna do, body check me if I make a break for it?

"I think, actually, I screwed up this interview back in the elevator. So I'll just see myself out. Thank you—"

"Sit down, Ms. McDaniel," King commands, his deep resonant voice like steel.

I stop in my tracks. Damn, he's even hotter when he's stern. Like in the elevator, my body responds, nipples getting hard, pussy dampening.

His nostrils flare as if he can smell it. But that's ridiculous. He's still sitting, but there's no question who holds the power in the room.

I reach for my chair, a bit wobbly. And not just because of my heels. "Yes, sir." I sink back down.

"Thank you. I asked you a question, and I expect an answer."

Damn the man. He's determined to make me suffer. I rub my thumbnail with the pad of my index finger` then drop my hands to my lap to stop fidgeting.

"Mr. King, I apologize for the things I said about you in the elevator—I was very rude and...disrespectful."

King's expression doesn't change. He watches me with that cool assessment. "Answer the question."

Okaaay. Guess he's just going to ignore my apology. I'd fight back with sarcasm, but I promised myself I'd keep a lid on it. "My knowledge of infosec is mainly practical. You won't see it on my resume, but I do know all areas of security—how to assess weak points, how to mask code. No code is impenetrable, except maybe yours."

"How long would it take you to hack the average guy's Gmail?"

I allow a tiny smirk to curve my lips. "That would be illegal, Mr. King."

"So do you, or don't you know how to hack?"

He knows. That's my first thought. I shift in my chair. He's figured out I'm Catgirl. *No, that's silly.* All infosec professionals probably know how to hack. Maybe it's a prerequisite. Like the way the home security companies hire busted burglars to improve their systems.

Not that a security system—physical or virtual—has ever been able to keep me out. Although my skills might be a bit rusty. My cat burglary days died with my dad.

"If I knew how to hack, Mr. King, I certainly wouldn't admit it here, and that's why you won't see it on paper. But if, in theory, I wanted to hack the average guy's Gmail, it might take me ten to twenty minutes."

Stu gives him a tight smile. "We do have a series of tests we'll give Ms. McDaniel, after the interview." He returns his attention to me. "Now, why don't you tell us about your programming experience?"

King looks as bored as I feel as I rattle off my programming accomplishments. Luis grills with all the standard kinds of interview questions: Do I work well under pressure? On a team? Am I willing to work nights and overtime when necessary? How do I feel about relocating to Tucson from Phoenix?

I answer automatically, studying Jackson King without making it obvious. He hasn't asked another question. What's he thinking? Is he still mad about what I said in the elevator?

"Do you have any questions for us?" Luis asks.

"How many candidates are interviewing for the position?"

Stu shuffles his papers as the other two men look to him for the answer. "Three."

"When do you expect I'll hear something?" Probably a bit presumptuous, but presumption is all I have left.

"In a few days. We're interviewing everyone today."

"Better get that elevator fixed, then," I quip, my voice lighter than I feel.

Stu stands. "Now, if you'll follow me, I'll take you to an office for the test."

Thank God. Tests I can handle. I don't dare look at King as I stand, my cheeks still burning. Ducking my head, I follow Stu. When I get to the door, I risk a glance.

King's looking at me, his lips quirking at the edges.

Sadist. He enjoyed making me squirm.

~.~

Jackson

I watch Kylie's long muscular calves strut out of the room, her ass a perfect heart-shape in the short, fitted skirt. My wolf is still going nuts, snarling to get out. I've never let him get so out of control, especially not in the office. But there's never been a temptation like Kylie.

I force my thoughts to business. At least the part of the business that concern her.

"I want the results of her tests sent to me."

Luis bobs his head. "Of course. Will you be sitting in on all the interviews today?"

"No." Luis probably wants me to elaborate, or to explain

myself, but he won't push. Everyone knows I'm a minimalist when it comes to conversation.

"May I ask...what did she say in the elevator?"

I shrug. "She insulted me. It's fine. I'm sure most of my employees have said similar or worse things about me behind my back."

Luis plays with his paper coffee cup on the table, too diplomatic to agree. "What did you think about her?"

"She's bright, that's obvious. Her resume isn't that impressive. How did Stu say he found her?"

"Headhunter."

"I wonder why the headhunter thought she'd be a good fit when she has no infosec experience on her resume."

"She's totally a hacker."

"Obviously. But how did the headhunter know that?"

Luis taps his paper cup on the table. "Good question. Want me to find out?"

"Yeah. And get me her test results."

"So did you like her?"

No one that hot should be so anti-social.

She thinks I'm hot. Yeah, I've heard it before, but never cared what humans thought about my looks. All shifters—well, all paranormals, actually—are more beautiful than humans. At least, I thought so, until I met Kylie.

"I found her... " *Fuckable? Intoxicating? Adorable in a tough-girl kind of way?* Right...the tough-girl thing is an alpha trait. If Kylie were a shifter, she'd lead the females of the pack. She had all the qualities of a top female.

Luis waits for my comment. What the fuck am I going to say? *Her scent is addictive. My wolf wants to claim her.*

"Interesting. I found her interesting."

I stand, wanting to prowl after Kylie into whatever office Stu has set her up in just to watch her work. My wolf doesn't want her alone with any other male. And I like a good hunt, especially if Kylie's my prey.

~.~

Ginrummy

He didn't expect Kylie to be so hot. Or poised. Brilliant, yes. But he pictured her mousy. Awkward. Socially anxious like him, perhaps with glasses and her hair pulled into an absentminded knot. Maybe with a nose-piercing. Not the cute diamond-chip in the nostril, but the bull-ring in the septum tough-rebel-chick kind.

He supposes not all computer geeks are misfits, but well, anyone who spent her entire childhood online and out of the real world shouldn't also be a certifiable brick house with high heels and juicy tits. Shouldn't be able to look that intimidating asshole Jackson King in the eye and run her own interview as if she was the one hiring.

She looks bored, now, as her fingers dance over the keys, solving the security problems they laid out for her.

In a way, this makes things easier. She's more like Jackson King than him. Dammit, Kylie—Catgirl—McDaniel is way out of his league. So framing her for the demise of SeCure won't hurt as much as he imagined. Because, in his mind, she's always been his cyber-girlfriend of sorts. Yeah, it's stupid, but she's female and he's male and they'd been accomplices in the hacker world since puberty when his raging hormones needed nothing more than the name "Catgirl" to get off.

They cut their teeth together as young hackers, sharing information and their successes, passing along tips, advising others. It was dumb luck he found her after she disappeared for the past eight years. But she re-surfaced on DefCon, the old secret hacker forum where they'd always interacted, looking for help with cracking into the FBI. Naturally, he'd assisted.

He'd been looking for her for a long time. Not just out of nostalgia, although he wondered about her. She's perfect for what he needs. There are very few hackers capable of breaking SeCure's code. And he happens to know Catgirl is one of them. She did it before—as a teenager, no less.

So when she resurfaced, he helped her with the FBI and then followed her through their doors to see what she was up to. She deleted files on three people—a deceased married couple and their daughter, vigilante burglars, known for stealing from the dirty. She also added evidence on another criminal, including tips on his whereabouts. By digging, he gathered enough evidence to surmise she was the daughter of the cat burglar team. It fit with the sorts of questions she'd posed years before—about security systems and safes. Based on the FBI's limited information, the criminal she'd set up for arrest had probably murdered her father during a job.

After that, it had been difficult, but he eventually found her IP address, and then it was a matter of sending a headhunter after her for a job at SeCure. Imagine his surprise to find out she lived a mere two hours away in Phoenix.

He watches her now, her glossy hair tucked behind her ear, whizzing through the stupid tests they made up for her. Oh, they were real tests—they would've been a challenge to anyone else, but he knew she'd pass with flying colors.

If that damned power outage hadn't thrown her together with Jackson King, hiring her would be a sure thing. But it sounds like she said or did something to piss the CEO off.

He sure as hell hopes King won't block them from hiring her.

~.~

Kylie

I push open the door to the house I share with my grandmother. My legs are stiff after the two hour drive back to Phoenix, and I'm ready to trash these heels. "Mémé, are you home?"

My grandmother appears from the kitchen, her lined face split into a grin. "Minette!" My pet name, *Minette,* is the French word for *kitty*. My parents came up with it. My mom was French—Dad met her on a crew working an art heist in Arles. It was love at first sight, the way he told the story.

"Well, how did it go?" Mémé always speaks to me in French, and I always answer in English. I speak five languages fluently, and French is one of them, but at home I'm lazy. Or maybe it's part of trying to be normal.

I sink into a chair at the kitchen table and kick off the evil black patent leather high heels. What a poor choice they were.

Mémé sits down beside me. "I'm waiting."

I blow a raspberry. "Not well. I screwed up, actually. Big time, Mémé. The power went out while I was in the elevator."

"No." Mémé gives an exaggerated gasp and covers her mouth in the animated way only people of her generation still employ. Mémé knows about my claustrophobia. She can probably guess its origin, although we never discuss my parents' profession or my former illegal activities.

"And I got stranded in there with Jackson King—*the* Jackson King."

Mémé gives me a blank look.

"He's the founder of SeCure. But I didn't know it was him—it was dark. And I said some not-so-flattering things about him."

Mémé looks sympathetic. "Ah. That's too bad, *ma petite fille*." She pats me on the shoulder and stands up. "I'm sorry. I'll get you some soup."

Of course. Because food fixes everything, doesn't it? Mémé's cooking is as good as therapy. She moved in after my dad died, and, for a few months, her crepes were the only reason I got out of bed.

Mémé moves to the stove and ladles the hot broth liquid into a bowl. Today's fare is French onion, my favorite. Mémé serves the rich brown broth with a baguette and Swiss cheese.

"Careful, it's hot."

I grin up at Mémé. After Maman died, I spent my entire childhood taking care of my dad—trying to keep him out of jail as he played Robin Hood, stealing from the rich to right the wrongs of the world. After all those years, it's sweet to be coddled by Mémé. Though she's tough when she has to be. I wouldn't have finished college if she hadn't convinced me. I'd always taken online courses—just for fun. But she insisted I take classes above board, from the same college and finish a degree. Get the diploma and put myself in the real world, even if it was under a false identity. So I did.

But I still barely have a social life. I'm too used to being a loner, keeping my secrets hidden. After what happened—after my father's... *Jesus.* I still can't think about it without a searing pain in my chest. His *murder*. His betrayal and cold-blooded fucking murder. Yeah. After that, I stopped all illegal activity. I erased our identities, not that Dad and I had ever been on the grid anyway. I went legit. With Dad's double-crossing murderer looking for me, I hid in plain sight, as an ordinary American citizen.

The heists were my parent's gig, anyway. They'd been a regular Bonnie and Clyde. But mom died in a car accident when I was eight, so I became Dad's new partner. I'd refused to leave his side, even though he would have preferred I sit safely in a boarding school or with Mémé in Paris. But his vigilante Thieves for Justice thing wasn't my calling. I just liked to hack.

That's how Mémé talked me into taking my current job for the gaming company. But I'm barely tied to the real world. I rarely leave home. I don't date or have any close friends. In some ways, I'm still Catgirl, lurking in the shadows.

Maybe that's why the elevator encounter threw me so much. I've never been touched by a man, much less a hottie like Jackson King. Frightening, how easily he breached my walls.

My cell phone buzzes, and I grab my purse to rummage for it. A SeCure number. "Hello?"

"Hi Kylie, it's Stu, from SeCure."

"Hi Stu." *Brilliant K-K, really brilliant.*

"I'm calling to let you know we were impressed with your skill set, and we'd like to offer you the job."

"Really?" Part of me wants to fist-pump the air in triumph. I gave the worst impression ever, and I still got the offer. *Take that,* Interviewing for Dummies.

The rest of me is skeptical.

"There's no second interview or anything?"

"Nope. You scored 100 percent on the test, and management liked you."

"Management?" He can't mean King.

"Yeah, Luis thought you were great. So the HR department will call you with the real offer, but I have permission to discuss salary with you. We're offering one hundred thirty-five thousand dollars plus moving expenses. Full health and dental insurance, profit sharing, and stock options add another third to the salary package."

Er...wow. I smile at Mémé, nodding. It's fifty K more than I make at the moment, and I never expected them to foot the bill for moving. *Probably too good to be true.* But I can't turn it down. "Thank you, that sounds great."

"So you'll accept the offer?" He sounds enthusiastic.

I should play hard to get, but fuck it. "Yeah. Absolutely. I'm thrilled."

"Great. HR will send you a written offer tomorrow. How soon can you start?"

"I don't know...a month?"

"I was hoping two weeks," Stu says.

"Really? That's pretty fast."

"We are paying for relocation, so that will simplify the move for you."

"Is two weeks a requirement?"

"Yes."

"Then I'll be there," I say.

"Great. We'll finalize the paperwork tomorrow. Welcome to the team."

I hang up and beam at Grandmere. "I got the job!"

Mémé throws her arms around me and kisses my temple. "That's wonderful! Congratulations."

I accept the hug, wondering what King thinks of my hire. At least he didn't veto it. That shouldn't excite me as much as it does.

2

Jackson

I sense the moment Kylie enters the building. Even if I hadn't already known it was her first day at SeCure, I wouldn't have missed her presence. My wolf senses prickle. A growl rises in my throat. Swallowing it back down, I move from my desk and pace to the wall-to-wall windows, gazing out at the Catalina foothills. My collar is suddenly too tight. I want to shed my clothes, take my wolf form. I want to run. To howl. To hunt.

When Tucson courted SeCure to move our headquarters to the city, I played hardball, pressing for tax advantages and new roads to the proposed location. But, in truth, it was a no-brainer. Tucson is perfect for a shifter—nestled between three mountain ranges, with a population of only a million, it gives me quick access to wilderness while retaining all the advantages for business. Attracting high-caliber employees wasn't hard—most professionals were delighted to relocate to the desert, even with the hot summers.

I built the headquarters at the base of the mountains.

My own mansion also nestles into the front range of the Catalinas so I can run and hunt at any time.

I pace in front of the windows, skin tingling. I'm actually considering shifting in broad daylight. My wolf wants out. He wants to hunt, to kill. Or fuck.

Mine.

Yeah, my wolf wants to fuck that hot little human on the sixth floor. If I were smart, I'd stay way the hell away from her. But I wasn't thinking with my brain when I recommended hiring her in the first place.

I can't get Kylie out of my head. Over the past two weeks, her scent comes to me at night. I see her in my dreams. The memory of her long legs and bat tits gets me hard every time.

How can a human be so attractive?

A tap on my door. "Mr. King? Your nine a.m. is here."

With a sigh, I sit at my desk. "Send him in." More business shit to deal with. Kylie will have to wait.

~.~

Jackson

I force myself to wait until eleven a.m. By then, my entire body twitches from the effort of resisting instinct. Shooting to my feet, I stride out of my office, past my secretary's desk.

She looks, surprised. "Your eleven a.m. is waiting, sir." She'd already told me once, and I'd asked for a minute.

"Yeah, I know. I'll be back in five." Or ten. Or however long it takes me to throw my little Batgirl up against the wall and fuck her senseless.

I shove my wolf back down. This is a bad idea. She's

human. Beautiful. Fragile. Breakable. At best, I'd bruise her. At worst... I'd break her.

But I have to see her.

I take the elevator to the sixth floor—the memory of touching her making my cock even harder. Thank fate we were stuck together. Thank fate I didn't realize how her scent called to me until after we were out of the enclosed space. Only years of control kept my wolf from taking over and claiming her right there. Control and being so fucking confused.

I've never felt this way before. I shouldn't feel this way. Especially not about a human.

I prowl down the hall, ignoring the way all the employees' conversations die when they see me. Most days, I welcome their nervousness. It satisfies the predator part of me. Today, I have different prey.

I don't need to ask where my little hacker is stationed. Her scent leaves a trail. Vanilla and spice, and a flavor I don't recognize.

My hunt ends at a tiny windowless office. Kylie sits studying her computer screen with a coffee mug at her lips.

Although I don't make any noise—shifters tread far more quietly than humans—she snaps her head in my direction before I step through the doorway, blinking as if she doesn't quite believe I'm real.

"Mr. King." She swivels in her chair but doesn't stand. My wolf likes that she's lost her fear of me. She crosses her long bare legs, and I thank the fates she's wearing another short skirt. "Or should I call you J.T.?"

So she's still annoyed at my little deception. Her voice holds a note of scorn no other employee would use, and damn, but it makes my cock twitch.

The sight of her thrills me, but I allow myself only a small grin. "You may."

Her gaze flicks to the doorway behind me, and only because I'm part wolf do I recognize a slight trapped animal vibe under the confidence. Like it makes her itchy to have the only exit blocked. Must be part of her claustrophobia. I step into the office and away from the door to give her an unfettered exit, and she relaxes.

I lean against the wall, crossing my arms over my chest. My wolf wants me to puff out my muscles, and run out to hunt and bring her back a rabbit for lunch. *Down, boy.*

Her scent hits me hard, bringing on the prickle of the shift. I will it back, hoping my eyes haven't changed color.

She arches a brow. "Is that what you go by?"

"No."

She sets her coffee mug down and stands. The skirt hugs her tight body, her heels making the muscles of her calves stand out in stark relief. A faded Spiderman T-shirt stretches across her chest. This girl has a superhero fetish.

Too bad I'm the villain. I want to yank the T-shirt up and drag my tongue up that flat belly to the perky tits.

"Listen, I want to apologize again for what I said. I didn't mean any of it. I was just...jealous." She sounds sincere.

I didn't expect another apology. The set of her shoulders says she's on the defensive, but the softness in her face and voice tells me she's actually trying to make nice. Which is...refreshing. My employees, business colleagues, hell, everyone in my life either sucks up to me, or talks shit about me behind my back. Or both. Only other shifters are real, but the Arizona packs don't love me. Which is my own fault.

"Jealous of what?"

She shrugs. "Your brains, I guess."

Another surprise. Most people are jealous of my success,

my money, my power. They seem to think I haven't earned them. I got lucky. "If you got inside my head, you wouldn't find much worth keeping," I say. Just a lifetime's worth of guilt. Any therapist would point out my obsessive career drive as compensatory. And if the psychotherapist knew what I'd done to deserve my self-loathing, they'd lock me up. But my mistake can't be undone. My mom can't be brought back from the dead, and my stepfather's death still came too late.

Kylie studies me.

What does she see? A giant, awkward geek? A creepy guy? Or does she see the wolf in my eyes, the predator that wants to put her on her hands and knees and fuck her senseless?

"You like my code." My voice is hoarse, guttural, this close to the change.

"I do." She gives a slow, sensuous smile, as if talking code is foreplay. Her teeth are perfect and white, lips plump and glossed. "Your eyes are lighter than I remembered."

Fuck.

I blink rapidly, forcing back the change. "They change." *Not a lie.* "I've been working on a new language." Jesus, this really was geek-talk. Next thing I'll be telling her a "once, at band camp..." story.

Her eyes light up, and she moves forward, invading my space. She's toned and leggy, but her tits and ass would make the perfect handful.

"I'd like you to test it for me."

Oh fates—what in the hell am I doing? I never let anyone see my work, especially not a brand-new employee whom I know nothing about.

She leans closer. "I'd love to."

Are her nipples hard?

"It would have to be after hours, on the side. I know Stu has other work for you."

"Sure, great." She isn't daunted by overtime, apparently. Definitely a legit geek.

"My office, six p.m." *Sounds like a date.* It must have sounded that way to her, too, because the scent of female arousal reaches my nose.

I ball my fists, pressing my blunt fingernails into my palms to keep from snatching her body up against my own. I imagine her naked, sprawled out on my desk with her legs open wide.

No. No, no, no. It can't happen. Some wolves are able to have sex with humans, no problem, but they wouldn't have the urge to *mate* with one. A human wouldn't—shouldn't—inspire the urge to permanently mark her with my scent. But it seems this one does. And that makes fucking her an impossibility. Because I can't mark her without serious injury or death.

Her berry lips part, as if waiting for a kiss.

I step forward.

"Am I forgiven?" Her whiskey voice goes straight to my cock.

I pin her with a cool glance. "We'll see."

The scent of her nectar grows stronger. She likes my authority.

I leave before I shove her skirt up, rip off her panties, and bury my tongue in her.

Not going to happen. Can't. Happen.

I walk away, body tense. My wolf wants to be unleashed.

Maybe I need to get outside. I use my cell to call my secretary. "Vanessa, cancel my appointment. I'm going out."

~.~

Kylie

Holy sexballs, Batman. Jackson King has a thing for me. Why else would he show up, all growly and intense, and invite me to his office?

He wants to show me his *code.* Is that what the kids call it these days?

Maybe he's just being nice, making up for his first impression. Maybe he wants to put me, a new employee, at ease on my first day. Throw me a bone. The big one in his pants. *Heh.*

But no. I'm not that girl. I've never even been with a guy. I didn't read *Career Advice for Dummies,* but I'm pretty sure sleeping with my boss is not a good idea.

Even if it's Jackson King...

After a few minutes of daydreaming, I shake myself.

No, K-K, I scold my libido. *Don't mess this up.* I've just landed my dream job. No more life of crime, or being on the run. No more hiding, the only excitement in my life discovering what Mémé made for lunch.

And Jackson King is probably a player. Maybe that's why there's no news about a girlfriend. He probably sleeps with his employees and pays them for their silence. Jerkwad.

If only he didn't have such pretty eyes. I thought they were green. Today, they were light blue.

I tap my keyboard, acting busy in case Stu interrupts me. Even though we can email or chat via the intranet, he drops into my office, often. I still haven't figured out why he was so gung ho to hire me. Glowing recommendations from college professors don't seem like enough.

I pull up Google to do a search on Stu, to see if I can learn more, and end up typing in Jackson King's name instead. There he is, unsmiling as always, in a photo shoot for *Wired* magazine. He stares through the camera, his thick hair mussed and jaw clenched. His typical *leave me alone or else* look.

It only makes me want to get closer.

Only a few more hours before I can go see his *code.* And I actually do want to sit and program with him, even if it means unpaid overtime. Maybe diving into a project will end the awkwardness between us. I'm standoffish and snarky in real life, but online, I'm Catgirl. Leaping tall buildings in a single bound. Solving the world's problems, one hack at a time. When my dad was alive, we moved so much between his heists—unable to stay in one place. The computer was my home. I didn't meet my friends at the mall. I met them online. And coding—the numbers just made sense. A challenge and a comfort at the same time. Something about hiding in plain sight.

For some reason, I think Jackson King would understand.

At six p.m., I leap out of my chair. My heart pitter-patters at a jaunty tempo as I take the stairs to the eighth floor—the executive level.

When I break out of the stairwell—which brings back bad memories, but not as bad as an elevator—I walk briskly. *Act like you belong, and people will assume you do.* My father gave better advice on blending in than any business book. As a thief, he would know.

I do belong here, I tell myself, as I head to the corner office. *For the first time in my life, I belong.*

King's executive assistant is packing up, pulling on a light jacket and slinging her purse over one shoulder. She's cute. And her blouse is unbuttoned way too low.

Holy cleavage, Robin.

I try to walk past her.

"Excuse me? May I help you?"

I whirl with a bright smile. "Sure. I'm here to see Mr. King."

The assistant shakes her head, bouncing her perfect blonde curls. "No. He doesn't have any appointments."

"Yes, he does. He asked me to look at some code." I extend my hand, doing my best to look friendly, despite the frosty reception. "I'm Kylie McDaniel, the new infosec specialist."

The young woman shakes her head again and ignores my hand. "Nope. It's not on his schedule. And Mr. King *really* doesn't like to be bothered. I can try to make you an appointment?" Her voice drips with doubt.

The door behind her pushes open. "Ms. McDaniel."

I shouldn't have done it. I could've just waited until the woman walked away, and gone in anyway. But something in me itches for a fight.

Eyes glued to the assistant's face, I answer, "J. T."

The assistant's eyes widen right before her face pinches up tight.

Fortunately, my over-familiarity doesn't seem to piss off Jackson. He doesn't explain himself to his secretary, but then he doesn't have to—it's his company. He steps back and gestures impatiently toward his office.

Only on him would authority look so hot.

"Nice to meet you," I tell the assistant as I swagger on by.

She ignores me. "Do you need me to stay, sir?"

No thanks, I'm not into threesomes.

"No."

So he gives others the monosyllabic answers, too. Good to know.

"Okay, good night?" the secretary says, a hint of desperation in her voice.

Without a word, he shuts the door. It shouldn't satisfy me, but it does. And now I'm alone with Jackson King.

"You're late," King growls.

He's taken off his suit jacket and tie. His collar stands open. His broad shoulders fill the dress shirt.

"Am I in trouble?"

He doesn't answer, only rolls up his sleeves.

Holy hotness, Batman.

"If you miss me, I'm only two floors down."

King grunts in answer and stalks behind a large, solid oak desk with a leather captain's chair. A retreat, but he's back in a seat of power. Two smaller chairs sit in front of the desk. I drop my bag in one but don't sit down. I'm not a naughty student visiting the principal's office.

Now, that's a fantasy.

King's office is impressive. Two entire walls of floor-to-ceiling windows showcase a breathtaking view of the Catalina foothills, which glow pink and purple in the setting sun.

"Your secretary sure is protective of you. Are you fucking her?" Oops, maybe a little too blunt. But if he's a man-ho, leching on all his employees, I want to know.

"Excuse me?" That stern voice warns me to settle down. Too bad it only makes me more excited.

I shrug. "She seems jealous."

"So you conclude I've taken her to bed?"

My face floods with heat. Once again, the first words out of my mouth are totally inappropriate. What is it about him that brings out inner thoughts? Around him, I can't hide.

He tilts his head to the side. "I don't think she's the one who's jealous. What did you think we were going to be doing up here, Kylie?"

I shiver when he says my name.

"Did you think we're going to sleep together?"

"No." My lie isn't very convincing. I should know. I was trained to lie. "Not at all."

His gaze drops to my breasts, and he raises his eyebrows, as if making a point. His eyes are light-blue again—almost silver. Mémé's change like that. Sometimes they look chocolate-brown, like mine, other times they are golden.

I look down. My freakin' nipples are standing out so far they show through my bra and T-shirt.

Damn.

I cross my arms over my chest to hide them. "Look, we're both adults. You invited me up here. Show me what you're going to show me, and I'll tell you what I think."

"You think you're ready?"

I saunter to his desk and plant my hands on it, leaning in. "King, I've been ready for you my entire life."

For a moment, King regards me. He pivots, squaring off to face me. He seems bigger, bulkier. His eyes burn into mine, ice blue with a black band around them.

A musky scent washes over me, spicy and masculine. My pulse picks up as I hear a low rumbling sound. It's coming from King.

I straighten. "You okay? You seem—"

"This isn't going to work."

"What?" I choke out, like he's punched me in the gut.

He closes his eyes, opens them, getting himself under control with visible effort. Whether it's temper or attraction, I can't be sure. I feel numb as he walks back to the door, presumably to see me out.

"Look, I'm sorry." I touch his arm. Electricity surges through my fingertips. King sucks in a breath. "I'll behave. I really want to see your code."

He steps back out of reach. "No. This was a mistake."

"Give me another chance," I plead. "I can act professionally, I swear."

He turns and hits me with the full force of his gaze. His eyes drift over my mouth, my breasts, down the length of my bare legs. Tingles spread through me. "Maybe. But I can't."

I shiver again. My senses go on alert, danger twining with excitement. There's a predator in the room, and he's got his sights set on me.

"You need to leave, Kylie."

Ouch. Not even his sexy voice can soften the rejection. I back toward the door, swallowing. The air in the office is electric, making the hairs on my nape stand up.

Something has happened between us. Something I don't quite understand.

"I'm sorry." I search for more to say. "I didn't mean to—"

"I'm not someone you should be alone with."

"What? I don't understand."

"This isn't a good idea." Head bowed, massive body outlined in red from the setting sun, Jackson King looks like a hero in a comic book, a being from another world.

"King," I say, and take a step forward.

His head snaps up, and he pins me with those blazing blues. "Get out."

My back hits the door, and I twist the knob, unwilling to look away from the big bad King. Muscles tight and eyes wary, he looks every bit as dangerous as he does sexy. But I'm not afraid. I want to seduce him.

I'm crazy. I don't know anything about seduction. These feelings are crazy. I try again, one last time. "I still want to test your code. You could email me. Or something."

"No," he says. "I can't." His lips twist into a miserable smile. "Leave. Now." His voice softens. "While you still have a chance."

What does he mean? I don't stay to find out. I close the door too hard, and it slams.

"And stay out," I mutter, my cheeks burning.

At least his secretary's not here to witness my humiliation.

As I walk away, a tortured sound rips from King's office. An inhuman sound. Almost like a howl.

~.~

Jackson

I pull my clothes off in the parking lot and throw them in my trunk. It's reckless. There are still cars in the lot, and it's not even dark yet, but I have to run. The moon is waxing, which makes my wolf' antsier than usual. That's the problem. Not that smart-mouthed, intoxicating little human who calls everything the way she sees it.

My chests shakes with a growl when I think about the danger Kylie is in. My wolf wants to protect her from all threats. But, of course, the only threat to her is me.

Garrett warned me this could happen. The Tucson alpha runs a tight pack. His wolves are all healthy, well-adjusted. He and I have a tenuous relationship—I am a lone wolf on the edge of his territory. Garrett keeps reaching out. Not just to assert his leadership—although he wouldn't be much of an alpha if he didn't try—but to save me from moon sickness. Wolves, especially big, dominant wolves, can go mad if they wait too long to take a mate. If I ever display the signs, Garrett has made it clear he'll take me down. I told him to bring his best fighters to be sure he could finish the job.

I can't be bothered with a mate. Hell, I don't even want a

pack, not after my birth pack banished me. I am a lone wolf, or I would be, if I hadn't taken in Sam. But that was different. Sam needs me, and my wolf likes the kid.

My wolf more than likes Kylie. It wants me to claim her, but claiming a human is dangerous. I know the consequences of letting my bestial nature run free. People get hurt.

I can't let that happen to Kylie.

I close my eyes and let the heat consume me. The cells tear apart. Rearrange. It's painless but requires concentration and takes energy. Dropping to all fours, I run behind the cars, out of the solar panel-covered lot, to the rocky dirt of the desert. I lope straight up the side of the mountain, racing to get behind the crest for cover.

Nose lowered to follow a rabbit trail, I let my wolf rule. No more being a CEO. No more company, or code. No more Kylie with scent, intoxicating and forbidden. The confused hurt on her face when I told her to get out...

For a long time, I run the mountain, dodging in and out of trees and scrub, stretching my muscles. The sun ducks under the horizon, and the moon rises, shimmery and plump, lighting the slope of the mountain.

I catch a familiar wolf's scent a moment before I see a flash of black and a pair of amber eyes. I tense my hind legs and leap to tackle the other wolf, knocking the young male onto his side and nipping his ear.

Sam is scrawny for a shifter—still large by wolf standards. My young pack brother yips and nips back until I growl and show my teeth. Sam tucks his tail and whines, offering his belly and throat.

I lick his ear and let the kid spring to his feet. Dominance and submission games are just that between us—play. It's the closest thing to fun I allow myself. If not for the kid—our pack of two—I wouldn't interact with anyone on a personal level—neither human nor shifter. But Sam refuses to leave. He remembers what it's like to be alone.

I lift my muzzle and trot off, knowing Sam will follow. Tonight, we'll run and hunt just like we did in the mountains of California, where I found Sam starving and half-mad, his human side almost lost. He seems to know what I cannot explain. Tonight, I'm the one who needs rescuing.

3

Kylie

It's been three days, and I haven't once seen Jackson King. Not since he threw me out of his office. Three days of reliving our conversation over and over. I tell myself to get over it, but I've been obsessing over King for years, and this crush has bloomed since the encounter in the elevator.

Work drags on. Stu keeps me busy with setting up new firewalls and other boring stuff.

Meanwhile, I've been wearing skirts and heels in case I see King again. Not that I want to impress him. I just want that big jerk to see what he's missing.

Oh, who am I kidding? I still want him to notice me. To come into my office and growl at me, bend me over my desk, flip up my skirt, and...*mmm*.

Holy horniness, Batman.

"Kylie? Are you okay?"

Stu and the rest of the team peer down the conference table at me.

"Of course." I sit up and try to remember the last few minutes of the meeting, but all I have are fantasies of Jackson King. *Dammit.* "Didn't mean to go on screensaver. I must need more coffee."

Someone laughs at my screen saver comment, but it's not a nice sound. I stiffen. I'm the youngest of this team, but I work as hard as anyone else. Maybe harder.

So much for finding my tribe.

"You were sighing a lot." Stu refuses to drop it.

"My heels are killing me." Which isn't a lie. I kick them off under the table and rub my feet against the legs of my chair. I've got to go back to the normal geek-wear of jeans and Chucks tomorrow. Screw King. I don't dress for any man.

The meeting ends, and I keep typing on my laptop, only closing it when Stu leans his hip against the table in front of me.

"Settling in all right?"

"Sure." I keep my smile cool. I like Stu, but his constant hovering is getting a little on my nerves. He keeps trying to make friends, but I get the feeling he only wants me around because he thinks I'm hot.

I guess that explains why he wanted to hire me.

"Bossman get you down?" Stu says, and I snap upright like he's thrown ice water over me.

"What?"

"I know he stopped by your office a few days ago. You haven't been as happy ever since."

Holy Stalker, Batman. Not that I'm one to judge, but still.

"You my big brother, Stu? Always watching?"

"No, uh." He flushes. Poor guy. He's obviously into me but trying to stay professional. Which is more than I've done with Jackson. "Just trying to show you the ropes. I feel responsible, 'cause I got you hired."

You hired my boobs. My snark self rears her head. *My brains are just along for the ride.*

"I know Jackson King is a big name, but he's not a nice guy. Kinda a jerk, actually. He's got a reputation around here for being a royal dick. The ladies always fall for him." Now, Stu sounds whiney and jealous. "But he treats them the same as any employee. Barely says a word that isn't rude."

"I'm fine, Stu. He didn't say anything rude. And I like working here, so far."

"Well, great." Stu casts about. "Got any plans for the weekend?"

Groan.

"Hanging with my boyfriend," I lie cheerfully.

Stu pushes off the table, away from me. Of course, I've been sending *I'm not interested* vibes for days, but now that he thinks a man has claimed me, he's finally taking a hint.

Jerk.

"Right," he says. "Well, I'm off to the meeting with Finance. We're setting a project to test their structure before the next 10-Q filings. Which is in a week. I might need you on it."

"Great." I fake enthusiasm at the promise of overtime and mentally upgrade Stu from *jerk* to *dickhat.*

"Okay." Stu shoulders his laptop case. "I'm heading up, now. You want me to hold the elevator?"

"No, thanks." I fight back a sarcastic reply. "Gonna take the stairs. Need the exercise." I let out a sigh when his footsteps fade away.

"Is Stu bothering you?" A low voice makes me jerk and almost spill coffee all over myself. King prowls in, looking like he's ready for the cover of GQ. "I'll have a word with him if he's being inappropriate."

"No. He's fine." Lordy, I'd forgotten how broad his shoulders are. "It's fine." I'm babbling. "He's just awkward. All geeks are."

"Are we?"

I arch a brow. "You, especially." *Crap. Here goes the truth serum again.* "The last time I saw you, you told me to leave. No explanation. No nothing. You tossed me out and didn't tell me why."

"You know why." His deep, quiet voice makes my cheeks flush and my pussy purr.

To hide it, I roll my eyes. "Stu just asked me the same thing about you. Wanted to make sure you weren't bothering me or being rude. Apparently, you have quite the reputation, Mr. Mean."

"What'd you tell him?" His jaw is clenched tighter than normal.

"I told him you huffed and puffed but didn't blow my house down. Relax." I smirk, and the tension in him eases a little. "I left out the part where you told me it wasn't safe to stay." I glance around the empty conference room. "Which reminds me. You said we shouldn't be alone."

A group of people pass the open door, chatting loudly.

"We're not alone. And we shouldn't." He fixes me with a look, and his tousled hair falls over his hollowed cheek. It should be illegal for a man to be so beautiful.

"I think I can handle you." *Maybe.*

Something flickers across his face. He looks away. "You don't know anything about me."

"I know you've never dated anyone," I blurt, mainly to distract him from the thought that put the pain in the expression.

"So you've mentioned. You still stalking me, little hacker?"

"No." *Yes.*

He smirks as if he knows it's a lie.

I grin back. "Thank you. I can handle Stu. But it's nice to have someone check on me."

"If anyone here harasses you, I want to know about it. Understand?"

A thrill goes through me, but I hide it.

"Wonder Woman today?"

"What?" I blurt, before I realize he's talking about my shirt. "Oh, yeah. Well, you're Clark Kent." I nod to his suit and tie.

"Ouch," he grimaces. "He was a nerd."

"He was Superman," I correct. "And you *are* a nerd."

He shrugs. "Billionaire nerd." A grin hides just out of sight on his mouth. He's handsome now; he'd be breathtaking if he'd smile. "Like Iron Man. Or Batman. He's more my style."

"Or Lex Luthor. Maybe you're not a hero."

The smile lurking in the corner of his mouth disappears, to my dismay. "Yeah," he mutters. "I'm definitely the bad guy."

"I was kidding. You're not a villain." I step closer, put my hand on his arm before I remember myself. "You act big and bad, but I know what you're really like. You're the one who comes to the rescue. I remember what you did for me in the elevator."

"No," he says. His eyes drop to my hand and up to my face. I remove it and step back, flushing a little. "You're mistaken."

My whole body heats from his nearness. He keeps shutting me down, but the fact remains, he's still standing here. I *know* he has a thing for me. He just has too much integrity to act on it. “So why are you here? Marking your territory?”

“Me? You’re the one who set my secretary back on her heels.”

“I did not,” I sputter, then grin. “That was just a little cat fight. And she deserved it.”

He holds up his hands. “All right, kitten. Sheath your claws.” Smirking, he strides off, looking almost...*happy*?

What was that all about?

~.~

Jackson

My wolf whines a little as I walk away from my little superhero, but he behaves. He wanted me to close the door and mark her with my scent so the likes of Stu will stay away, but he’s satisfied that we got to see her at all.

I shouldn’t risk getting near her, but I can’t help it. At least I proved to myself I can be in the same room without jumping her. I love that she’s not afraid to tease me.

You’re Clark Kent.

If she only knew.

I skip the elevator, take the stairs two at a time.

My secretary gives me a bewildered look as I pass. I realize the strange feeling on my face is a smile.

“Mr. King?” I turn, and my secretary’s perfume hits. The downside of having a sharp nose.

“Yes, Vanessa?”

“You have a call from Garrett. No last name. I wouldn’t bother you, but you said to put him through—”

“I’ll take it.” Ever since Kylie sparred with her, my secretary’s been subdued. I still get rock hard when I think of the encounter. If Kylie was a shifter, she'd be an alpha female. Perfect for my wolf. Strong enough to stand up to my rule, sexy enough to keep me wrapped around her little finger. Sweet enough to keep me hard, just thinking of putting my cock in her. Of long nights running under the full moon. Just the two of us at first, but, one day, there'd be pups...

Shaking my head, I pick up the phone. I must be moon mad if I'm thinking about pups.

"King?" The Tucson alpha sounds like he's making his voice deeper. At twenty-nine, he's one of the youngest alphas in the states. It helps that his father runs a big pack in Phoenix, and backs Garrett's claim of the territory. "Just wanted to check in."

Most alphas have a protective streak. Garrett is no different. But I'm not one of his pack. If any alpha tried to claim me, I'd be obliged to make it clear I'm no one's wolf. Quickly and violently. My wolf tolerates Garrett's "check-ins" because it thinks of the young alpha as a kid brother, kinda like Sam. Still, Garrett and I are careful in our interactions. In a fight for dominance, I'd win, but I have no interest in taking over his pack. And it'd be a shame to best him, because I like the guy.

"Garrett," I answer. "Full moon this week."

"That's why I'm calling. My dad's hosting mating games on pack land near Phoenix. Wanted to invite you to run with us."

"You going?"

"Yeah. The guys want to sniff some she wolves. They won't mate, but they'd like to get laid." There are fewer than twenty members in Garrett's pack, all young, unattached males, like him. And they all live in the same apartment building. Bit of a fraternity.

"Appreciate it, but I can't make it. I'd send Sam, but I promised him we'd run our own property."

"Dad says you're always welcome," Garrett says affably.

My money is welcome. I'm barely tolerated, standoffish even for a lone wolf. I'm dominant enough to hold my territory, but that doesn't mean I want a pack. I've avoided gatherings since my birth pack banished me.

"There aren't a lot of single females, but you might find one you like."

"Tell your dad thanks but no thanks. Maybe in a few years, if Sam wants a mate." I don't want to insult the Phoenix alpha, but I find it best to be blunt. Maybe not the most politically sensitive, but I'm big enough, people tiptoe around me.

"Look, King, I don't give a shit if you mate or not. Obviously, I haven't taken a mate, either. But three males in my dad's pack have gone moon mad in the last few years. It's my responsibility to make sure you at least mingle with some females, since we don't have any down here."

What he really means is: *You're a lone wolf past the age of thirty, and a dominant, and more susceptible to going moon mad unless you take a mate.*

Also, there is at least one female wolf in Tucson. Garrett's beautiful younger sister is a student at the University of Arizona, but I can't fault the guy for leaving her out of the equation. Not that I'm interested in her, anyway. The image of Kylie's Batgirl stretched tits rises in my mind.

Not a wolf.

Garrett goes on, "I'm bringing up my pack to give them all a chance to at least run off some tension."

"I didn't know matchmaking was part of the alpha's job description," I drawl.

"I know your wolf is dominant. Without a pack to run, it must be dying to bring a she-wolf to heel."

Every muscle in my body clenches, imagining bringing my little hacker to heel.

"Besides, with birth rates among shifters so low, it's good for the pack if the most dominant of us settle down and have pups as soon as possible." He sounds like his father. "Why put it off?"

I scoff. "Says the chronic bachelor. What, did your mother call asking for grand pups, and you decided to pass the advice onto me?"

Any other alpha might bristle and take offense at my jab, but not Garrett.

"You caught me." I hear his grin, and it goes a good way to mollifying my wolf, who's annoyed at having this conversation in the first place. "I figure if she has your wedding to coo over in the shifter society gossip pages, she'll leave me alone."

"I'm onto you now. I'll think about it next moon. Sam should definitely get a girlfriend."

"All right." Garrett laughed. "We'll look for you. See you around, King."

"One more thing, Garrett." I drop all joviality. With my wolf's newfound attraction to a human, I'm suddenly not so certain about my own stability. "If I do ever go moon mad, promise me you'll protect Sam. And bring your whole pack in to stop me. Whatever it takes."

"Whatever it takes," Garrett vows. The silence hangs cold and serious between us. We both hang up without saying goodbye.

I drum my fingers against the desk, the warning a weight in my chest. Garrett did the right thing, bringing up moon sickness in the most tactful way possible. It irks me that it took this reminder to make me back off Kylie. The animal inside me is dangerous and just looking for a moment of weakness so it can break free.

No more tests of my control. No more games like today. I have to stay away from Kylie. For her own good.

I open my laptop, ready to immerse myself in work, when the chat pings.

Batgirl4u: *Hey*

For a second, I catch my breath, thinking I've found my nemesis at last—Catgirl, the hacker who broke my code years ago.

But no. It's Batgirl, with a B. And it's on our intranet, the private network my employees use. Except I only allow connections with my executive team. Which means I've been hacked.

King1: *Who's this?* I type, although I can guess.

Batgirl4u: *Who do you think?*

I shake my head. King1: *Cute trick, kitten. But if you have time to hack our intranet, I need to get Stu to give you more to do.*

Batgirl4u: *Just proving my worth. You could send me that code you wanted to show me*

The cursor blinks at me.

This isn't a good idea. I want to watch over her, but I can't. Today, I had a weak moment. I have too many of those around her. Like it or not, I am dangerous. Deadly. She thinks I'm not a villain.

She's wrong.

I power off my computer. Time for another run.

~.~

Kylie

After an hour waiting for King's reply, I power off my laptop and head home. I shouldn't have taunted him like that. I was showing off and, if I'm not careful, he might connect the dots some day and figure out I'm Catgirl.

Infuriating man. One day I think he's going to bend me over his desk and fuck me senseless, the next he's throwing me out of his office. Then he's back to flirting. And then he ignores me online. I can't keep up.

"Holy mixed messages, Batman," I mutter as I close my front door and pull off my heels. One thing's for sure, I'm not wearing these shoes for him again.

"Mémé? You home?"

A note on the table in my grandmother's loopy scrawl tells me she's run to the store, so I pick up the mail, pulling out the large manila envelope with no return address. I pry the flap with my thumb and rip it open.

A thick packet of papers emerged, with a typewritten cover letter.

Oh fuck.

My heart stops beating.

We know who you are, Catgirl, and have the proof to put you away.

To ensure our silence, you have twenty-four hours to install the code on this thumb drive into the main drive of SeCure.

If you do not comply, if you corrupt the files on the thumb drive in any way, or if you speak of this to anyone, we will send this packet to your new employer and the FBI.

No.

I struggle to breathe as I flip through the rest of the pages of the packet. They include all the evidence from my break into SeCure years ago, as well as IDs and photos of me and my parents under various aliases.

None with my real name.

Hell, even I've forgotten that.

My head throbs, and the room spins away. Someone found me. Maybe not *him*, but this is a huge threat.

First things first. Is there anything in this packet that can put me in jail?

I flip through the pages again.

No. But it will raise flags. SeCure will fire me, for sure. I'll lose the chance to work with Jackson King, not that it looks like we'd be working closely, but still. Goodbye to my chance at being normal.

But I can't do it and stay. If I give in to these guys, I'll be their bitch forever. Next, they'll ask me to hack into the credit card vault. Then somewhere else. I can't do that. I have to disappear. Like I've done a million times before.

I stomp to the bedroom, grab a suitcase from the closet, and fling it onto the bed. Without thought, my hands move, packing the necessities. Black clothes, one pair of each thing. A simple bag of toiletries.

Running again. It doesn't matter how hard I try to outrun Catgirl and my parents' legacy, the past always catches up with me.

But what about Mémé? We've moved so many times, I don't want to drag her on the road again. This time, our lives aren't in danger. It's not fair to make her pick up and move. Can I leave her?

She's the only family I have. Ditching her to keep her safe feels like what my father did to me, when he tried to stick me in boarding school after my mom died. I wouldn't let him, and I'll bet Mémé won't like being left behind, either.

Okay, so we'd both move. Mémé can make soup anywhere.

We have to run. We have to hide. What other choice do we have?

So much for my chance at normal.

I wrench open my drawer. The Batgirl shirt stares up at me.

"I can't," I say. "I'm not a superhero."

I'm definitely the bad guy, Jackson told me. If only he knew. I'm his arch-nemesis, as bad as they come. I thought I was clear of my old life. I thought wrong.

In the past, I'd hack my way out of any problem—mine or my dad's. We were in it together. Always on the run, but together. I'd felt safe. Powerful, even. But the Louvre shattered that. Stabbed in front of my eyes, my father gone forever. I almost died in that air-conditioning shaft, suffocating on my own panic. I've never felt safe in a tight space again.

Except in the elevator, with King.

I remember the pressure of his arms around me, the triggering of the calming reflex. I'd looked it up when I got home. All I found was reference to yoga postures that involve locking the chin into the sternum for calming.

Jackson's big hands had been so much better than a yoga pose. They'd radiated warmth and safety.

If anyone harasses you, I want to know about it.

It's not real. It's not safe. I can't trust him.

But what if I can?

I shove the papers back in the envelope, write a quick note for Mémé and run to my room for a new outfit before I can change my mind.

I've built my life on lies.

Maybe it's time to try the truth.

~.~

Jackson

The moon shines silver, lighting the mountainside. I usually run and hunt most of the night when the moon is so close to full, but my instincts screamed to go back early. It wasn't because of the rain, either.

Sam chases me, nipping at my hind legs, but I turn and snarl at the young wolf, causing him to tuck his tail and whine. I don't want Sam's company—I never do, but the kid is my self-appointed permanent shadow. When we reach the back side of my property, we both freeze. The rain makes it impossible to scent anything, but the high-pitched tone set at a frequency only canines register tells us my alarm system has been tripped.

Sam snarls, his upper lip lifting to show fang. He charges forward, rounding the corner.

I fly inside, through the dog door in the back, to check the interior. I scent nothing unusual. I shift and yank on clothes as I jog to the control room to look at the security feed.

A lone bike stands propped outside the iron gates that surround the front of my property and a small dark figure trudges through the rain toward my front door. A growl reverberates, low in my throat.

Who in the hell?

Sam arrives at full speed, fangs gleaming, and leaps through the air, his front paws landing on the intruder's shoulders and knocking him or her to the ground.

Take that, motherfucker.

Dark fury pumping through my veins, I leave the control room to confront the unwelcome guest. I jog down the slippery steps and across the rain-soaked gravel.

"Easy Cujo." The shaky sound of her voice shocks me like a live wire.

Kylie.

A jolt of fear tremors through my body. "Off. Get *back*," I snap.

Sam doesn't move, his wolf side not giving way to human reason, his instinct to protect and defend his home turf too strong. Thank the fates, Sam hasn't torn her flesh.

My little hacker's smart—she's gone perfectly still beneath Sam.

I grab the scruff of my pack brother's neck and haul him back. "I said *off*."

Sam gives his head a shake and tucks his tail at the sound of his alpha's angry tone. He takes a few steps backward.

I gaze down at our intruder. Even soaking wet, in a sweatshirt and jeans, she's beautiful. She lies in the mud, not looking nearly as afraid as she ought to.

"What in the hell are you doing here?"

She groans and starts to move, but winces, reaching for the back of her head.

Well, hell. A good-sized rock lay near her. She must've struck it when Sam knocked her down.

"I had to talk to you," she croaked.

Anyone else, I'd grill right there, while they lie on their back in the dirt at my feet. But not Kylie. That new, strange prickly heat takes over and screams at me to protect her—from Sam, from the rain, from the rock, from myself.

I pluck her from the ground and set her on her feet, forgetting to pretend she's heavy.

Her eyes roll, unfocused, as if the movement pains her head. "Ugh. Wow."

I reach around and cup the back of her head, fingers questing until I find the growing goose egg.

She flinches when I touch it.

"You're hurt." I turn and glare at Sam, who ducks his head.

She eyes my housemate, too. "Good thing you were around, or I think Cujo would've eaten me. Is that even a dog?"

"He's part wolf."

"Part wolf, part what? Gargoyle?"

I suppress a smile. I love that she pulls out the wry wit despite her injury. But then, it's her default defense mechanism, as I learned in the elevator.

I study her. I ought to call the cops, or somehow scare her into respecting my boundaries. "Are you going to tell me why in the hell you broke into my place?"

She rolls her eyes. "Please, if I was breaking into your place, I wouldn't trip the laser sights to announce my presence. Forgive me, but I didn't see the doorbell out there."

What woman knows about laser security systems? And doesn't scream when a giant wolf pins her to the ground?

"I don't recall inviting you. How the hell did you even find me?"

"I'm a hacker, remember?"

"Or a stalker."

"Same thing." Her hand goes to the front of her sweatshirt, and I hear the crinkle of paper. "I have something to show you. It couldn't wait until tomorrow."

I take her elbow and lead her up the slick Italian tile steps and inside the mansion. Kylie moves stiffly, as if more than just her head hurts from Sam's attack. It doesn't stop her from looking around my place as I escort her to the guest bathroom on the second floor. Somehow, I doubt she's missed a thing, either. Why is she here, really?

I angle her through the bathroom door. I intended to grab her a towel and leave her to freshen up, but I find myself gripping the hem of her soaked sweatshirt.

"What are you doing?"

I tug the fabric upward. "Getting you out of these wet clothes."

Color infuses her cheeks, making her eyes shine bright. Strands of her wet brown hair cling to her cheek and neck, a drip of rain runs down her throat. I want to lick it off.

She lets her arms go slack and follows the movement of the sweatshirt, letting me pull it over her head without protest.

My cock throbs painfully against the zipper of my jeans when I catch an eyeful of skin. I remove her undershirt with the sweatshirt, and she stands in nothing but a lacy red bra and wet jeans.

Her chest heaves, and she keeps her gaze intent on my face, as if waiting to see what I'll do next.

What *will* I do?

I know what I want to do. I want to peel those tight,

soaked jeans down and bend her over the bathroom counter. I want to plow her from behind as much as I want to get into that whip-smart mind of hers and find out what makes the unique female tick. And dammit, yes, I want to sink my serum-coated fangs into her flesh and forever mark her as mine.

Which can't happen.

I drop the sweatshirt on the floor and hear the rustle of paper again.

Kylie's focus snaps to the discarded clothing, and she lunges for it, breaking the stare-down between us. Trapped between the layer of shirt and sweatshirt lies a manila folder, which she retrieves and hugs to her chest, covering those perfect tits from my view.

She licks her dry lips. "Mr. King, before I share this with you, I just want to tell you when I did what I did, I was a cocky teenager trying to prove my worth to myself and the hacker world. I never took anyone's credit card numbers, and I never sold any information. It was simply a—"

The realization hits me like a fist in the gut. *"Catgirl."*

Of course she's fucking Catgirl. The only person who ever hacked my code. No wonder she was nervous about interviewing at SeCure. What in the hell kind of game was she playing, showing up at my headquarters, at my home, for fuck's sake?

The one breach in security that haunted me for the past eight years just blew up in my face. Again.

I snatch the manila folder from her hands and dump the contents onto the bathroom counter.

"I'm sorry." Her voice sounds small.

Dammit.

I hate hearing her diminished, even to me, a natural

alpha who demands submission from everyone. Even when I'm pissed off with her.

"What the fuck is this?"

I flip the stack of papers and read the one on the top. *Fuck no.* Rage sharpens into a deadlier sense of awareness.

Blackmail.

Someone wants to sabotage SeCure.

Or is this some elaborate game Catgirl's playing? Because anyone as brilliant as she could have some unseen strategy going here.

This girl's trouble and my judgment about her has been clouded by lust.

She stands perfectly still, her small hands clenched into fists. "I'm sorry," she repeats.

I toss the papers back down the counter. "What the fuck? What do you want? Why are you really here?"

I hate seeing tears fill her eyes, but I steel myself against my instinct to yank her into me or slay her foes. Those instincts can't be trusted.

She shakes her head. "Nothing. I don't want anything." Her voice wobbles on the first word, but then she regains control of it. "I just figured if I confessed, myself, the jack-asses would lose their leverage. I don't want to negotiate with terrorists, you know?

"I just offered you all the information you need to hand over to the FBI to build a case against me. Obviously, I'm hoping you'll settle for my resignation."

"No," I growl, surprising myself by speaking before I knew what I was going to say.

But I'm not going to let her off that easily. In my world—in the shifter community—transgressions are dealt with head on. They aren't handled by cops or resignations.

Punishment is swift, usually physical. Or else recompense is demanded, or offered, and accepted.

She flinches, her slender shoulders sinking. "What are you going to do?" Her voice sounds hoarse.

Blood rushes to my cock at the thought of taking her to task. *Firmly.* I lower my voice to a dangerous level. "What do you think I should do?"

"Well"—she licks her full lips, the intelligence returning to her face— "if I were you, I'd want to catch these motherfuckers. So I might keep me as bait."

Damn, I almost trust her. An enormous mistake.

"You know, monitor me closely to make sure I don't misbehave, but wait to see who makes contact and put a stop to these guys."

Yeah, I'll monitor you closely.

Monitor the way those red lace bra cups lift her perky breasts. Monitor the scent of her arousal, the changing shape of that lush mouth. Kissable lips. "I see. And how should I punish your previous *misbehavior?*" My voice is definitely deep and raspy. If she doesn't know what I'm thinking, then she's a complete innocent.

But her eyes dilate, nipples pop through the fabric of her bra. *That's right, baby.*

"No pity for the kitty?" She loses her breath on the word *kitty*, which makes it sound twenty times sexier.

"Right." I spin her around and bend her over the counter. My palm connects with the wet pocket of her jeans before my brain even knew the plan. It makes a loud crack, satisfying on every level. My cock hardens at her gasp.

Kylie tosses her head, looking over her shoulder, teeth bared. She likes it. Judging by the scent of her arousal —a lot.

I smack the other cheek, harder.

Fuck, I want to pull those wet jeans off her, find out what color panties she's wearing before I tear those down, too. But if I see her naked ass, there'll be no holding back the beast. Even this mild contact over her clothing has me harder than a fucking rock and my teeth lengthening.

Since she didn't freak, I keep spanking, hard slaps that echo off the Italian tile. "You hacked me, Catgirl?" I smack her again and again. "What were you—like twelve?"

"Fifteen," she gasps. "I never took anything—I swear —*ung*."

The last sound from her lips sounds too much like I'm fucking her instead of spanking, and my vision tunnels, my wolf clawing to take over.

I stop spanking, struggling to slow my breath. I keep my hand on her ass, because, well, the thought of *not* touching her kills me. "Just wanted to see if you could, baby?" Now that it's set in, the fact that she's Catgirl turns me on even more. This girl hacked me *as a teen*. She's a fucking genius, and I'm swooning for her brains almost as much as her sexy little body.

My eyes meet hers in the mirror. Her face is flushed, eyes dilated and glassy. I reach around and cup her right breast, squeezing and pulling her back up against my chest.

"Bad girl," I whisper in her ear, and she lets out the cutest little moan.

I *have* to fuck her. As in, I'm going to die if I don't get my cock inside her now. I need to own her completely. Punish her with the roughest fucking of her life until she screams my name and learns I'm the only male who will ever crack *her* fucking code. Then I'll start over again, slowly. Lick the pain away. Make her come over and over again until she weeps.

But I don't trust my control around her, so I settle for

flipping her back around, picking her up by waist, and plunking her down to sit on the counter. "Did you like your spanking, baby?"

"Y-yes."

I love her honesty. I shove her knees apart and bring my thumb to the seam of her jeans, right over her pussy.

She arches into me and catches my shoulders, her head falling back. "Jackson..." she whispers.

I push the hard fold of fabric into her seam, rubbing up to her clit.

She jerks and lets out a needy cry. Her fingers come down and cover my hand, urging me to give her more.

My mental faculties slip away. I yank open the button of her jeans and lower the zipper, parting the two sides.

Matching panties. Red lace, like the bra. I knew it.

My satisfaction is short-lived because a storm of rage blows hot on its heels. "Who's seen you in these, baby?"

"Wh-what?"

"Who has seen you in these cute-as-hell panties?" I get right in her face, teeth showing. "Who do you wear these for?"

She pushes at my shoulders, but, of course, I don't budge. Human female strength against shifter alpha male? No comparison. "What gives, Jackson?" There's real fear in her eyes, and it drops me like bullet. The flash of anger evaporates, replaced by the need to soothe and protect my female.

Shit. I already consider her my female.

I lean my forehead against hers. "Sorry," I murmur. "Is it wrong to want to kill the guy you bought those for?"

She lets out a shaky laugh. "You're crazy."

Because I'm a stubborn bastard, I wait, still wanting her to answer my question.

"No one's seen them," she mutters.

Holy hell, is she blushing? Maybe she's more innocent than I thought.

"No one?" I'm unable to keep the incredulousness out of my tone.

She pushes again, but I'm back to my original purpose. With an arm wrapped around her waist, I pull her off the counter to stand, and delve my fingers into her pants and panties.

Hell, yes.

The moist heat of her core slicks my finger, sending a kick of lust through me so strong I have to drag in a sharp breath.

"Jackson."

"Yeah." She can call my name with that husky voice anytime.

I rub my middle finger along her weeping slit, spreading moisture up to the swollen bud of her clit.

I'm still pondering the blush. Is she embarrassed she hasn't been with anyone recently? Considering the way she clings to my neck and moans the moment I touch her perfect little pussy, I think that's a distinct possibility.

Some ridiculous male pride surges through me. I'm going to be the one to satisfy her. I force myself to slow down as I circle her clit, my free hand slipping around to grab her ass and pull her pelvis closer.

She grinds down over my finger.

"Greedy girl," I murmur. If I had her panties off, I would have spanked her pussy, but the fit's too tight.

Her breath stutters as I screw one finger inside her tight channel. I work the heel of my hand against her clit.

She rises up on her tiptoes and claws the back of my neck, fingernails scoring me like a female shifter marks her mate. My teeth sharpen in my mouth, and I clamp my lips closed to keep from marking her, myself.

Her pelvis undulates forward and back in greedy thrusts.

I work a second finger inside her. "You're so. Damn. Tight."

She stiffens slightly, even though I meant it as a compliment, but I stroke her inner wall and hit her G-spot.

Her muscles squeeze, and she grows even wetter. "Fuck...no...I mean, yes. Oh please!" She hangs from my neck, her breasts pressed into me as she pumps her hips over my fingers.

I feel like a pubescent wolf, ready to come in my pants. But this is for her—not me. I thrust in and out of her, letting my knuckles bump with force until she squeals and clamps her inner thighs together. Her internal muscles contract, and she comes all over my fingers in the hottest display of female orgasm I've ever seen.

I did that. My wolf grins with satisfaction.

When her orgasm fades, I ease my fingers out and claim her mouth, prying her lips open with my tongue. I wrap a hand around the base of her head to hold it hostage and plunder, command her to submit.

She does. She opens for me, presses her killer body against mine, kisses me back.

Damn.

With great effort, I break off the kiss.

She gazes up at me, beautifully disheveled from the rain and my assault. "Does this mean we're square?" She sounds breathless.

"Not even close, baby. You owe me, and I intend to collect."

Her gaze drops to my stiffy. "How?" She doesn't wait for the answer, but sinks to her knees.

The creak of a floorboard in the hallway makes me curse inwardly. I yank her back to her feet before we give Sam a show. Why in the hell didn't I shut the bathroom door?

Although the sound is soft enough I thought she'd miss it, Kylie startles, craning her neck to see around my shoulder. Every cell in my body screams for me to reach for the door knob, shut the door and tell her to please continue.

But no—Kylie is human. And my employee. Because I am keeping her on, where I can watch her.

Keep your enemies closer.

I've already gone way too far with her. Any further, and I'd mark her, and then I'd have a world of new trouble on my hands.

Forcing restraint, I pull a clean towel from the cabinet and toss it to her. "Get in the shower and warm up. I'll find you some dry clothes."

I turn her around and propel her toward the shower stall, delivering another smack to her heart-shaped ass.

She makes a low purring sound in her throat and looks over her shoulder with heat.

I bite back a groan. It takes all my willpower to turn around and walk out, shutting the door behind me.

4

Ginrummy

His cell phone beeps. It's eight p.m., and he's still at SeCure, but that isn't unusual. It isn't unusual for half the employees there. They work flex time, and a lot of programmers do their best work at night.

It's Mr. X calling.

Yeah, seriously. The asshole calls himself Mr. X.

He doesn't know how many people he has under him or behind him. He did his best digging and all he came up with was that Mr. X doesn't exist. He's part of some powerful organized crime ring.

Well, whatever. He'd do his part and become a rich man. Maybe he would even warn Kylie back into hiding before the FBI pick her up. Or not. He still hasn't made his mind up about her. He is both more attracted and repelled by her now that he's met her in person.

He swipes his screen. "What's up?"

"Looks like your threat wasn't convincing enough."

Not a surprise. She is Catgirl, after all.

"How do you know?"

"Her bags are packed. We picked up the old lady she lives with, though. We'll take it from here."

His breath stalls in his chest, and he feels sick to his stomach. *Well, duh.* Of course these guys wouldn't be above kidnapping. Jesus, they probably aren't above murder, either. A chill runs through his limbs. What will they do with the old lady? What will they do with Kylie?

Fuck.

He doesn't want to be a part of all this. But he does want the fifty million dollars and safe passage out of the country promised to him. And this is why he's partnered with men like Mr. X. They are willing to do the hard stuff. All he had to do was write the code.

And it's too damn late to back out. Yeah, he has a feeling the only way out of this now will be through a bullet in the head.

~.~

Kylie

My legs wobble as I step into the shower. I may still be wet, but I'm sure as hell not cold anymore. *Holy finger fucking, Batman.* And now I see the advantage of a real live sexual partner. They do things to you you didn't know are possible.

All this time I'd been perfectly content with watching porn and using my battery operated boyfriend. I shimmy out of my wet jeans and take off my bra and panties.

Who has seen you in these cute-as-hell panties?

Did he really turn agro over some imaginary other man? A shiver runs through me, and I step under the spray of water. Is that a total red flag? Maybe he is as creepy as I'd portrayed him in the elevator. Would he keep me locked in a closet for whipping?

Oh God. Just the thought of confinement in a small space makes my solar plexus twist. I erase the thought, focusing instead on the whipping part.

He *spanked* me.

A grin splits my face and I reach back to palm my ass, which burns a little under the spray of warm water.

Yummy.

Seriously, that was the hottest thing that ever happened to me.

Okay, yes, it's the *only* hot thing that's ever happened to me.

My V-card has never been punched. I've lived such a strange existence, never able to trust anyone. I started college at age sixteen, had a few unsatisfying hook ups in which I abandoned my goal of punching the card and gave blowjobs instead. So, yeah. That's my sex life in a nutshell.

Total virgin, finger fucked by Jackson King in his bathroom after confessing to hacking him as a teen.

The fact he satisfied me and not himself is an argument against the creep factor. But who or what stopped him when I was ready to suck him off? He heard something in the house.

Does he have a roommate? Secret girlfriend? Housekeeper? Pool boy?

Even though I didn't enjoy either of my early experiences with men, I was so ready to blow Jackson's mind. My mouth watered to taste his cock, to pleasure him like a porn star.

Hopefully there will be another chance. I run my hands over my ass again, replaying the spanking. Leaning my forehead against the tile, I bring my fingers between my legs.

Ohhh. I've never been so slick and swollen. I imagine Jackson stepping into the shower with me, his huge frame crowding me back against the wall. He'd order me to place my hands on the wall and slap my ass until I beg him to stop, then he'd grip my hips and plow into me from behind. I pull up on my fingers, undulating them between my legs.

A second climax rips through me, and my head swims from the heat. I breathe deeply until the stars clear then I shut off the spray.

When I step out, my wet clothes are gone, and a towel and a neatly folded MIT sweatshirt sit on the counter.

A flush of embarrassment washes through me. Did he come in while I was masturbating? I grab the towel and dry off then pull on the warm sweatshirt. It's huge on me, falling to mid-thigh like a sweater dress, which is good, since he didn't leave me any panties. I love wearing something that belongs to him. I pull it to my nose, breathing in his faint scent.

I can't stop thinking about his thick fingers moving inside me, and I'm suddenly dying for the full package. Getting my V-card punched by Jackson King would be the ultimate hacker girl fantasy fulfillment. But no, this isn't about checking a box, or having a famous person.

It's about the sheer animal attraction between Jackson and I. I felt it in the elevator before I even knew who he was. I loved the take-charge way he handled me there as much as I loved being bent over his bathroom countertop for a spanking.

I search for a brush, but this seems to be a guest bathroom. There are no personal items anywhere, just cleaning supplies and toilet paper. I tear my fingers through my wet hair and head out.

The house—mansion, really—is enormous. I follow the curved staircase downstairs and follow sounds of movement to a huge, open kitchen.

The man standing behind the enormous granite-topped island eating cold cuts from the container with his fingers isn't Jackson, though.

"Oh, hey," I say inanely, giving a small wrist wave.

He's young—my age or younger—with blond hair that is straggly and wet like mine. The lean muscles of his arms are covered with tattoos, and both his ears are stretched with rings. He has the still bearing of a predator, and he watches me approach without moving.

I tug down the hem of Jackson's sweatshirt. "I'm, uh, Kylie," I offer, hoping to get an introduction back.

"Sam." Somehow I get the feeling he doesn't like me.

Fuck. Is Jackson gay? "Are you and Jackson…?"

His cold demeanor cracks with a flicker of a smile. "He's my brother."

I gape. Clearly not a blood brother. They look nothing alike. "Looks like you were, um, out in the rain, too."

The young man doesn't answer.

"I see you've met Sam." Jackson's deep voice sends tremors through my body, like after-quakes from my climax. Climax*es*. Plural. Because he was certainly responsible for both.

I look from Jackson's huge mountain man frame and dark hair to the lean muscled fair man, and I'm not convinced they're not lovers. Especially because Sam shoots Jackson a *What the fuck?* look.

Why does that make me desperate to stake my claim on

Jackson? But it's not my right. I am in big trouble with my employer and my blackmailers, and we need to make a game plan.

"Do you want to see what's on that thumb drive?" I ask. The envelope with the threat and thumb drive disappeared from the bathroom while I was showering. Even though nothing terrible has happened yet, I'm still not sure I made the right choice coming here. Trusting someone other than family. I remember how badly that turned out for my father.

Jackson gives me a cool nod. "Yeah. I'll take a look at it," he says dismissively.

I hate getting the dis on this. I mean, I'm a hacker through and through. I need to see the code, know what they were planning. Especially because it involves me. "May I see it?"

Jackson considers me for a moment. "You didn't look before you brought it over here?" Despite the fact we just shared the hottest and most intimate moment of my life upstairs, he's returned to Mr. All Business. His face could be carved out of granite.

I shake my head. "Want to look at it now?" I don't add the *together* that's on my lips.

"I want to look at it first," he says. "Alone."

Alarm bells go off. Did I make a mistake bringing this here? Not handling things on my own? Now my fate is in his hands, and I still don't know how he's going to play things. "I'm pretty good with hacks, too."

His eyes narrow. "So I recall." He looks at Sam. "My new employee turns out to be the only hacker who ever busted my code."

I can't figure out if he's still pissed or if I detect a note of admiration there.

"And she allegedly just received a blackmail letter asking her to install malware into our system in exchange for silence about her hacker identity."

Allegedly. The blow hits me like a hand grenade in the solar plexus. He doesn't believe me? Of course not. Why would he? Just because we both would like to get each other naked doesn't mean we should trust each other.

Except I do want to trust him. And it's probably just my misguided teen crush, but I desperately want Jackson to trust me back.

But hell, maybe his plan is to turn me over to the cops just as soon as he knows what he's dealing with.

~.~

Jackson

Kylie pales when I say she allegedly has been blackmailed. If not for the hurt I read on her face, I might have stayed on the fence about her. But it's so palpable, I swear I can scent it.

And then this new mate-driven part of me has to step closer and make up for wounding her. She's standing on opposite side of the island from Sam, who's eaten three packages of cold cuts since we've been standing here. I sidle next to her and give Sam a warning look about the meat. He immediately sweeps away the empty packages, dumping them in the trash, which, of course, only draws more attention to his carnivorous appetite.

"You were hungry," Kylie observes.

My wolf hearing detects the sound of her stomach grumbling. I don't want to feed her. Well, that's a lie, but I need to get her out of my house before I do something unforgivable to that hot little body of hers. She's standing in nothing but my sweatshirt, which looks incredibly hot, slipping off one shoulder. Knowing her bare pussy is just a hand-reach away has me balling my fists on the countertop.

"Are you hungry, Catgirl?"

She hesitates for a moment then shakes her head.

I cock my head, annoyed that she lied. If Sam wasn't standing there, I'd give her a second spanking for it. "Say it out loud," I say softly.

"What?"

"You're lying. I want to hear you say it out loud so I know how it sounds when you lie."

She flushes to her ears and, this time, I enjoy making her squirm. I've watched hundreds of employees or other wolves fidget under my dominance, but it's never turned me on like this. I want to strip her, tie her up, and interrogate her with a riding crop.

And that image is not helping me stay disengaged. At all.

But she rallies, lifting her chin. "I didn't come here to eat."

"Sam, get her something," I command. As soon as I say it, I realize it will sound off to her. Without the lens of pack dynamics, she'll see him exactly as the whipping boy she described in the elevator.

To make it worse, Sam flicks me a condemning look before he obeys. He pulls out a package of cold cuts, bread, and condiments and starts making a sandwich without asking what she likes.

It annoys me more than it should, but Kylie's stomach complains again, and she looks appreciatively at the food, so I figure it's okay.

"I'm going to take you home. You're going to come to work tomorrow, like nothing happened. Let me know if they make contact again," I tell her as Sam makes the sandwich.

She lets out an impatient puff of air, but lowers her chin. "Yes, sir."

My cock goes rock hard. Hearing those words, the same ones that normally annoy the hell out of me coming from kiss-ass employees, feels like a total win. This time I picture her on her knees at my feet, gazing up with those beautiful, gold-flecked eyes, waiting for my command.

Sam slides the plate across the counter to Kylie.

"Thank you, Sam." She picks it up and eats with enough gusto to satisfy the itchy part of me driven to tend to her comfort.

"You need me to do anything?" Sam asks.

"Bring her bicycle in from outside the gate and put it in the back of the Range Rover."

He nods and leaves, and I turn on Kylie. "If you say one goddamn word about him being my whipping boy, I'll bend you over and spank you again."

Her lips stretch into a wide smile, and she flicks the last crumb of sandwich from the corner of her mouth with her tongue. The flash of pink makes my cock surge again. I'm barely keeping it together with this girl.

"He's an adopted brother. I took him in as a homeless teen."

"Hmm." She takes another bite. "That's a fact that has never been reported about you."

"I don't owe the public any part of my private life."

"I'm good at keeping secrets—usually." She flushes again.

I arch a brow, trying to figure out what made her blush.

"For some reason, being around you is like drinking truth serum." She can't quite look me in the eye, and I find it so damn appealing, I reach for her, pulling her body up against mine with one arm around her waist and one hand behind her head.

"You'd better never lie to me, babygirl, or I'll make you very sorry."

Her breath catches, full lips part. The heady scent of her arousal wafts up and sets my wolf howling. Heat prickles my skin. "You like to punish." She sounds breathless. "I got that much right."

"You did."

Before tonight, I would have denied it, but I sure as hell enjoyed spanking her perfect ass. I nip her lips, tasting the sweetness there. With great effort, I pull away and cup her chin. "So, the truth. Who do you think left you the envelope?"

A line creases between her brows. "I don't know. That's why I want to see the code. I might recognize the style."

I nod. "Okay. Maybe tomorrow. After I take a look." I still don't trust her fully, and I need to look at the malware when I'm not distracted by her intoxicating presence. "Let's go."

I have to get this female back in her clothes and out of my house. Before I lose my mind completely.

~.~

Kylie

I don't want to ride home with Jackson, but I'm too exhausted for another long bike ride in the rain. The thing is—I don't like riding in other people's cars. I'm fine in my own. I know the exits and can control the vehicle. I can roll the windows down if I get itchy.

I'm relieved to see it's a Range Rover and not some tiny sports car. I climb in the passenger side and give him my address. I keep my hand on the door handle.

Jackson turns into Mr. Silent again, nearly giving me whiplash with the hot and cold thing. I *know* he's into me. Even as inexperienced as I am, I'm sure of it. But it's like he doesn't want to be. And it's not about trust, because he was like that even before he knew I'm Catgirl.

He pulls out of the gated driveway and onto the road. "What happened to you?" he asks softly.

I swivel my gaze to him, and he lifts his chin toward my white knuckles on the handle. "The confined spaces. Something happened." Without my asking, he cracks my window an inch, even though it's raining.

My throat closes. I've never talked about it, not even with Mémé. I'm not even sure I can. But Jackson is my truth serum.

"Yeah," I mumble. "Something happened." I close my eyes against the memory of the panic. The walls closing in on me, my shoulders compressed, head unable to lift, darkness all around.

He says nothing, and the space between us stretches like an invitation, a pool of *real* I could jump into if I only dared.

Can I? Be real with someone who isn't a family member?

No. My father's death proved you can't trust anyone but family. But my lips move anyway. "I got stuck in a tight space once. There was no one around to help, and it took me hours to get out." I'm gripping the door handle so hard I might tear it off.

Jackson reaches over and squeezes my hand. "I'm sorry

that happened to you. You're safe now, baby. You have your own exit. I'll pull over at a moment's notice if you needed to bail. Okay?"

Something tightens in my solar plexus as the torment of that particular trauma tries to come out. I suck in deep breaths. No fucking way I'm going to start bawling in Jackson King's car. Damn him for dragging this out of me.

"Hey." He releases my hand and contorts his arm to push on my solar plexus, the way he did in the elevator. "You're okay." He starts to pull over, and I shake my head.

"No. Keep driving. It isn't the car," I choke.

"Tell me the rest," he demands. His voice is hard, like he's suddenly furious. At what, I can't fathom.

I shake my head. "Drop it."

"Not going to happen. Tell me, or I'll pull over and help you, baby."

I had no idea what *help you* meant, but I didn't want this to be a big deal. "Something bad happened. Right before," I blurt.

His hand tightens on the steering wheel.

"Not what you're thinking." I realize he might be going with some sex abuse or child molestation thing because his face turned absolutely murderous.

"Not sexual." My throat works. "I saw a murder."

Murder. The word has a jagged edge to it that charges the confined space of the vehicle with danger. The danger I've been in ever since that night. "I had to stay hidden. And then, afterward, I couldn't find my way out. I guess shock confused me."

Jackson curses. "How old were you?"

"Sixteen." A year after I hacked SeCure and thought I was the smartest girl in the universe.

He eases the pressure off my sternum and slides his hand behind my head. "Thank you for telling me."

I roll the window all the way down and let the rain pelt my face, hiding the rogue tear that slipped out. Actually, unbelievably, I feel lighter. Like speaking the words freed the lock on the darkness I trapped in my chest eight years ago. It lifts from me, still hanging in the car, still sobering and depressing but less intense. I imagine it getting sucked out the window, back to the ether. Whatever ether is.

"I've never told anyone," I say finally, my voice slightly raspy from the withheld tears.

"Now you have."

A deep sense of comfort settles over me like a blanket. For the first time in years—since my mom died—I don't feel like I'm carrying the weight of the world on my shoulders. Alone. Someone shares my secret, and the world hasn't imploded.

Not yet, anyway.

Maybe I'll pay for this later. I lean my head back against the headrest, cooled by the splattering of rain, soothed by the shush of Jackson's wipers.

He pulls up in front of my house. "See you tomorrow."

For one moment, I consider running again. I've done the right thing by giving Jackson the thumb drive, but if things are going to get hot, if the blackmailers are going to call the FBI, it would be better for me to leave town.

Except the thought of *not* seeing Jackson tomorrow is too much. I push open the door and step out. "Yeah. See you tomorrow."

~.~

Jackson

I'm stunned by my need to protect Kylie. I want to slay every dragon that ever showed its teeth to her. To fix the wrong she suffered. And I must be crazy because, as soon as I get home, I research her, checking law enforcement and social work databases with her name and social security number. Not surprisingly, I find nothing.

The name and social she used on her employment application was probably falsified. A girl like her, a hacker of her caliber, would have the ability to create believable false identities. She could access any Department of Motor Vehicle, the Bureau of Vital Statistics. The power she could wield is stunning. And yet she never stole anything from my clients when she'd hacked SeCure. It was a game. She was just a kid.

Whatever her story, her life hasn't been easy. No teen walks away from witnessing murder without some scars.

I should know.

Not satisfied, I vow to keep digging until I find out exactly what happened to my little hacker. But, for now, I have something far more pressing to research. On a power-washed laptop I keep solely for testing code, I open the thumb drive and study the malware Kylie was supposed to infect SeCure with.

It doesn't make sense to me, so I start brainstorming what angle they're going for.

And wish I'd let Kylie stay so we could look at it together.

Tomorrow. In a public place where I'm less tempted to touch her. Tomorrow, we'll work on it together.

I don't question the rightness of the way that feels, because nothing about Kylie's effect on me makes sense.

Only Kylie. Kylie alone makes sense to me.

~.~

Kylie

The lights are on in the little house we rented near the university. I chose that locale because it's hip and there are plenty of restaurants and shops within walking distance. I always pick places where it's easy to blend in.

"Mémé?" I push open the door and then stop. Something feels off. Hairs prickling on the back of my neck, I step in, trying to identify what's different.

Nothing seems out of place.

"Mémé?" It comes out sharp, and I hope she's not in bed already.

I look around the kitchen and see unpacked grocery bags on the floor. Alarm bells go off full force.

My phone rings. I dig it out of my pocket and stare at the words *number blocked*. Normally, I would never answer, but something's not right, so I swipe the screen and put the phone to my ear. "Hello?"

"You did not follow our instructions." The voice is computer generated. A surge of anger rips through me.

"Fuck your instructions."

"We're fucking your grandmother. You should have done what you were told."

Ice floods my veins. I sway on my feet. "Mémé?" I scream, running through the house.

"Install the code, and you'll see the old lady again." The call ends before I can rip them a new one. I'm not sure what I would have said. Most likely, *I'm going to kill you motherfuckers!*

My hand shakes with fury as I race through the house again. Of course, I know it's fruitless. She's gone. They have her. And I have no choice but to bring down Jackson King's multi-billion dollar empire to get her back.

I want to retch. And scream. Mostly, I'd like to get my hands on whoever thought kidnapping an old lady was a good idea and ram a meat tenderizer down their throat.

5

Kylie

I'm sorry, Jackson.

My crush-induced idiotic decision to go straight to Jackson instead of getting the hell out of Dodge with Mémé last night has more than backfired.

I placed the one person I love, the only family member I have left, in terrible danger. I'll never forgive myself if something happens to her. So, despite the compelling moments I've had with Jackson King, despite my desire to make a genuine connection with him, to trust he could bridge the giant gap I'd set up between myself and the rest of the world, his company will be going down by my hand. Mémé is more important.

I have to get the thumb drive back from him without arousing suspicion. I decide to go with direct.

It's definitely a Chucks day. Wearing a short jean skirt, an anime T-shirt and my black sparkle Converse, I march into SeCure at 6:45 a.m. I figure it will be open, and I'm banking on Jackson being in early to stay on top of the threat. I take the stairs to the eighth floor.

The lights are off, doors locked. I plop down on the floor in front of Jackson's office, lean my back against his door, and pull out my personal laptop. I'm out of things to research—I stayed up all night trying to trace the blocked phone number from the threatening call to an IP address, but haven't locked it down yet.

How did they find me? I've been so careful, all these years.

The elevator dings. I look up from my screen, fingers still flying over the keyboard, seeking data strings.

Jackson stops when he sees me. "Couldn't sleep?"

I scramble up to my feet. "Nope. You?"

"Not at all."

"What'd you find?" I'm going with the *let's pretend we're allies and in this together* tactic. He lifts a brow to let me know I'm out of line. He's in charge, and we're not a team. "Sorry. Am I supposed to kiss your ass and call you Mr. King at work?"

"I liked when you called me *sir,*" he says, unlocking his door and stepping past me.

"I'll bet you did," I mutter, the memory of his dominant handling of me last night flooding back. I trail in behind him, making myself at home in his ginormous office by plopping down in a chair and pulling my laptop back out. "I brought my personal computer to load the malware. I'd like a chance to study it, if you're ready to let me take a look." Fear and necessity have brought back the old Kylie, the one capable of lying to anyone, even Jackson King, my personal kryptonite.

He ignores me, his face unreadable as he pulls out his own laptop and drops it into the docking station.

Too fidgety to sit there and wait for him to deem me worthy of answering, I ask, "Should I make the coffee?" He must have his own personal refreshment station on this floor.

He stops moving, his eyes lighter in the sunlight that streams in through his wall-to-wall windows. There's something predatory about the way he looks at me. Like my offer to make coffee turned him on. Well, maybe he has a master-slave fetish thing going. He gets off on being served. He definitely was bossy with Sam, his housemate.

"Cream, no sugar."

"Where is it?"

"Around the corner to the right. You'll find it."

Funny, but I might have the flip side of the same fetish because it turns me on to fetch his coffee.

Grateful for the expenditure of the manic energy that's ruling me, I slip out of his office and make the coffee. It's freshly ground beans from Peet's, and there's real half and half in the fridge below. I make myself a cup, too, and head back, just as his secretary arrives.

If looks could kill, I'd be in twenty pieces on the floor.

"Don't worry about his coffee," I say breezily. "I already got it."

She gives me the up-and-down sweep of the eyes, her lip curling when she sees my sneakers.

I flash my brightest smile as I head into Jackson's office. "Your coffee, sir." I walk around to his side of the desk and stand too close as I lean over like a sex kitten to deliver it.

His secretary gapes in the doorway.

"Watch it, kitten, or I'll punish you here, too," he growls in an undertone.

"What?" I ask innocently.

"Cancel all my appointments and close the door,

Vanessa. We have a situation to deal with here," he says to his secretary as he opens his desk and pulls out a wooden ruler. He lays it on the desk between us, shooting me a meaningful look.

Despite it all—despite the lack of sleep and worrying sick over Mémé, despite my daunting task of getting the thumb drive and hacking into SeCure's system within the next twelve hours, a charge of pure sexual desire runs through me.

Hell, yes, he can spank me again.

He's going to want to do far worse when he realizes what I'm going to do. And that thought sobers the lust right out of me.

I hold out my palm. "Thumb drive?"

I'm really not sure he's going to hand it to me, but, after a moment, he pulls it out of his pocket and tosses it in the air.

I snatch it, and he smiles at my quick reflexes.

"You'll stay in my office while you work on it." He lifts his chin toward the chair across from him.

Shit. How in the hell am I supposed to hack into SeCure and load the damn malware while sitting in his office working on a computer that's not linked into the system?

I settle into a chair and plug in the thumb drive. It's a sophisticated program, and I'm not entirely sure how it works, but I can't concentrate on figuring it out. Instead, I'm reviewing everything I learned about hacking SeCure eight years ago. Of course, I know nothing will be the same this time.

Fuck, I've only been on the job a few days. How do they expect me to get this installed? I haven't been given security access to anything yet. Unless...

What are the chances of getting on boss man's computer? Here I am, sitting in his office. If he's logged onto the system, I can grab his password, or maybe even load the code from his computer. The man will have to use the restroom at some point, right? Or leave for lunch?

My heart pounds as I contemplate the treachery, and Jackson looks up, like he hears the rampaging beat.

I keep my head down, as if I'm studying really hard.

I'll have to make a run for it the moment I finish, or else I'll be leaving in handcuffs. I consider the exits. Stairwell leads to the back of the building. I might make it to my car.

And then where do I go?

The asshole blackmailers didn't even tell me how to get in touch. How will I get Mémé back?

A terrible, horrible fear strikes me like an electric shock to the spine. *What if they don't intend to give her back?* What if she's already dead, her body lying in the desert somewhere? I should've demanded to hear her voice. What in the hell is wrong with me?

Once I load the malware, I'll have no leverage whatsoever. Mémé and I will both be expendable. I'll take the fall for the attack, and Mémé dies.

"What?" Jackson's voice cuts across the office.

I jerk my head up to find him staring a hole through me. His nostrils are flaring like he smells something distasteful.

My heart pounds harder. Did I say something out loud?

"I sense your agitation. What did you find in the code? Do you know who did it?"

Jesus, he *senses my agitation?* No wonder this man built a multi-billion dollar company out of nothing but a laptop. And I'd always thought he was socially stunted. Maybe he stays away from people because he can read them all too well, and they bore him.

My mind races for something to give him. "I-I think I was set up."

His lip lifts with scorn. "I thought we knew that part."

"I mean from the inside. How did I get this job? A headhunter called me out of the blue. I never saw it posted anywhere. Never applied to SeCure."

Jackson pales, and I swear his eyes change to blue again. He stands up with a grim expression. "I'll be right back." He walks out the door, shutting it behind him.

I count to five, steadying my breath. Then I walk swiftly to Jackson's desk and sit in his seat.

I learned in my heist days to disconnect fear when on a job. Time was always of the essence, and, if you lost your head, the job was as good as over. I learned to dive into a black hole of concentration. I focus on nothing but the task at hand. That's the headspace I find now, my vision narrowing to the prompts on the screen as I sift through login screens to pull Jackson's password. I find twenty, with no discernable pattern. He must have a different one for every login. Smart man.

I work to get through the firewall and into the infosec code. I do not allow myself to think of what will happen if Jackson comes back before I've succeeded. Or if I can't get in. Or if they don't let Mémé go.

I only see the characters on a screen. A puzzle to solve.

Sixteen minutes later, I'm in.

No time to celebrate. I grab the thumb drive and insert it into his port.

I'm sorry, Jackson. I'm so fucking sorry.

It auto-launches, code unfolding before my eyes with lightning speed.

I get up from his chair, pick up my things, and walk swiftly out. I don't acknowledge his secretary. I travel down the hall, like I'm headed for the bathroom, and slip into the stairwell.

Eight stories. Then a parking lot, and I'll be in my car.

Except I already know I've been had. They're not letting Mémé go. How could they frame me if an old lady is telling a story about being kidnapped?

So I just committed another felony act and destroyed the only company I've ever admired for nothing.

Worse—I've destroyed whatever I had going with Jackson King. And that...that almost hurts as much as the thought of Mémé being dead.

~.~

Jackson

The way I see it, this attack had to come from someone in my infosec department.

Unfortunately, that narrows it down to 517 people, located all over the world. Only 137 of them are in this building. But I can start with Luis, my CSO, and Human Resources, to get some answers about Kylie's hire.

I head straight to Luis' office and barge in without knocking. He's on the phone, with his wife, probably, because I can hear the female voice on the line, telling some long, drawn-out story.

Luis sits up straight, giving me an attentive look as he tries to interrupt the monologue. "I'm sorry, honey. Mr. King just stepped into my office."

"Oh! Okay, call me later," she says quickly.

"Yep." He hangs up and gives me a sheepish look. "My wife is all worked up about getting our kid into the school talent show."

I have to hand it to Luis. After all these years of me stonewalling all personal discussion, he still makes the attempt. It's like he wants me to remember he has a family and is human, so I don't ask too much of him.

Not that it ever stops me.

"What did you find out about the new hire in infosec?" I ask.

Luis' brow wrinkles. "Kylie McDaniel? What do you mean?"

"I asked you to look into where we found her. Who vetted her? How long was this position open?"

"We always have open positions. You asked me to double our infosec team three years ago, and I've been working on it. It's hard to find new hires. It takes an average of three months to fill a position."

"And this position was posted?"

"It's not posted, no. We use a headhunter. It mitigates wasted time sifting through unqualified applicants. She's been actively searching for candidates for the last year."

"And how did she find Kylie?"

Luis shrugs. "I'm sorry. I haven't looked into it. It's well known the hacker boards are tapped for these jobs. It makes sense to hire from the pool of those who truly understand what we deal with. We make special exceptions for candidates like Kylie. For example, the official job requirements demand twenty to twenty-five years in the field. But her demonstrated skills, based on the test Stu administered, are used in lieu of the years of experience."

It all makes perfect sense and even sounds plausible. But, Kylie was right. It was too much of a coincidence that she was sent the blackmail note immediately after starting with SeCure. If the hackers were looking for an in, it would have taken them longer than a few days to identify and get the dirt on each employee.

This looked like a first-class frame to me.

"I'd like the name and number of the headhunter."

"Is something wrong, sir? I thought you liked the girl, despite her cheekiness."

"It doesn't matter whether I like her or not. I want to know more about the headhunting practices used to fill the most sensitive positions at my company," I snap, using my most authoritative voice.

Luis instantly puts on his calm, placating face. "Of course, sir. I understand. I will call HR right now and get you the information." He picks up his phone.

"Never mind," I say. "I'll go there myself." I need to see people's eyes, be close enough to smell their fear when I interrogate them. I head out, striding purposefully to the elevator and ride down to the fourth floor to see the director of HR.

I get no further with her, other than receiving the name and number of the headhunter.

By this time, my wolf is scratching at the surface, telling me something about Kylie. I'm itchy to see her. Needy almost.

Damn. Is it possible for a shifter's true mate to be human? Because there's no other explanation for the way I feel.

Unless it's just my instinct warning about her potential danger to me.

With that thought, I take the stairs two at a time back to my office, unwilling to stand quietly in an elevator. Her scent is everywhere, filling my nose as if she's in the stairwell with me.

I get to my office and fling open the door.

My computer is open, and a program is scrolling quickly over the screen.

Oh shit.

My heart chokes me, stuck somewhere between my collarbone and my throat. My palms go clammy; my vision tunnels with rage.

Tell me it's not what I think it is. Tell me—

Fuck!

With a roar, I pick up my laptop and throw it against the wall, shattering it into a million pieces.

"Mr. King!" Vanessa runs into the office.

"How long ago did she leave?" I'm surprised how calm I sound.

"Oh! Um... about ten minutes, sir. Why? What happened? Sir? Is something wrong?"

I ignore her and run past Vanessa.

The stairwell.

The fucking stairwell. No wonder I thought I smelled her in it. That's how she got away.

~.~

Kylie

I make it to my car and peel out of the parking lot. I head in the direction of downtown, but I have no idea where to go.

The cops will look for me at home. It's time to bail. I've done this at least twenty times. I know how to erase my existence and put up a new one in another city. Another country, even. But I'll be damned if I'll leave Tucson without Mémé.

So, I just need somewhere to lie low. To wait for the blackmailers' phone call that I fear isn't coming.

I drive to Bank of America, where I have a safety deposit box. Maybe I can get in before the FBI puts an alert on anything to do with my present social security number. I walk briskly into the bank, tugging the hem of my T-shirt down, wishing I'd worn the heels today.

I withdraw all my savings in cash, give them my ID, and ask to have my safety deposit box. They send me to an office to wait. Three minutes go by. Five.

Please let this one thing go right for me.

The overweight manager with a nineties hairstyle returns with the box.

Thank God.

I open it and take everything out. I have passports and IDs in there, along with more emergency cash. I put on my most businesslike demeanor and resist the urge to stuff everything into my purse and run. I keep my movements clean and crisp. Not a wasted gesture or moment, while maintaining the cool, calm, and collected exterior necessary to avoid suspicion.

"Thank you very much," I say to the bank manager with a bright smile. As I head out, I nearly crumble.

If I run now, I will be utterly alone. No Mémé. No friends. No chance of maintaining the normal lifestyle I'd adopted.

But, if I stay, I'll end up in federal prison. Instead of getting in my car, I start walking. Downtown Tucson is small, but there are people everywhere, and I fit in. I hoof it up Congress Street, not heading in any particular direction, just needing to move. To think.

My phone remains agonizingly quiet. Surely the blackmailers know by now the code has been installed.

So, yeah. They have no intention of setting Mémé free.

I find a cafe and pull out my laptop to work once more on tracing the phone call I received the night before. Just having something familiar to do lowers my stress level. I work the rest of the day without luck. By the time the windows darken and the barista is giving me dirty looks, I know there's no hope.

They're not going to call.

I'm somewhat surprised someone from SeCure or the FBI hasn't at least tried to ring my phone, not that I'd answer it.

I leave the cafe and walk back to my car. It's not surrounded by cop cars or impounded, but I walk by it, anyway. Not worth the risk. Instead, I call Uber and use a dummy account to take me to a cheap hotel off the I-10 frontage road. I book a room with my new identity and credit card.

In the hotel room, I kick off my shoes and sit on the bed with my best and only friend, my laptop.

Think, K-K, think.

What do I do now? Drive out of town? Get on a plane out of the country? What can be done about Mémé?

I'm a smart woman, but no answers come to me. I draw my knees up to my chest and rock back and forth.

~.~

Jackson

I squeeze my temples with one hand as the other moves over my keyboard. It's four a.m.

Every employee in infosec and myself have been working all day and night to isolate the fucking malware, but it's gone everywhere. I implemented emergency measures of transferring the financial data of millions of users to new secure servers, but I doubt we are quick enough. They probably already have enough to do major damage. I still don't even know what they're after. This seems bigger than getting at the credit card data. There would be easier hacks than SeCure if that's all they wanted.

"Tell everyone in the department no one's going home tonight until we have the transfer complete," I snap at Luis. "And if anyone breathes a word of what we're dealing with here, I'll have their ass. Understand?"

"I've already told them," Luis says with his infinite patience. "At what point are we getting the FBI involved?"

"Not until we have this entire situation managed. I don't even want the rest of the executive team to hear about this until it's contained."

Luis looks doubtful, but nods. "Yes, sir."

My directive makes perfect sense. We're sitting on an emergency of epic proportions. If word of it gets out to the press, SeCure's stock will plummet, and the nation's populace will turn frantic about their money and information being stolen.

But I have another reason for refusing to involve law enforcement.

I want to deal with Kylie McDaniel personally. She betrayed me, and I need to look in her eyes and understand how I made such a mistake. I need to make sure it never happens again.

And, there's something else. Something I don't even want to admit is a motivator, but it is.

Kylie wouldn't survive in jail.

She's claustrophobic. It would kill her.

So I'd rather take wolf justice on this one. Find Kylie and make her pay the traditional way. Punishment and repayment.

She *will* fix this.

Even if I have to keep her my prisoner until she does.

"Do we know how they got through, yet, sir? Do you suspect the new hire? I heard she disappeared today."

"I'll deal with the people behind this. You stay focused on containing the disaster."

"Yes, sir."

"You stay here and supervise. I'm going to find who did this and make them pay." The predator in me needs to hunt my prey. I have to find Kylie.

Luis must see the fierceness of my wolf because he pales and bobs his head. "Yes, sir."

6

Jackson

The hairs on the back of my neck stand up as I walk to the Range Rover in the solar panel-covered parking. I lift my nose to the air and sniff, but all I smell is the cool spring air of the desert.

The moon beckons me, makes me itchy to shift and hunt for Kylie.

I reach the vehicle and stop.

A dark head is visible in the passenger seat of my car. I know immediately it's her.

My body surges into emergency mode, the shift upon me. I don't know what to think—someone's murdered her and put her in there. Or that she's waiting to kill me. Or she's committed suicide and left her body for me to find.

I know it's Kylie, and getting to her is a goddamn emergency. I rip open the door.

She's not dead. She's not even hurt. And she's not holding a gun.

All I find is a pale, tear-streaked face punctuated by huge, miserable eyes.

Relief and fury simultaneously flood my veins. I haul her out of the car by her wrists and slam the door.

I don't smell fear on her, but she's docile, like she knows she deserves my wrath. Obviously she's delivered herself to me, which makes no sense logically, but the wolf in me approves.

"Kitten, you have to be crazy showing up here tonight."

A single tear tracks down her face. She bites her lip and nods. "Yeah. I'm crazy."

"You have thirty seconds to explain yourself." I don't expect her to have an explanation—I can't fathom anything that would possibly excuse her behavior, but I need to hear what she has to say.

"When I got home last night, my grandmother was gone. They'd taken her." More tears well up in her beautiful eyes, and the scent of them does something to my wolf. Every cell in my body screams at me to protect her, to fix whatever has made her cry. "They called, and a computer-generated voice said I should have done what they instructed me to do." Two more tears track down her cheeks.

I'm ready to tear these fuckers apart with my teeth. I wouldn't even need to shift to do it.

"Mémé is all I have. Stupid me. I thought they'd give her back if I installed the code. But, I'm sure she's dead. I've been perfectly set up to take the fall for ruining SeCure. I'm sorry, Jackson. I screwed you, but I'll do anything to help you fix it. I know you have no reason to believe me. I know you have even less to trust me. But I'm here. I'm offering myself up to you." She holds her wrists out like I have handcuffs. "Call the cops, if you want. But you know I'm more useful to you outside of jail. And I sure as hell want to make them pay for what they've done to—" Her face crumples, and I'm helpless to do anything but pull her against my chest.

The rightness of her body against mine soothes the wolf. "She may not be dead."

Kylie bunches my button-down shirt in her fists as her tears wet it. "Why would they keep her?" she chokes.

The scent of her anguish fucking slays me. She's right. Her grandmother probably *is* dead.

"Get in the car," I say, more gruffly than I mean to. I throw open the door. "You're my prisoner until we figure this out. You won't leave the mansion. You won't do anything but eat, sleep, and trace this fucking code to shut it down. Got it?"

She nods and slides into the passenger seat. "Yes, sir," she whispers. She sounds so forlorn and lost, but my wolf still takes her deference as a win.

Mine.

She came back to me. Mine to handle. Mine to punish.

Mine.

~.~

Kylie

Jackson doesn't speak as he drives to his mansion. I can't believe he didn't wrap a fist around my neck and squeeze. Or call the cops.

He's angry, still. I sense his fury, simmering underneath the tightly-leashed control. But it didn't stop him from wrapping me up in his arms and letting me cry on his shirt.

I was right to stay in town. It's the first right decision I've made in a long time.

I've never trusted anyone but family before, but something about Jackson King keeps me coming back, checking my insecurities at the door, and offering myself up on a silver platter. It's crazy.

Because he truly holds my life in his hands now. It would have been so easy for him to turn me over to the police. They could make an ironclad case against me. And maybe he still will, after I help him quarantine the infected data.

But, somehow, I don't think so. Jackson feels like safety to me. Like home. The opposite of the utter loneliness I experienced walking down Congress Street contemplating my future.

"Thanks," I say hoarsely.

He turns his serious gaze on me. "I'm glad you came back."

"Do you believe me?"

"Against my better judgment, yes. I do."

I settle back against the seat, exhausted, but relieved. "I'll do anything to help. I won't rest until I've fixed it. Okay? I promise."

He reaches over and brushes my cheek. "I will help you, too, kitten. I'll hire a private investigator tomorrow to look into your grandmother's disappearance."

It's a sweet gesture, but I doubt a PI will be able to find anything a hacker couldn't. Still, tears of gratitude leak from the corners of my eyes.

Jackson's nostrils flare, and his glance shifts from the road to my face. He rubs away one of the tears with a knuckle. "Tell me about your grandmother. She lives in Tucson?"

I draw in a steadying breath. "We moved here together. We live together. I've been living with her since—" I stop because I've already told him too much about myself. I don't want him to piece it all together.

"Since when?" he asks sharply, like he already knows.

"Since my parents died. She's all the family I have. Had," I modify, my stomach lurching.

"Is she dead, kitten? Do you know it in your gut? Reach beyond the fear. Yes or no?"

No.

Relief slips around me like a blanket. "I don't think so," I croak. I'm fascinated by Jackson's reliance on gut instinct over logic. A man with a brain like his? If he trusts it, so do I.

Jackson gives a single nod. "Then we need to crack this code and find her."

I square my shoulders, the mantle of purpose returning. My brain launches into dissecting what I've seen of the malware. I pull out my computer. "Mind if I work in the car?"

"I'd be pissed if you didn't."

We drive another ten minutes in silence with me studying the unlaunched code I copied from the thumb drive earlier. When we reach Jackson's mansion, the automatic gate swings open, and he pulls into the drive. I snap my laptop closed and shove it in my bag, looking up at the house.

Jackson's black wolf dog stands on the step looking down at us as the car rolls past. His greeting lacks the waggy-tailed joy of a normal pet. There's an aloofness to it, an eerie quality that makes the hairs on the back of my neck stand up.

"I'm not sure wolves should be kept as pets," I mutter as he pulls into the garage.

Jackson arches a brow. "I won't let him hurt you."

I won't let him hurt you is quite different from *he won't hurt you.* The capacity to maim or wound is definitely there.

"What's his name?"

Jackson hesitates, like his dog doesn't have a name, or he doesn't remember it. "Wolf," he says finally.

"Wolf? That's original."

"Keep up the sass, kitten, and I'll add to your punishment."

A shiver runs through me, although I don't think it's fear. "Punishment?" I give myself a mental high five for saying the word without my voice quavering.

"Mmm hmm. But we'll deal with that later. Right now, we have work to do."

We get out of the car and enter through a laundry room and into the kitchen. Wolf meets us there. He bares his teeth at me, growling. He's even more frightening in full light. He stands as high as my waist, and the black fur at his nape is ruffled with anger, amber eyes staring right at me.

"Enough." Jackson doesn't sound nearly as worried as he should, as far as I'm concerned.

I freeze. "I don't think he likes me much."

Jackson prods my back from the door, still unconcerned. "He's just protective." To the dog, he says, "Kylie's staying with us. You'll be watching over her, got it?" He bats Wolf's muzzle away, and the dog turns and slinks out of the kitchen.

I exhale a shaky breath. "Tell me again why you have a wolf for a pet?"

Jackson ignores my question. "Come on. I'll take you to your room."

I push back the disappointment that I have my own room. But what did I think? Jackson would take me into his bed and cuddle me after what I did to his company?

A blow like this may not end SeCure but even if we isolate the potential damage, a loss in reputation may eventually undermine the entire company's well-being. Even with my help cleaning up, the damage will persist.

I follow him up the stairs.

Jackson leads me to a guest bedroom and switches on a light. The room is tastefully appointed, but, like the rest of the house, lacks any personal touches. I have a feeling he hired a decorator. "You'll stay in here. I'm going to catch a few hours of sleep before I have to get back to the office."

"I'll stay up," I say immediately. There's no way I can rest, especially now that I believe my work can help recover Mémé. I pull my laptop out again. "I need into your system, please. To know how this thing works and spreads. And I need to know what your team is doing to contain it."

He cocks a brow. "Thought you'd already hacked it. But, no, you went the easy route and used my computer. I must be the biggest idiot on Earth to have left you alone in my office."

He's already leaning over me, punching in the password for his Wi-Fi then logging me into SeCure. He smells divine. Like pine trees and...masculine strength. Yeah, I know that's not a smell. But that's what his scent evokes.

"No, you weren't an idiot. You thought you could trust me. I'm going to make it up to you."

He cups my chin and lifts my face. "I love it when you grovel, kitten."

A flush spreads across my chest and up my neck. "I'll bet you do," I say drily, blushing further when I remember I have a punishment coming.

What will it be this time? Another spanking? I hope it's something...even more intense.

He explains the orders he's given his infosec team for

quarantining and moving SeCure's data. His plan sounds solid to me. "It looks like they have it well in hand, so I'll work on tracing the malware back to its source."

"Good." He drops a kiss on the top of my head. "Wake me up at seven a.m. if I'm not already up."

OMG. I'm playing house with Jackson King. The directive goes straight to my naughty parts as I imagine pulling the sheets off his naked body and arousing him.

Mind out of the gutter, K-K. There's work to be done.

7

Jackson

I wake up with my fangs dropped and Kylie's scent in my nostrils. No wonder I dreamed about owning her hot little body the entire two hours I slept. I must have marked her in every position in my sleep. I shouldn't feel rested, but the sexual frustration pumps me with energy.

Claim. Mate. Mark.

My wolf fucking *loves* that she's in my house. I force myself to get in the shower with the spray on ice cold so I won't go hunt her.

It doesn't help. I'm still ready to dominate her when I get out. Chase her up a rocky mountain, knock her to the ground, and sink my teeth so deep into her flesh, she'll scream...

Yeah, and that would kill her. She'd be screaming, all right, and it wouldn't be *yes, Jackson.*

I skip the suit and tie today, opting for a button-down and khakis. My employees have been up all night working, I don't need to show anyone up.

Kylie's scent hits me hard the moment I walk out of my room. My cock swells against the zipper of my pants. I find her in her room, still working.

She has a pen stuck in a messy bun on top of her head and looks no less beautiful for not having slept all night. If anything, the sight of her up, working hard for me—for the benefit of my company—sends a fresh kick of lust rocketing through me. Of course she's not doing it for *me*, she's doing it for her grandmother, but the wolf doesn't care about that.

All wolves need to dominate their females, but I never knew how turned on I would be by having one under my paw, so to speak. At the same time, the urge to take care of her rises up strongly. "Good morning. Are you hungry, kitten? I should have told you to help yourself to anything in the kitchen."

She flashes an easy smile, the kind that has no intent behind it but could topple nations. "Oh, I would have. I was about to go in search of coffee."

"Find anything?"

"It's a complex sequence. There's something familiar about the style, but I can't put my finger on it. I've been cross-checking old posts on the DefCon board but so far I haven't figured it out. Your employees have all your data secure now, but I'm guessing the blackmailers had access to at least 250,000 records before you got it quarantined."

I've already heard the same thing from Luis and Stu, but it's good to know my little genius concurs.

"Come on, let's get you some breakfast. Your body needs fuel after staying up all night."

Damn. Why am I talking about her body? It's a torture enough to me without mentioning it.

"I'll be down in a minute." She taps her finger against the edge of her screen as she reads.

Downstairs, I find Sam sitting at the breakfast counter. Apparently, none of us slept much last night.

"What's going on?" he demands the minute I walk in. I called him when I stayed late last night, and told him what Kylie had done, so my showing up with her in the wee hours of the morning must've seemed incongruous.

"The blackmailers kidnapped her grandmother. She turned herself in to me. We're working on getting a trace on the code to find any clues."

Sam shakes his head, his mouth screwed into a judgmental ring. "I don't like it. You're not acting right, Jackson. She's a fucking *human*. Why in the hell did you bring her here?"

A growl erupts from my throat, the wolf in me ready to defend my chosen mate to the death.

Sam's jaw goes slack as he stares. "Are you fucking kidding me?"

"What?" I ask tightly.

"You do realize she's triggered your mating instinct?"

I ignore him and pull out a carton of eggs, then break them into a bowl. "I need you to stay here and keep an eye on her. Don't let her leave the mansion under any circumstances."

Sam doesn't answer, which forces me to look over. He watches me with narrowed eyes.

"And don't hurt her."

"I'm to hold her prisoner here, but I'm not allowed to hurt her." His tone drips with doubt.

Another growl erupts from my throat, but I manage to cut it off as my wolf senses detect Kylie coming down the stairs. She shouldn't have been able to hear our conversation, but, when she enters, her expression is sharp.

"So Sam's my keeper?" she asks brightly.

I purse my lips. *Damn.* She has superhuman hearing. I need to remember that. "Right. I forbid you to leave the house while I'm gone."

"You *forbid* it." Her tone matches Sam's perfectly with the doubt-infusion.

I arch a brow. "You have a problem with that?"

"You're the boss." She shrugs.

Damn right.

"House arrest with Sam. I can't think of anything more fun."

"Watch the sarcasm, kitten," I say, but my wolf isn't happy. I can't fucking stand her using the word *with* and another male's name, even if it is by my orders.

She peers into the bowl of eggs. "Whatcha making?"

My innate sense of confidence wanes, the need to please my female, to feed her, swelling in importance. "I was thinking about french toast. Does that sound okay?" Fates, I don't even recognize myself. When do I ever ask anyone if something is okay?

She flashes that picture-perfect smile, and the wolf relaxes. "Sounds great. Thanks. Is there coffee?" She looks around.

"Help yourself." Sam points to the full pot.

I'm simultaneously grateful to Sam for making it and pissed that he gets to offer it to her.

She pulls down two mugs and fishes the half and half out of the refrigerator. She hands me a full mug. "Cream, no sugar, right, boss?" Her husky tone, along with her act of service, sends desire kicking through me.

Mate her.

I want her here every morning, making me coffee while I cook her eggs. I want to watch those gold-flecked eyes peeking over the top of her mug as she tells me something brilliant. I want to earn that easy smile by saying something humorous.

Record scratch. I'm not a funny guy. I never say anything humorous. Except I had in the elevator. I'd made her laugh then. Around her, I turn into someone else. Someone better.

You're not the bad guy.

I dip four pieces of cinnamon raisin bread in the egg batter and drop them onto a heated skillet doused with melted butter.

"I'm going to head into the office after we eat. I want hourly updates. Unless you're sleeping." I whirl around to pin her with my sternest look. "You do plan on getting some sleep?"

She lifts her mug of coffee in the air. "Not for a while. Don't worry. I do my best work when I'm half-delirious."

"Not on my watch. You need rest."

She rolls her eyes, and I smack her bottom as she passes by. My cock hardens at her yelp.

Sam stares out the window like he's never seen such a fascinating view.

"Come on, boss, I need to work. Please." Her begging melts me. "I prefer catnaps to a solid eight hours anyway. "

I flip the french toast, delirious with the need to know if that's true. I want to know every single detail about this woman. *Need* to.

I pull out my cell phone and hand it to her. "Give me your number." She scrolls to my contacts and adds herself with remarkable speed as I plate the french toast and pull the maple syrup from the refrigerator.

I see she's entered herself as "Catgirl," and it makes me smile. "What's your real name, kitten?"

She tenses, and her hesitation wounds me more than I care to admit.

"Why is it a secret?" I ask softly. "Because of the murder you saw?"

She pales, and I immediately regret pushing her, but, if she's in danger, I have to know. The need to protect her from any and all her enemies is a tearing, consuming beast in me.

"Yeah." She picks up a plate of french toast and butters them.

Sam must finally realize he's a third wheel, because he stands from his perch at the breakfast bar. "Holler if you need me. I'll be around the house, Catgirl."

"I don't think he likes me, either," Kylie says after he leaves. She doesn't know Sam can still hear every word.

"He's just protective. What do you mean, *either*?"

"Like Wolf. Your monster-sized dog." She forks a piece of french toast, and a low rumble, almost like a purr, rises in my chest. I like feeding her. Too damn much. "Where is he, by the way?"

"He's probably out. He needs a lot of space to roam." *Not a lie.*

"Okay, so I'm your prisoner, and Sam's my keeper." She takes another bite, her tongue flicking out to catch a bit of powdered sugar, and I almost groan. "I'm to update you every hour. Any other orders?"

Jesus, I get so hard when she plays submissive with me. And, believe me, I know it's play—a choice, not her personality. The girl is all alpha if I've ever met one. An alpha female who only submits to her male.

A tug of longing pulls at my chest. I finally meet a female who interests me—both sides of me—human and wolf—and she's human. Fragile. Unable to withstand a marking.

How will I keep her? I have to.

~.~

Kylie

The food and the coffee help. I spend the morning breaking into the FBI's system to get all their files on known hackers. The malware used to infect SeCure wasn't the most sophisticated thing I've ever seen. Which is good—it enabled Jackson to contain the threat. The downside is I have to look for the suspects in a much larger pool.

Jackson messages me to say that he hasn't hired a private investigator because he doesn't trust anyone not to fuck with me, but he's working on a plan.

By noon, I'm nauseous from lack of sleep, but now I'm so wound up from the coffee and adrenaline, I doubt I'll be able to rest. I get up to stretch my legs and wander through the upstairs rooms. I haven't heard Sam—my guess is that his room is somewhere downstairs.

I'm drawn to search Jackson's room. Hackers are by nature stalkers, and I'm dying to know more about my crush.

I tap lightly at a closed door and push it open. *Bingo.*

The large master suite must belong to Jackson. I pick up his scent, and it calms my over-wired system immediately. I've always had an overdeveloped sense of smell. My dad used to tease me about it.

Like the rest of the house, the room is elegant but simple. There isn't much to look at, but I wander around, peering on the dresser top at his loose change, checking the wastepaper basket for anything interesting, but there's nothing.

"What are you doing?"

I gasp and jump, my overtaxed system nearly sending me into cardiac arrest. "Jesus, Sam. You scared me."

His eyes narrow. He doesn't look like the kind of guy to

tangle with. He may be lean and wiry, but the tattoos decorate hard muscles, and the piercings give him a don't-fuck-with-me vibe. I remember Jackson had to give him the directive, *don't hurt her.* Kinda like his wolf-dog, the violence is there, right below the surface.

I go for the truth. "I'm snooping. Trying to understand Jackson better."

Sam gives a quick shake of his head. "His secrets aren't for you to unwrap, Catgirl."

I like that he calls me *Catgirl.* The name still has a power to it, evokes the invincible teen I once was. *Before.*

I lean a hip against the dresser, holding my ground. "So there are secrets?"

Sam folds his arms across his chest and leans against the doorframe. "Everyone has secrets."

I try a different tack. "I never wanted to hurt him. I'm here to fix things, not make them worse."

"Your being here definitely makes things worse."

Now it's my turn to narrow my eyes. "What's your problem with me?"

"Look, I can tell there's something special about you. Jackson wouldn't be interested, otherwise. But he can't be with you—it's not going to work. And your being in this house is going to be a problem for him."

I turn his words over in my head, but they don't make sense. The only thing I can come up with is that he and Jackson are a couple and he's warning me off.

"Is he gay?"

Sam's brows twist in puzzlement. "*No.* What makes you think that?"

"I was just trying to figure out if you and he—"

Sam laughs. "No. I told you, he's my brother."

Relief floods me. *Down, girl. He's still not yours.* "How did you meet?"

Sam's face sags and, for a moment, he looks thirty years older, weary from whatever happened in his young life. "I was wandering in the Santa Cruz mountains, lost, and he found me."

"What were you doing in the mountains?" I picture a lost Boy Scout, but it doesn't fit.

"I was a runaway. Figured I could survive there on my own. But I was starving. Half-crazy—I'd been alone so long."

"How long?"

He shrugs. "I don't know. A few months, maybe. Jackson saw me, and I ran. He chased me down. I fought him. I didn't want to return to civilization, but he forced me to come back with him. Promised not to tell anyone he'd found me."

A rush of sympathy floods my chest. Sam's been in hiding, like me. Someone out there wants something from him. An abusive family, probably. He's right. We all have secrets.

"How long ago was that?"

"Seven years. I was fourteen."

"I'm glad he found you. And I won't tell anyone."

"I'm not worried anymore," he says. "But, thanks." A reluctant smile tugs at his lips, and he steps toward me, holding out his fist. I bump it and follow him out of the room, glad to have unearthed another small piece of the Jackson puzzle.

~.~

Jackson

When I get home, I find Kylie crashed out on the sofa, her open laptop tilted against her chest.

Sam's in the kitchen, eating a stack of ten hamburgers. I pick one up and take a bite. "How long has she been like that?"

"Couple hours," Sam says with his mouth full. "I found her snooping in your bedroom. She said she wanted to know your secrets."

A niggling sense of worry tickles me. What if I'm still being played by this girl? But that didn't make sense—what more could she want or need? She'd already done enough damage to bring me down.

No, hackers have boundary issues. They get an inflated sense of power. They can spy on anyone and anything. Read emails, cancel credit cards. Check high school grades. Kylie's snooping around my room was an extension of that. She hasn't been able to hack me personally because there's nothing to find. She's not the only one who knows how to create or erase an identity.

"What's your plan with her? You can't keep her here forever."

I stab my fingers through my hair. "I don't know," I answer honestly.

"You *can't*. Keep her here," Sam repeats.

"Why the fuck not?" I snap, even though I know he's right.

He raises his brows. "You planning to mate her?"

I scowl. We both know that's not possible. A werewolf bite to a human could kill her. Would cause serious scarring and damage, at the least. And that's assuming Kylie's willing. Which would mean telling her—a clear violation of pack rules. And if I tell her and we don't mate, she'll have to be eliminated. Pack rules. Or have her mind erased by a vampire. I can't risk either of those things happening to her.

So, yeah. Sam's right. I can't keep her here.

But I sure as fuck can't let her go, either.

"Just until this blows over," I promise.

Sam's pursed lips tell me he knows it's a lie. "You know what happens to a wolf who ignores his mating instinct?"

Nausea twists in the pit of my stomach. *Moon sickness.* "That's not what's happening here. She can't be my fated mate—she's human."

Sam shrugs. "I realize that, but you're acting like a male ready to mark. And the moon is full tomorrow."

"I have the situation under control." *And pigs fly.*

Sam polishes off his fifth hamburger and shoves the plate of remaining burgers my way. "I'll see you. I'm working at the club tonight." He sometimes works as a bouncer at Eclipse, Garrett's nightclub.

Don't rush home.

My wolf wants Kylie alone. Which is probably the worst idea ever.

~.~

Kylie

I wake to the sound of Sam's motorcycle pulling away and Jackson's angry voice from the kitchen. "Who leaked it to the press? I will have their ass. Well, find out and terminate them before I get my hands on them. Understand? Good."

Damn. Jackson's shit storm just got worse if one of his employees leaked the situation to the press. I wonder if that means I've been named as the perpetrator? How long before the FBI is involved? I climb off the couch. The windows are dark, which means I must've slept all afternoon. I check the time on my laptop. Seven p.m.

Jackson's starts up again—he must be making phone calls. "Get me Sarah, in PR."

I jog upstairs, determined to take a shower and make myself presentable before he sees me. I fail miserably, because he walks out to the living room and watches me ascend the stairs while he yells at his public relations director.

I wince and give him a wave of surrender, mouthing the word *shower.*

He nods and continues with his tirade.

When the FBI gets involved, will he turn me in? I slip into his guest bathroom and the memory of what we did in there two nights ago comes rushing back.

I strip and climb into the shower, letting my fingers slide between my legs like last time.

I have another punishment coming.

I'm suddenly desperate for it. My time here may be limited. If the FBI is looking for me, I may have to leave in a hurry. And my business with Jackson feels unfinished.

I want his touch, his mastery, one more time.

Right, and he's downstairs in crisis-control mode.

But maybe a little distraction is exactly what he needs, too. I could give him that blow job I didn't get to start last time. It could be my penance for what I've done.

I rub my clit, excited by the prospect. But I don't want to finish myself off. I'd much rather have Jackson's skillful fingers there.

I shut off the water and step out, toweling off.

Yep, there's only one way to play this. I wrap the towel

around my waist and sashay downstairs, my bare breasts puckering in the cool evening air.

Jackson's still on the phone, but, when he sees me, he stops speaking. He lifts one finger and points at me. I don't know what it means, but I keep coming.

"You know what to do. Don't call me until it's done. Got it?" He hangs up. "Kitten." His voice sounds strangled. "What in the hell are you doing?"

I play the coquette and bring one finger between my teeth, biting down. "Is it time for my punishment?"

"Fuck." It comes out in a burst. His eyes look bluer than I've seen them—a pale blue. No sign of the green at all.

He points to the couch in the living room. "I'll be right in."

My palms are clammy. Despite my bravado, I have no idea what I'm doing. Seduction is a new game for me, and punishment is completely foreign. No, that's not true. I've watched my share of fetish porn. But I've never experienced real pain. I'm not sure how I will like it.

Jackson returns holding a wooden spoon, and my stomach flips.

I bite my lower lip and work to keep my breath calm.

He sits down on the overstuffed brown suede sectional and pats his lap. "Lose the towel, kitten."

My pussy clenches. I'm not sure whether I'm more excited or nervous, but either way, I'm going forward. I drop the towel to the floor and climb over his lap, offering my ass up for his punishment. I pray a wooden spoon isn't the worst implement of torture in the world. It probably isn't, since it was used regularly on children's butts in the days when spanking was considered a useful and acceptable form of punishment. Not that I agree with such measures.

"Oh, kitten." It sounds like a lament, a groan almost.

Jackson runs his hand up the back of my thigh and over the curve of one cheek. I feel his hard length press against my hip.

I part my thighs.

"Baby, I'll take care of that ache between your legs soon. But, you're right. It's time for your punishment, now." He gives my ass a slap, but it's just with his hand.

"Mmm," I encourage him.

He slaps the other side and rubs away the sting. A few more slaps right and left and I start wiggling, wanting more.

He leans over and bites my ass, and I shriek and giggle. He chuckles, too.

"Okay, let's say...twenty with the wooden spoon."

I have no idea if that's a lot or a little, since I haven't felt the spoon yet, so I keep my mouth shut.

He leans over. "If it's too much, baby, I want you to tell me."

"Yes, sir."

He groans. "I love it when you call me that."

"Is that why you became a CEO?"

He pops me with the wooden spoon. It's definitely worse than his hand, but not horrible. "No, baby. I don't want anyone else to call me *sir.* Just you." He starts spanking rapidly, one side then the other.

I roll my hips, jerking with the impact.

"I only love it from you. The rest of them can go fuck themselves."

I squeeze my ass together. It hurts. A lot. But then it's over. Twenty spanks in twenty seconds. I'm almost sorry it was only twenty. *Almost.*

Jackson strokes his palm over my twitching ass, and I moan softly. "I'm not sure that was enough," he muses. "I didn't know how you'd take it." His fingers delve between my legs, and my thoughts scramble.

"Should we do another round, kitten? Twenty more?"

"No."

Heat flushes everywhere; my pussy weeps for him.

"No?" His touch is so beguiling, fingers sliding up and down my slick folds. My brain can't compute that he's threatening me with more of the wooden spoon.

"Yes?" I say.

He growls, low and sexy. More like an approving rumble. "I like spanking you, kitten. Love having you spread across my lap for punishment."

"Who else?" I choke, because, for some reason, I'm a jealous bitch when it comes to Jackson.

He stops moving. "Excuse me?"

"Who else have you spanked?"

His low chuckle goes straight to my erogenous zones, tightening my nipples, making my pussy squeeze. "Just you, baby. Only you." He picks up the spoon again and pops me with it.

I definitely don't like it this time, since I'm already sore from the first spanking, but I'm also not willing to say it's too much. He applies another rapid-fire round, and I squirm and squeal over his lap. "Ouch, please!" I shout at the end, but he was stopping anyway.

His fingers immediately slip between my legs, and I can tell I'm three times as wet as before. I guess I did need a second spanking.

"Jesus, this cute little ass bobbing over my lap makes me want to do this all night."

"Noooo," I moan. I'm definitely not down for round three.

He chuckles and flips me over. He's a big guy, and I know

he's strong, but I swear he makes it seem like I weigh less than three pounds. With one huge palm wrapped around my thigh, he pulls it open and lifts my hips. His mouth hits my core, ripping a scream from my lips.

Holy cunnilingus, Batman. His tongue circles my inner lips. He sucks and nips on my labia, suctions his lips over my clit.

I buck and claw at him, closing my mouth around the screams that won't stop coming.

He growls, penetrating me with his thumb as he continues his earth-shattering torture of my lady parts.

I come unglued, a climax ripping through me with enough power to fuel a rocket ship.

"Fuck, kitten." Jackson removes his mouth and pumps his digit in and out of me, watching my face as I finish.

One part of me thinks I should be embarrassed that he's seeing my O-face, but the rest of me doesn't care. Or, rather, believes he deserves the privilege, since he's the one to produce it.

"Fuck, fuck, fuck." There's desperation to Jackson's tone. His eyes glow light blue. He flips me over again, this time onto my knees on the couch with my torso hanging over the arm of the sofa. He slaps my sore ass, and I hear the rustle of clothing.

I realize I'm about to lose my V-card. Things are moving so fast. Jackson's breath is erratic, his movements jerky. He rubs the head of his cock over my sopping entrance. I don't think he put a condom on. Part of me is thrilled to have inspired this much passion in him. The other part is—*ouch.*

I gasp, tears spearing my eyes when he shoves into me, breaking my resistance.

He freezes. "Kylie, *no*."

I'm still holding my breath.

"Baby, *no.*" His torso covers mine, and he strokes my hair back from my face, trying to see me. His cock fills me, stretching my opening. Now that the initial shock of pain is gone, it feels good. I want him to start moving.

"I'm so sorry. Did I just—"

"Yes. I'm okay. Go on."

He curses and eases out.

"Don't you dare," I snap. "You're not taking this from me. Finish what you started, big man."

He strokes my hip. "Kylie." I hear the regret in his voice, and it pisses me off. I'm not a fucking china doll. Or maybe he doesn't want to have sex with a virgin. Maybe it's a total turnoff and he's lost his erection.

"Don't you dare," I whisper again, and my voice breaks.

"Kylie." His hands are gentle this time. He lifts me and tries to set me on his lap, but I'm too humiliated. I lurch off and run up the stairs. My nudity isn't sexy anymore. It's just...vulnerable.

Jackson's right on my heels, but, to his credit, he doesn't touch me. "Kylie. Kylie, wait. I'm sorry. I'm so fucking sorry."

I run into my bedroom, but when I try to shut the door in his face, he stops it with his hand.

Tears of frustration leak from the corners of my eyes.

"Kylie, please." He puts his entire body in the doorframe, so there's no way I'm closing it. I give up and walk to the bed, pulling on my day-old clothes.

"I'm sorry. I totally lost control. I didn't even have a fucking condom on, and I had no idea you were a—"

I whirl around and glare at him, which stops the word from coming out of his mouth.

He shakes his head. "I never planned to have sex with you. I was just going to give you a little pleasure. But you were so fucking hot, and I lost control." He shoves his fingers through his hair, making it stick up in all directions. "It's better this way, kitten."

Why does he look like he's breaking up with me? I want to throw something at his sympathetic face.

"I'm glad something stopped us. I...can't have sex with you."

What in the hell is this? First, Sam tells me it's not going to work, now, Jackson.

Why can't he be with me? Why? Is he married already? Subject to seizures? I just can't fucking figure out what makes it impossible for us to be together.

But I'm too fragile to drag it out of him now.

"I need to be alone, now," I tell him.

His face falls. "Right. Okay. But, are you hurt? Promise me you're not hurt."

I lift my chin. "Definitely not hurt." *Not physically.*

Jackson, on the other hand, looks like he's in enormous pain. I notice his cock still bulges in his khakis.

Well, good. Serves him right for stopping. I hope those blue balls hurt him all night long.

~.~

Jacqueline

Jacqueline rolls over in the dirt and groans. She's too old for this crap. If her granddaughter wasn't in terrible danger, she would let herself die out here in the desert.

It would be so easy. She suffered so many bullet wounds. Four, at least. Not even a shifter should be able to survive a bullet to the head.

But she's still breathing, so that must mean she survived.

How long has she been out here?

An entire night and day, at least. Could be more; she was in and out of consciousness.

But the cat in her rallied, pushing the bullets out of her flesh, closing the wounds. There's one still stuck in her head, though. And she's lost a lot of blood. She just wants to sleep.

But Minette. Her *petite fille* is in danger. The men who kidnapped her have plans for Minette. She has to get help. If only she could shift.

Usually, if a shifter is badly wounded while in human form, their body will naturally shift to beast for protection and healing. Why she is still in her weak, human form, she doesn't know. It must have something to do with the head wound.

She needs to get to other shifters.

They've only been in Tucson a week, but she paid a visit to the wolf alpha, Garrett, to introduce herself a few days ago. She needs to get to him. He'll be able to help.

She forces herself to her hands and knees and then to her feet. Her clothes are stiff, covered in blood and dirt. She can't scent her way to civilization because nothing but the smell of blood fills her nostrils.

Maybe it would be best to wait until morning, when she can judge the direction of the sun. But she doesn't want to spend another night out in the cold. Not in human form.

Shift, dammit, shift.

Why can't she shift?

~.~

Jackson

I am the biggest ass. I pace in my bedroom, listening for every creak or movement from Kylie's room.

I feel horrible about taking Kylie's virginity without asking. Without even using protection. Even worse, if things had continued, I would have marked her. I was already half beast. No thoughts were moving through my brain, other than to take her. Claim her.

Mark her as my mate.

Yes, if I hadn't hit her virginal resistance, I might have sunk my coated teeth right into her shoulder, tearing her delicate human flesh, possibly even killing her.

But the fact I wounded her pride—insulted her by stopping—made the situation insufferable. How did I not realize she was so inexperienced? In retrospect, it should have been obvious by her blushes, yet she carries herself with such confidence, sexual and otherwise, I never guessed.

The wolf in me preens over being her first, which disgusts me even more. I didn't even make it good for her. It was a negative five on a scale of one to ten.

And yet, I can't figure out how to make it better. I can't finish what I started. If I learned anything tonight, it's that I can't trust myself. Especially with the moon full.

Kylie's emotions aren't my only problem tonight, either. Someone leaked the story to the press, naming Kylie as the culprit. I will have feds at the office tomorrow, wanting to investigate her, and I sure as hell can't let them find her.

I log onto my computer to check how the story is coming out in the press.

Art Thief Vigilante's Daughter Hacks SeCure Corporation.

Art thief? I pull up the story to read about Kylie.

"Daughter of Robin Hood-style art thief Jacob Anders, Kaye Anders, also known as Kylie McDaniel, may be responsible for

hacking into SeCure Corporation and stealing hundreds of thousands of credit card numbers. McDaniel was hired by the company just days before she hacked the system and installed malware.

"Sarah Smith, Public Relations Director from SeCure corporation says owners of the accounts breached will be notified as soon as possible, and they are recommending the cancellation of all credit cards affected by the breach.

"Smith says it is unknown whether McDaniel staged the breach as another vigilante-style heist, following in the footsteps of her father. Jacob Anders was best known for reclaiming art and other antiquities stolen by the Nazis during World War II and returning the treasures to their rightful owners or to museums. His body was discovered in The Louvre in 2009 with multiple stab wounds that law enforcement officials believe to have been inflicted by a partner during a heist. The Degas painting 'Elegant Dancer,' a painting reportedly confiscated from convicted Nazi war criminal Hedwig Model and donated to the Louvre, was discovered missing from the art museum at the time.

"McDaniel, whose other aliases include the hacker moniker Catgirl, *has been wanted for questioning since the 2009 murder but has not surfaced again until now.*

"FBI officials were not available for comment, but the spokesperson from SeCure Corporation says they will work hand in hand with law enforcement to aid in McDaniel's arrest and will press charges to the full extent of the law."

Kylie, an art thief, in addition to the most talented hacker in the world. My beautiful, talented little cat burglar. But Jesus, she watched her father murdered before her eyes. No wonder she has PTSD. I've got to protect her.

A growl rumbles in my chest, my wolf ready to go on the

hunt. No one is going to touch my kitten. I don't know how to fix this, but I sure as hell am not going to let Kylie—or whatever her real name is—take the fall.

I hired a hacker and thief into my company. The PR is going to be hell.

A whimper sounds from her room, and I surge to my feet, flying out the door to stand outside hers.

Another whimper.

I gently push open the door. My little hacker's asleep on her side, one arm tossed over her head, which she rolls back and forth fitfully.

Bad dream.

I ease onto the bed behind her, curling my much larger body around hers. "Shh, baby. It's just a dream."

She whimpers louder. "Can't get out can't get out can't get out." Her breath drags in and out, too fast, the way it did in the elevator.

I rest my hand on her ribs and give her a gentle shake. "Kylie. Kitten. Wake up, baby."

She startles awake with a scream.

I start to cover her mouth but realize it will only make the claustrophobia worse, so I go for her sternum again. "Breathe, baby. In. Out. You're safe. It was a dream. Just a dream, kitten."

She lets out a tremulous whimper, and I roll her to her back to see her face in the dark.

Her arms loop around my neck, and she clings to me, trembling.

I rub her back. "Shh, baby. You're okay. I'm not going to let anyone hurt you."

As quickly as she turned to me, she pulls away, scrambling off the bed and onto her feet.

I follow her up. "Kylie."

She ignores me and paces back and forth, her shoulders hunched, her head bent like she's thinking hard.

She's rejecting my help. Fighting her problems on her own—as she has since she was just a teen. Maybe all her life. I want her to come back to me. Desperately. But I don't know how to get through.

"You saw your dad's murder."

She stops pacing, and her breath leaves her with a whoosh.

"In the Louvre? Where were you? In an air duct?"

Her knees buckle, and I catch her as she stumbles back. I pull her up into my arms, but she fights me. The scent of her tears hits me, salty and filled with pain. I don't let her go.

She needs me, even if she doesn't want to accept my help.

"Stop fighting me," I murmur as she shoves at my chest. "I'm on your side, baby. Stop fighting."

She collapses against me, tucking her face against my neck, wetting my skin with her tears.

"Damn you, Jackson. Damn you," she sobs.

"Why, baby?" I stroke her head. "I know I'm an asshole, but why are you mad?"

"I don't want you to take care of me so well."

I find her mouth, capture those tender lips, twine my tongue with hers.

She shifts in my arms, holds my neck, and swings one leg around to straddle me. My cock grows heavy, pressing in the notch of her legs, the heat of her core sending darts of lust through my bloodstream. I'm not going to lose control this time, though.

My female needs me. Needs comforting. Gentleness. And, wonder of wonders, my wolf submits. The need to protect her trumps his need to mate. My teeth stay human sized, even as my cock grows.

"Don't tell me you can't have sex with me." She tears open my button-down, popping the buttons.

Oh fates and all things sanctified.

I carry her to my bedroom and lay her down gently on her back. I shove her skirt up and yank the gusset of her panties to the side, placing my mouth where it always wants to be. Right on her core. Tasting her sweet essence, giving her pleasure. Satisfying her.

She arches, pulling her knees up to open wide.

"That's right, baby. Let me make you feel good."

She reaches down to help, rubbing her clit as I penetrate her with my tongue. "I want your cock, big man. I need it here." She taps her pussy.

I groan.

Can I do this?

I have to.

She's my female, and she needs me. Even the wolf understands.

I grab a condom from my dresser.

"Clothes off," she commands. "I want to see all of you, Jackson King."

I smile and peel my clothing off with purpose, standing in the light of the nearly full moon through the window. "I'll let you give the orders, just this once, kitten." I roll the condom on my length, grinning at her wide-eyed attention. "Because I fucked up earlier. But don't forget who has the wooden spoon."

Her face flushes, and the scent of her arousal fills the room, even stronger than before.

I grip the base of my cock and point it in her direction. "Like what you see?"

"No wonder it hurt," she says, but she's wearing a grin.

"Clothes off, kitten. That will be a rule. You should never be wearing more clothing than I am."

I take the musical ring of her laugh as another win.

I'm going to take care of you, baby.

She shimmies out of her clothing and lies back. I see why I was fooled. There's nothing innocent about her peach-tipped breasts, the curve of her hips, her neatly trimmed mons, and long, shapely legs. Even with a blush on her cheeks, she gives me *come hither* eyes. I don't know how she made it this long without having sex, but my wolf is doing double backflips in celebration of being the first.

I want to groan. I want to sing. Worship at the altar of her body for the rest of my life.

I *will* keep it together this time. I owe her.

~.~

Kylie

JACKSON KNEELS BETWEEN MY LEGS. His body is even more incredible than I imagined—cut from solid muscle. His chest is covered in dark curls, and his cock... sizable.

He nudges my entrance with the sheathed tip of his cock and I arch, pleasure spiraling out, inner thighs trembling with anticipation. He's breathing harder than normal, but he goes slow, easing into me, even though he already plowed the path open.

There's no pain this time, only satisfaction. He fills me, holds still for me to adjust. I lift my hips impatiently. *Not fragile, buddy.* I need this. I deserve it.

Jackson groans and climbs over me, leaning his weight on his fist beside my head.

He's huge, looming over me.

Before I can control my reaction, I stiffen and lurch away from him, needing to see the exit.

Still buried inside me, he rolls our bodies so I end up on top. I suck in a breath, my muscles relaxing.

He shows me his open palms as if to prove he doesn't have a weapon, then he shoves them under his butt. "You're in control, kitten."

I nibble my lip because he's made it plain he likes to be the one in charge. And I *love* his dominance. I just can't stand being crowded. Still, riding him feels good, and my hips start moving of their own accord, rocking over his huge, hard manhood. I tip my pelvis forward to grind my clit down over him, rubbing harder and faster.

His lips peel back from his teeth, and he squeezes his eyes shut, breath dragging in and out audibly.

A surge of power rockets through me, knowing I'm affecting him so much. It spurs me on. I slide up and down faster, my tits bouncing over his chest. I dig my nails into his shoulders, taking him deeper.

"Fuck, kitten. *Fuck*," he roars. His face contorts. His hands fly free of his self-imposed position and grasp my hips. I'm grateful for him to take over because my muscles are shaking, straining for release.

He yanks me over his cock, up and down, and then he shouts, his hips lifting off the bed, carrying me with him, even as he holds me to angle deeper than I thought possible.

I cry out, too, muscles contracting around his enormous cock, milking it for all it's worth in a pumping motion beyond my control.

Out of breath, trembling, I fall down over him, molding my body to his, nuzzling his neck.

He wraps his strong arms around me and holds me tight. This time, there's no fear. Only platinum satisfaction.

"Kiss me, baby."

I turn my head, and he captures my mouth, kissing me aggressively, letting me feel teeth and tongue, owning me.

Yes. That's what I like. Jackson in control.

It brings back that sense of home. Belonging.

His cock swells inside me. Lordy. Is he really ready for round two already?

He groans. "You'd better get off me, kitten, or I'll be throwing you on your back and fucking you into oblivion. And you're probably already sore."

I am. I ease off him, checking out his cock to see it's still just as big. "Jackson?"

He reaches down to grip it and surges up, meeting my eyes. "The condom came off!"

I flush, like I've done something wrong. I'm not stupid. I've read *Cosmo*. I know it happens. I also know I'm now at risk of pregnancy.

Jackson takes charge, pressing my hips to the bed and delving his fingers inside. *Holy embarrassing moment, batman.* He retrieves the condom. "Shit. I'm sorry, baby."

"It was probably my fault," I mumble, attempting to roll away.

He catches my hip and rolls me back to face him. "Hey. I'm in this with you. Whatever happens. I wouldn't be sorry if you had my pup."

My heart pounds, but I snort. "Pup?"

"Kitten," he amends quickly. "I'd love for you to give me a little kitten-girl." He gives me a devastating smile.

I roll my eyes. At least he didn't say, "I'll pay for your

abortion" or freak out. But yeah, this is all too much to absorb. I just had sex for the first time. Twice, because the first time was an aborted mission. Then a rubber gets lost in my hooch. And now I could be knocked up by none other than the guy I've been lusting after since I was a teen. Oh, and I may be on the run from the FBI.

If I could just grab a breather and more than a couple of hours of sleep, I'd probably be able to deal.

8

Kylie

I've never slept with a man in my life before now. I had no idea how incredibly wonderful it would be. The *rightness* of being nestled against a man's body—not just any man's, but *Jackson King's* body—with his heavy arm draped over my waist. How safe and comfortable I'd feel.

I don't want this impossible, short-lived romance to end. But reality calls. I'm wanted by the FBI for robbing my new lover's company. So, yeah, hiding out at his house isn't going to work for long.

The first rays of light illuminate the windows. Jackson's cock twitches against my backside, sending a fresh kick of lust shooting through me.

I wonder if he's into morning sex because I *totally* am. Yeah, I was a virgin until yesterday, but morning is my masturbation time.

I push my ass against his manhood, and his cock responds by lengthening, sliding between my thighs. Jackson's large hand coasts up my side and palms my breast. He pumps his hips, fucking the gap between my legs and running his hard length along my slit.

"Mmm, kitten. Is this pussy wet for me again?" He rolls my nipple between his two fingers.

It would seem so.

He pinches my nipple, and I writhe in surprise at the pain.

I reach between my legs to pull his cock tight against my core. A slow undulation of my hips grinds my clit over it.

He groans and bites my ear. "You want me inside you, baby? You need me to fuck you awake this morning?"

"Yeah," I rasp. I adjust my hips and angle his cock at my entrance.

"Fuck, baby, I don't have a—." He slides into me. I shudder with pleasure, my muscles clenching around his cock.

A condom. Oh yeah.

"Oops," I say.

Jackson's breath rate increases, and he holds my hip, thrusting deep into my channel. I know I should stop him, tell him to get the condom, but it feels. So. Good.

"Pull out before you come," I tell him.

He makes a pained sound. "I'll stop now," he says, but continues plowing into me with cruel, delicious force. His grip on my hip is bruise-worthy; his loins slap against my ass.

"Jackson—" I gasp.

He shoves me onto my belly and mounts me from behind, capturing my wrists above my head.

Thankfully, the claustrophobia doesn't kick in. Maybe because the view in front of me isn't blocked. I lift my ass to him, loving the new angle, wanting more, wanting everything. Every position, every variation, every rhythm.

An eerie, animalistic growl erupts from Jackson, and I twist to look over my shoulder.

And scream.

I scream at the top of my lungs, and I don't stop screaming.

Because Jackson is a fucking vampire. Fangs have punched out, and his eyes are ice-blue. *Ice-blue.* Not green at all. And the sound he's making isn't human. He's going to bite me and turn me into a vampire. I feel like I've tumbled straight into a horror movie.

Like the claustrophobia, my terror is a living thing. No thought, just pure adrenaline-fueled fear.

Thankfully, my scream surprises him, and he pulls back enough for me to scramble out from under him. I grab my clothes from the floor and run downstairs stark naked. Barefoot.

I fly out the back door, pulling my shirt over my head as I run. I thought it would exit into the garage, but I must've been confused—I'm out in the desert that leads straight to the foothills. I hear Jackson calling behind me, so I bolt straight up the foothills toward the mountain.

"Kylie!" Jackson shouts. He's outside, and he sounds furious.

I realize now, they'd been trying to warn me off. He and Sam both said he couldn't be with me. Why hadn't I listened? I stop long enough to yank my jean skirt on and keep running. I'm not going to make it far without shoes. It's all rock and cactus, and my feet are already bruised. I turn to look over my shoulder, but I don't see Jackson following.

Thank God. Maybe he went back in to get dressed. Then an enormous shape bounds up the hill. A silver wolf. And it's coming straight for me.

Oh Jesus. Jackson's not a vampire. *He's a wolf.*

I can't decide if that's better or worse. Do werewolves infect you with their bite and turn you into one, too? Or is that vampires? No, vampires drain your blood. So, yeah. Werewolves infect. I still feel like I'm stuck in that horror movie, only it's becoming campier.

The wolf is upon me in no time, but it doesn't pounce the way...*Jesus*. Was that *Sam* who attacked me outside the mansion? This one is definitely Jackson. I can tell by the ice-blue eyes. He nudges my hand with his nose.

"Get. The fuck. Away from me."

He lowers to his haunches and whines. He's enormous. Twice the size of a normal wolf with a thick, silver coat. A beautiful wolf, but definitely deadly.

I blink, and he's a man, again, crouching beside me. Naked. "Hey. You're safe. I'm not going to hurt you, kitten."

"Don't call me that!" My strangled voice sounds slightly hysterical. I'm generally someone who prides herself on keeping it together, but this situation has thrown me for a total loop.

I run up the hill. In my periphery, the wolf appears, trotting by my side, like he's decided to become my pet. "Go home," I command. If only he were a simple dog I could send running home.

Of course, he keeps trotting along beside me.

I glare at him. "So, you're a werewolf? That's your big secret? And what? You have to bite someone on the full moon? Something like that?"

Jackson—or rather, the wolf—whines again.

"What do you want with me?" I sob.

He licks my moving calf.

"No!" I shout. "Don't touch me. Stop following me. Go. Home." A rock twists under my foot, and I go down on my knee, hard. Pain shoots through my entire leg. I squeeze my eyes shut, trying to ignore it.

When I open them, Jackson's in human form again. Naked. He scoops me into his arms.

"No," I protest. "Put me down."

He walks stone-faced down the hill. "You're hurt."

"I'm not going back inside that house with you." My stubborn side has risen up, immune to logic. If he's a dangerous werewolf, waiting to turn me, he's not going to care where I want to go.

But Jackson stops. His shoulders sag. "Okay, fine." He starts running up the hill at incredible speed.

I clutch his shoulders. "Where are you taking me?" I gasp.

"I have a cabin up on the mountain."

Great. He's taking me somewhere even more remote so he can turn me. Except, I'm no longer afraid. Now that the initial horror has worn off, my brain is starting to get back online.

"Jackson, what happens when you bite someone?"

"A serum coats my teeth. It leaves my scent in your skin."

"And turns me into a werewolf?"

"*No.*" He keeps moving at dizzying speed, his bare feet and long strides eating up the mountain. I can't imagine how his feet don't get torn up. "We don't change people," he says stiffly, and I realize, with a bubble of amusement, that I may have offended him.

"But I am in danger? What does the serum do?"

He stops running and closes his eyes in resignation. "When a wolf picks his mate, he marks her with his teeth. A mating serum coats his fangs and permanently leaves his scent on her, so other wolves know she's been claimed."

I gape at him. Illogically, a hot pulse starts up between my legs.

"Did...do you want to mark me?"

"I *can't,*" he grits, once more ascending the mountain. "A human couldn't withstand such a bite. Shifters heal quickly, but a human would lose blood, maybe even die. Shifters don't mate with humans."

A cloud seems to roll over us. "Ah. That's why Sam said you couldn't be with me."

"Right." He clenches his jaw so hard I swear it will shatter.

A small log cabin comes into view. He retrieves a key from the top of the doorframe and opens the door. Inside is a beautifully appointed mountain cabin, simple but comfortable. He carries me to the leather couch and arranges me on it, with my back against the armrest and legs elevated on the cushions. My ankle has doubled in size from the swelling, and my knee is cut and bruised as well.

"I'll get some ice." Jackson disappears around the corner. When he returns, he's pulled on a pair of jeans and carries a dishcloth wrapped around a cold pack. He crouches by my feet and applies the pack.

"I'm sorry I freaked out on you."

He gives an impatient shake of his head. "No, I'm glad you did. I would've bitten you."

I stare at my throbbing ankle, unable to look at Jackson. "Well, I'm flattered, I guess."

He lets out a harsh laugh that doesn't sound amused at all. When he stands, he stabs his fingers through his hair like he did last night.

"Now, you understand. I'm dangerous to you, Kylie."

I study him through narrowed eyes. "I'm not afraid of the big bad wolf."

His eyes look haunted. "Learn to be. Listen, I need to get to the office. I have the feds to deal with." He walks to an old-fashioned desk and pushes the lid up. Inside, the comforting lights of a wireless router flash. He pulls out a laptop and brings it to me. "You can work from here. Or I'll go back and get the car and drive you down the mountain."

"Here is fine," I say quickly. For some reason, I'm not ready to go back to his mansion.

"There's food in the cabinets. I'll bring you things so you don't have to get up."

He leaves and returns with a loaf of bread and peanut butter and jelly, along with a can of oysters. "I wish I had a painkiller to offer you, but shifters don't use them."

Shifters. It's still setting in, but now that it has, it makes him all the more fascinating and attractive. No wonder I'd had a teen crush on Jackson King. He is superhuman.

"I'm really sorry about freaking out. I'm embarrassed. I wish we could have a do-over, and I'll be uber cool about it. Can we try?"

A reluctant smile tugs at Jackson's lips. "How would it go?"

"I'd be like, *oh, you're a werewolf. That's cool. Don't forget the condom.*"

A shadow descends over his face, perhaps at the reminder of the condom mishap. "I'm bad for you," he says tightly. "This...can't work."

Something tightens in my solar plexus. I want to grab him and tell him I'm not afraid, but he snatches me first, stamps his lips over mine, twisting over my mouth with an intensity I find dizzying.

I sense the desperation in the kiss.

The goodbye.

"Don't message me. I don't want anyone to trace you through me. I'll be back tonight. As soon as I can. Do you want me to send Sam up to check on you?"

I shake my head, swallowing down my disappointment. "No, I'm solid. I will keep working on the malware. Jackson?"

"Yeah?"

"Why haven't they contacted me if my grandmother's still alive?"

He frowns. "Maybe they're hanging onto her in case they need more leverage on you?"

I shake my head. "No, they leaked my history to the press. This was definitely a frame."

He touches my shoulder, and I swear I feel his strength transferring into me, warming me. "I don't know, but my gut says she's alive, too."

He kisses me again and shucks the jeans. His cock is still hard, mouth-wateringly impressive.

I watch this time as he transforms. There's a shimmer in the air and then he drops to all fours, a huge, beautiful wolf. I dare to stretch a hand out to touch his fur, and he licks it then licks the wound on my knee clean. It tingles. I remember a doctor in Mexico recommending I get a dog to lick a cut on my hand to make it heal faster. My dad and I had laughed at Third World medicine, but, of course, I'd researched it later, and there is something to it. I wonder if a werewolf's saliva is even better?

I stroke his silky ears. I want to bury my hands in his fur, but he spins and trots toward the kitchen. I hear the swing of what must be a dog door and he's gone.

So. Jackson King is a werewolf.

Now I know.

I'm surprised at how protective I feel over his secret. I will work even harder to straighten everything out at SeCure now that I know the company's brilliant CEO is as vulnerable to being exposed as I was.

~.~

Jacqueline

Jacqueline opens her gritty eyes, blinking against the morning sun. Still in the desert. Still in human form. She drags herself to her feet and checks out the angle of the sun. It is rising over the far mountain range, which means the Catalinas. So she's in the Tucson Mountains on the west side. Probably out in Marana somewhere, where the crack-heads cook their meth.

She isn't the only one who knows how to research things online. Her Minette thinks she's only capable of making soup...

Minette.

She starts walking east. Her gait is clumsy at first, but after a dozen steps, her coordination returns. Her sensitive hearing detects the sound of cars in the distance. *Dieu merci.* Too bad she's covered in blood. It will make it hard to explain if she flags down a car.

If only she could shift.

She drops to all fours and closes her eyes, willing herself to shift. The trouble is, she hasn't shifted often enough in recent years. To stay nimble, shifters must shift back and forth as nature calls. A shifter who stays too long in beast form, will forget how to become human again, and vice versa. Living with Minette, her halfling granddaughter who never manifested as a shifter, she wasn't able to run wild as often as she'd like. Especially when they were hiding in cities. Now, weak, hungry, and injured, it is even harder to call up the magic.

Remember. Remember what it's like. She thinks about

her first shift at puberty, the joy of chasing her sister through the French countryside. *There.*

The magic shimmers around her. She stops to pull off her bloodied clothes so she won't have to fight them after the shift and transformation. Now, to stay hidden from human eyes as she runs downtown. At least she remembers the way.

Garrett showed her a map of their territory on the west side once. His pack runs in Saguaro National Park West. Close to downtown and his headquarters. All she has to do is follow the Santa Cruz riverbed south.

~.~

Jackson

I walk into the office like a fucking gladiator. Every employee who sees me takes one look and averts their eyes. Even humans know to submit when the dominant is out for blood.

"The FBI is in with Mr. Anderson, sir," Vanessa says, pointing toward my CFO's office. Luis is in there, too. I already knew this from the fifteen phone conversations on my drive in, but I give her a curt nod.

No one from SeCure has admitted to leaking the information about Kylie, which could mean she's right, it came from her blackmailers. Although the blackmailers could be on the inside, too.

I can't stop the prickly awareness that there's still *more* to this attack we haven't seen. Would a hacker go to the trouble of kidnapping an old lady and framing someone for less than a million account numbers? Maybe. But it was risky. I don't know how much money they managed to divert, but their window was short. We closed it on them yesterday.

I march into Anderson's office and take a chair. My executive team is sweating. This is more pressure than I've ever put them through, and it's not nearly over yet.

Luis has given the feds Kylie's file and is bobbing his head up and down, agreeing with something they're saying.

He looks over. "Mr. King, the FBI have their own infosec team they'd like to deploy on our system."

I nod. "Good. Show them the breach and everything we've done to shore it up."

One of the agents stands and hold out his hand. "Special Agent Douglas."

I shake it. "Jackson King."

"Mr. King, I understand you were asking questions about Kylie McDaniel before the breach. Did you have reason to suspect her?"

I go for the truth. If Douglas is smart enough, he'll follow my logic. If not, we're no worse off than before. "Actually, I was wondering how she got hired into the position. The assumption was she was a hacker, but nothing on her resume would have told us that. I wanted to know who flagged her for this position and why."

"You think she has a partner on the inside?"

I shrug. "Maybe. Something's off with this whole thing, and it's more than a twenty-four-year-old hacker who called herself Catgirl as a teen."

"She's long been associated with vigilante thieves. This could be an organized attack from that direction."

I consider the man. He seems sharp. "Mr. Douglas, I'd like to share some information with you in private."

My team looks outraged, but I stand and walk to the door, knowing Douglas will follow. I take him to my office and toss the packet Kylie brought to me the night everything started.

"Ms. McDaniel turned herself into me after she received this," I explain.

Douglas shuffles through the papers, assimilating the information quickly. "But she still installed the code. From your office, I understand."

I rub my forehead. "Yes. I brought her into my office the next day and asked her to decode the malware on an un-networked computer."

"But she used the opportunity to load it onto yours."

"Yes."

"So what do you think happened?" He holds up the packet. "This was a ploy to get into your office? Save herself the trouble of having to hack through your firewalls?"

I shake my head. "No. She contacted me later to tell me her grandmother had been kidnapped and was being held hostage. The grandmother wasn't returned after she loaded the malware, so she offered her help."

"Contacted you how?" he asked sharply.

This is where it gets dicey. I sure as hell don't want them looking for Kylie at my place or around me. "She was waiting for me in the parking lot."

"The hacker who took down your system was waiting for you in the parking lot, and you didn't call the police? Something's definitely off with this story, Mr. King. What aren't you telling me?"

The need to protect Kylie makes anger curl in my stomach. I don't answer.

"Oh, I get it. You have a thing for Ms. McDaniel, don't you?" There's no missing the note of scorn in his voice. "I heard the two of you were trapped in the elevator together on her first morning. Think that was a coincidence?"

A chink of doubt sticks in my chest. Would Kylie orchestrate such a thing? Why? To get close to me? Seduce me?

But no, her terror in that elevator had been real. No claustrophobic woman would choose an elevator to stage a seduction.

I pace the office, shoving my hands into my pockets.

"So she met you in the parking lot and offered to help. What did you do?"

"I let her go." I'm facing away from Douglas, staring out the full length window. Lying isn't my forte, and I don't like the dishonor of it, but I'll do anything to protect my mate.

Fuck. Not my mate. Can't be my mate.

"Bullshit. Where is she, Mr. King?"

My fingers tighten into fists. "She's trying to find her grandmother," I snap.

He stares at me a long moment. "Okay," he says finally. "We'll follow up on that lead."

I force my teeth to unclench.

"And when you're ready to tell me where to find your mysterious Catgirl, "I'll be waiting." He tosses a card on my desk. "My cell phone is on there."

I nod.

He picks up the packet. "All right for me to take this?"

I'm surprised he asks for permission, but it's probably just a courtesy.

"Yes. Let me know what you find on the grandmother."

He pauses on his way to the door. "Am I working for you Mr. King?"

I clear my throat. It's not in my nature to grovel, so this makes twice today. Once to Kylie, once for her. "Please."

The ghost of a smile plays around his lips. "I'll keep you posted."

I sink into my chair when he leaves. The alpha in me wants to tear things apart and howl.

The moon is full. My company's under attack. My female's in danger. A human knows my secret, which means by pack law I must do something about her. And while telling Kylie should have ended our relationship—now that she understands why we can't be together—my wolf won't stop seeing her as my goddamn mate.

~.~

Ginrummy

The plan is unfolding. Kylie hacked SeCure and installed his code. That much worked. As did the leak to the press to get the FBI onto her. He didn't care whether the FBI found her or not—the point was just to throw them off his trail.

Mr. X said they took care of her grandmother. He didn't ask what that meant. He knew.

Time to issue the next blackmail threat. He shifts around in his seat, heat building under his collar. The feds are all over the building, and everyone is talking about the private meeting King had with one of the agents.

What in the hell did it mean? What could King have to say to the agent that he wouldn't say in front of his executive team?

He doesn't like it.

He spent all morning answering the same questions about Kylie four times to different agents. Now, he's supposed to give them access to the SeCure system so their infosec people can do their own investigations.

He has nothing to hide. Kylie uploaded the malware; his IP or prints aren't on anything.

He checks his phone. A message has come through from Mr. X.

Making the call to King, now.

A muscles twitches in his cheek. This is the part of Mr. X's plan that goes way beyond cybersecurity and credit card numbers.

They're making a play to take down the entire company. The credit card number theft was a diversion from the true infection into backup data, which granted the X team the capacity to wipe out every record stored by SeCure. So asking SeCure to transfer five hundred million dollars to restore the files won't be too much. If successful, it will be the biggest ransomware attack in history. If not, they already stole a half billion in credit card transactions.

~.~

Kylie

At dusk, I limp to the shower to clean up before Jackson shows. He hasn't contacted me all day, and I'm itchy to see him. To touch him. My body feels achy from the sex and my run up the mountain, but all I can think about is having Jackson's hands on me, having him take me roughly the way he wants to—biting me and marking me as his own. It's like the full moon has affected me, too.

The scrapes on my knee look a week old instead of a day. I guess werewolf saliva *is* better than dog spit.

I spent the day hacking into multiple credit card company sites to get the data on the stolen card numbers. By my estimate, around five hundred million dollars was stolen in the twenty-four hours before the owners were notified and cards frozen. It must have been all automated. Using the small vendors' merchant accounts stolen, they charged random amounts under a few thousand dollars on each credit card. Again, it suggests an insider, someone who knew what data they would find and how it would be configured in order to have pre-programmed such a complex formula.

With no contact from Jackson—although his reasons for limiting it are sound—emptiness sets in. He doesn't think he can be with me. He wants to—I know that much—but he believes he'll harm me.

I'm not afraid, though. He pulled back when I screamed. Went to his belly, even when I gave chase. He has way more control than he believes. And I'm not afraid of being marked. In fact, the idea thrills me. Maybe this is why ordinary men never interested me. I needed a superhuman.

I want to know everything about his shifter life. What it's like, how it works. What happens on the full moon. Which is tonight.

The bathroom door opens and closes, and my heart picks up speed. Through the foggy glass door of the shower, I see Jackson's wide frame. "Jackson?"

A moment later, he slides open the shower door. He's naked, his sheathed erection even more pronounced than it was this morning. Blue eyes burn from his face. His hands ball into fists at his side, his expression dark, furious. Hungry.

I catch my breath. "Jackson?" My voice wobbles.

He steps into the shower with me. I half expect to see elongated fangs when he opens his mouth, and I tense, not sure whether I'm going to let him mark me or not.

"I've wanted to fuck you in the shower since the night

you first showed up at my house." His voice is low and gravelly. "You think I didn't see you touching yourself through that fogged-up glass door?"

A shiver of pure desire runs through me, shooting down my inner thighs, curling my toes.

He catches my wrists and spins me to face the shower wall. His touch is reverent as he presses my palms against the tile. "New rule," he murmurs in my ear. "You don't touch that pussy without *my* permission. Understand?"

I don't, but I'm too turned on to speak.

"I need to hear a *yes, sir.*"

"Yes, sir." The words slip out of me before I even know I'm going to speak them. Heat blooms in my core at the bossy edict.

"Do you know why?" His voice is like a rumbling purr in my ear.

"N-no."

He reaches around to cup my mons, sliding two fingers along my wet slit. "This pussy belongs to me. I get to pleasure it. *My job.* Got it?"

Oh Jesus, fuck. My legs tremble from desire. I can't do anything but moan my assent.

"Good girl." He rewards me with a quick shimmy of the pad of his finger over my clit.

My knees buckle, but it doesn't matter, because he wraps an arm around my waist, catching me and holding me up as he penetrates me with two fingers. I throw my head back on his shoulder and close my eyes, lost in the ecstasy of his touch, his heat.

"You left me blue-balled this morning, kitten."

I cry out as he grinds the heel of his hand over my clit.

"I'm going to have to punish you, now."

"Yes," I breathe. *Punish me. Fuck me. Keep me as your play-*

thing. I want to be owned by Jackson. Marked by him, no matter how much it hurts.

He pulls his hand away from the notch between my thighs, and I moan with disappointment. "Ass out, baby."

I immediately obey, pushing my ass backward for his punishment.

He slaps it, and I shriek. The water makes it sting so much harder; the tile makes the crack of his palm echo. He spanks my other cheek then repeats, right and left. I'm in heaven, the cacophony of sensations—the water of the shower, the pain of his spanks, the pleasure of his touch all mingle to bring me right to the edge of orgasm.

Jackson groans. "Fates, I love spanking you. I ought to take a belt to your ass for the state you left me in today." His voice is a deep rumble that seems to enter my body through every pore.

When I don't disagree, he curses. "I'm going to fuck you so hard, kitten, you won't be able to walk right. Then you'll remember who this pussy belongs to."

I steal a glance over my shoulder, checking for fangs. The domination is hot, but it's also way over the top, tonight, and I'm not sure if he's in control. When I shift my weight, the pain in my ankle twinges.

Jackson surges forward and catches under the thigh of my hurt leg, hoisting my knee up to the tile wall. His body molds against my back, the head of his cock prodding my entrance. "Are you okay, baby?" His lips brush my ear as he speaks.

If possible, my pussy turns even more molten. He's in control. Protecting me. Like he's done from the start.

"Yeah," I pant.

"Reach down and guide me in."

I obey, reaching between my splayed legs and directing his cock to the sweet spot of entry.

He eases forward, parting me, filling me, inch by delicious inch. The position is so lewd, his dominance so extreme, I feel like the star of a porn movie. Jackson makes an approving hum behind me and then thrusts upward. "Take all of me," he growls.

I cry out. It's the good kind of hurt—deep and delicious. His cock stretches me, hits the front of my passage on each ramming instroke.

"Oh God," I moan.

"Not yet, baby." Jackson must be talking between clenched teeth. He braces himself with one hand against the shower wall by my head and continues to plow into me.

Need coils tight within me. "Please."

"Oh fates, baby. Are you begging? Keep fucking begging. That makes me so hard for you, kitten."

Tears sting my eyes. I'm desperate for release. My one standing leg shakes so hard, it's a wonder it holds me up. "Please, please, Jackson," I plead.

An inhuman sound rips from his throat, and I freeze. He fucks me so deep and hard, I see stars. Another roar blasts against the shower walls, and Jackson plunges deep, lifting me off my feet, spearing me with his erupting cock. He catches me around the waist, still holding my lifted knee with his other hand.

I clench around him, release spiraling out of me in a divine series of squeezes and shudders, until I'm wrung out and limp with pleasure. All the time, I'm waiting for the bite, but it never comes.

I can't decide if I'm disappointed or relieved.

"You take my cock so well, baby." His lips are right at my

ear again, his deep, rasping voice seductive. "Open your eyes and look at where you are."

Are my eyes still closed? It seems they are. I allow them to flutter open. I'm still nose to tile with the shower wall, Jackson's hard muscled body pressed against my back.

"This is a tight space, don't you think?"

My heart hiccups. It is a very tight space. And the exit is blocked. And I'm not the least bit afraid.

I let out a puff of laughter. "It is."

He nips my ear. "You survived it." He eases out of me and gently turns me around. His eyes are still blue, and his teeth do look sharper than usual, but he is clearly Jackson the man, not the wolf.

"I'm not afraid when I'm with you." It's true. Not a twinge of claustrophobia.

He shakes his head. "You don't ever need to be afraid again. You've conquered it."

I'm not sure I share his confidence in me. This situation is special. Next time, I probably won't have a goddess-worthy male fucking the daylights out of me to make me forget to be scared. But I love that he remembers. That he cares.

I smile up at him. "Maybe we should practice a little more to be sure."

Agony flits over his expression. "I'm not sure I'll survive it. I need to get out of here and run. Otherwise, I'm going to end up tying you to the bed and fucking you for the next eight hours. And that's if you're lucky and I don't lose control."

And bite me. Mark me as his.

Fresh heat spikes in my core. I've never felt so desirable in my life. Yeah, I know I have a hot body and have even used it on occasion to my advantage. But this animal side of

Jackson, this crazed, I can't-stand-being-near-you-without-fucking makes me feel like Helen of Troy. Or the most irresistible siren.

He tugs off the condom and steps out of the shower to dispose of it. When I come out, he opens a towel for me. Doesn't just hand it to me but waits for me to step into it then wraps it around me. There's a familiarity to the gesture—like we're a long-time couple, easy with the little sweetnesses. Suddenly I want that so badly—want to stay and have Jackson King be my normal. My pack.

But he's already said it can't happen. He has to mate another shifter. Not me.

The pain of it nearly blinds me. I turn away so he won't see it on my face. I need to rescue Mémé and leave town. Guilt for even thinking about a man when she's missing squeezes my stomach.

Yes, finding Mémé and leaving town is the only ending to this story that makes sense. I just pray she's still alive. She's the only *home* I have.

~.~

Jackson

I don't know how I survived fucking Kylie without marking her. My teeth were down, serum coating my fangs, but I somehow kept the wolf in check. Because I had to. To protect my female.

Yeah, I just flipped the bird to moon sickness. Taking the female my wolf wants desperately to mate without biting her ought to win me a medal of achievement. But my entire body itches to shift now. And I don't know what will happen after I've given the wolf free rein.

I wrap a towel around my waist and stalk to the back door where I jam the barricade in the giant doggy-door. The last thing I want is to come in after running under the full moon and attack Kylie.

"Do not let me in if I'm on four legs," I tell her.

She's followed me out, also dressed in a towel. It occurs to me that she could really use a change of clothes—she's been wearing my clothes or her same jean skirt and tee for three days now—and I feel like an asshole for not remedying the situation for her. A small one compared to her missing grandmother. Her eyes are wide, but she nods bravely. No surprise there. My little hacker thief, stealing million dollar paintings by age ten.

Somewhere out on the mountain, Sam howls, calling me out to run. "I have to go. Lock the door after me and don't open it. Understand?"

Another nod.

I grab her for a rough kiss, our mouths melding, tongues twining with enough heat to draw my fangs down again. It takes all my effort to pull away from her, shift, and run out into the night.

~.~

Kylie

I wake to the sound of howling right outside the cabin. The hairs on my nape stand up at the eerie cry. One wolf.

I look at the clock—four a.m. I passed out in the large, comfortable bed in what I assume was the master bedroom right after Jackson left. And now, it seems, he has returned. But he's on four legs, which means I can't let him in.

Thud. That sounded like a body being thrown at the

back door. He's trying to get in. I slip out of bed and limp to the kitchen at the rear of the cabin. I'm wearing nothing but one of Jackson's T-shirts, which I found in the dresser. I peek out the window and see Jackson, in his giant silver wolf form, heaving himself at the barricaded doggy door.

The black wolf—must be Sam—appears behind him and nips at his hind quarters.

Jackson turns on the smaller wolf and attacks. The two roll on the ground, their horrible growls filling the air. It seems like more than play. Jackson's teeth snap, Sam's answering whine sounds pained.

Jackson once again runs and heaves his enormous body at the door. He seriously is trying to huff and puff this door down. The fact that he doesn't just shift and use the doorknob tells me he's incapable of it. And this is why he told me not to let him in.

A shiver runs through me that has nothing to do with the cool mountain air.

So what's Sam doing? Trying to protect me? Keep Jackson away? It would seem so, because the smaller wolf once more comes after Jackson, nipping him and running away before Jackson can bite him in return. When Jackson ignores him and goes after the door again, Sam repeats the action.

This time, Jackson moves faster, taking a bite out of Sam's flank. The wolf yips pitifully, and my hand flies to the door handle. I need to stop this before Sam gets hurt. But I'm no wolf. What do I know about stopping a wolf fight? Maybe this is just full moon play.

But no. Jackson stays on Sam, even when Sam rolls over and gives him his belly. The great silver wolf goes for his throat. I scream at the same time Sam transforms into human form.

"Jackson." The urgency in Sam's tone scares me.

Dear God, if Jackson's jaws snap on Sam's throat in human form, will it kill him? I fly out the door, needing to help.

Sam's amber gaze swivels to me, alarmed. *"No!"*

Jackson whirls and leaps to the steps in a single, impossible arc. His shoulder hits my waist and knocks me against the door.

"Ooph."

Sam transforms back to wolf and makes a similar graceful leap, landing on top of Jackson and throwing him off the steps. The two tussle again.

I cage my scream. Common sense tells me to run back inside the cabin and lock the door, but I can't let Sam stay out here and get hurt for me. *I can't.*

"Jackson!" I yell to distract him.

His head jerks up with a ferocious snarl, and he charges me once more.

Sam moves quicker, leaping through the air and landing between us. Once more, he shifts to human form, reaching for the door knob. "Get. Inside."

Jackson shifts too, and slams Sam against the wall, choking him with a forearm across Sam's windpipe. His eyes are ice-blue, eerily inhuman. "Stay. Away from her."

Sam's palms fly up in surrender. "You're...a danger," he wheezes.

For a moment, I think Jackson will kill Sam, but his eye color starts to bleed into green, and he releases Sam, who gasps and clutches at his throat. Blood drips down Sam's leg from the earlier bite.

"Sam," Jackson rasps, regret laced through the single syllable. He cradles Sam's head and leans his forehead against the younger man's. "Fuck. Thank you. I'm sorry."

"You okay?" Sam asks, which seems backwards, since he's the one who's hurt. But I know he's asking if Jackson's in control.

"Yeah." Jackson grabs my arm and spins me around, giving my ass a pop. "Get inside, female. I told you not to open that door."

Butterflies take off in my belly at the hint of punishment to come.

"You want me to stay?" Sam asks as I head inside, as told.

"No, I'm back. Thank you, brother." There's a solemnity to the way he speaks, as if he's uttering a solemn oath or vow. A shiver of recognition of their pack roles gives me gooseflesh.

Jackson steps in, his cock fully engorged, swinging as he walks. He's an incredible sight—wild, smelling of pine and dirt and the night air. His muscles bulge and shift as he stoops to throw me over his shoulder. His expression is dark. Ravenous.

"Jackson. *Jackson.* Are you okay?"

He carries me to the bedroom and sets me on my feet. "I don't know. You tell me. Is it okay to disobey me?" He rips the T-shirt off me in a swift tug. Wraps a fist in my hair and pulls my head back.

I'm unbelievably turned on, and a smidge scared, because he's not quite Jackson. There's a fierce hunger in his face, a controlled violence just below the surface.

He kicks my feet apart. "Spread your legs."

I obey.

His palm connects with my pussy, a punitive slap. "Wider."

I spread wider. He slaps my pussy again, still controlling my head with my hair.

"Answer my question. Is it okay to disobey me, kitten?"

Any minute, I'm going to tell him to take it down a notch, make sure this is play and not real. But, apparently, I don't want that, because my molten pussy aches for his touch and, "N-no," is the only sound from my lips.

Another slap. Another. It hurts and sings at once. *Slap. Slap.* He continues spanking my lady parts. My legs tremble, and I wonder if I can come from pussy spanking alone.

I don't get to find out. "Bad girl," he murmurs in my ear. His huge palm kneads my ass. He doesn't sound the least bit angry. All I hear is excitement. Seduction. He wiggles a finger between my cheeks and presses on my anus.

I jerk in surprise, tightening my cheeks in embarrassment.

"I'm going to have to fuck your ass for this."

He releases my hair and stalks around the bed, throwing the pillows in the center.

My poor wobbly legs barely hold me up, and my tummy is all flutters. "Jackson, I don't think—" I trail off, staring at his enormous erection. *No. Way.* "You're too big. I don't think I can take you."

He stalks out of the room, and I hear a dark laugh. When he returns, he's holding a bottle of olive oil from the kitchen. "Oh, you'll take me, little girl. You'll take every inch of me. That's your punishment. When you disobey, kitten, you get it in the ass."

It sounds like a horrible idea. A terrifying, wonderful, horrible idea. But I can't bring myself to refuse. My body is wound up in a tight coil, desperate to be sprung.

He slaps my ass. "Lie over the pillows, baby. I'm going to own that hot little body of yours."

Something akin to a mewl comes from my lips, but I find myself obeying, tottering to the bed and climbing over the pillows. Presenting my ass to him like a cake on a platter.

There's a dark rumble of approval. I watch over my shoulder as he sheaths his cock and pours a generous amount of oil over it then trickles another stream along my crack.

He crawls over me, one hand fisting his cock, the other massaging oil into my ass, around my anus.

"There are consequences for disobeying your alpha." He pushes the head of his cock against my anus and waits.

I tighten against his touch, but, a moment later, the muscles give. As soon as they loosen, Jackson pushes forward, penetrating my tight hole.

I let out a keening cry.

He stills, stretching me wide, waiting for me to calm down. The care he takes reassures me that he's in control, and I yield, willing my pelvic floor to relax. He pushes in farther and the stretch becomes more intense, then eases.

"There. That's the head. I'm in, baby. Now, take the rest of me."

I whimper but let all my muscles go slack, arch my back a little, and wait.

"Good girl," he rumbles, one hand coasting up my side, stroking my skin.

The praise sends curls of warmth through me, and I arch some more.

"That's it, baby. Take it like a good girl, and I'll kiss that ripe pussy when I'm through." He eases in and out, giving me a tremendous sense of urgency each time he fills me.

My ass is stuffed full of his cock, but my pussy feels tragically empty. I reach my hand between my legs to remedy the situation. My flesh is juicy, swollen beyond recognition, even to my familiar fingers.

Jackson growls and catches my wrist, pulling my hand out. "*Mine.* What did I tell you about touching your pussy?

Only I get to master this sweetness." He covers my body with his, reaching around to cup my mons. It's exactly what I need. The tremors start through my body.

"Jackson." The hoarse cry doesn't even sound like my voice. "Jackson, please."

"That's it, baby. Beg me." He picks up speed, plundering my ass while his fingers fuck me from below. I'm dizzy with lust, drugged with need. The cabin spins and tilts.

"Jackson!" The room fills with keening cries, which must be mine.

A snarl and a roar cut across them, and Jackson plunges deep. I grab his fingers in my pussy and push them deeper and hold them there as I come, too, my vaginal muscles squeezing, anus tightening around his huge girth.

He pulls out too soon, stumbling back, and I twist to see what I already know will be there. Fangs.

He tears off the condom and discards it. Then comes for me.

~.~

Jackson

If I don't get enough of Kylie, I'll die. I need to possess her in every way.

Fates, I almost killed Sam out there. My wolf smelled Kylie in the cabin and needed to get inside with a desperation that rocked me. When Sam tried to interfere, the wolf thought he was challenging me for her. Thank fuck he shifted, or I would've gone moon sick for sure.

Even now, the fact that I just orgasmed doesn't ease any of the fierce need sifting through me. I pray if I just keep claiming her, pleasuring her, fucking her, it will appease my wolf enough he won't mark her.

I pull the pillows out from under her heart-shaped ass and flip her over. Shove her knees apart. Apply my mouth to her core, licking and sucking like my life depends on it.

She's limp at first, her knees falling open, still languorous after her orgasm. But her fingers come to my hair when I tongue her clit, and she lets out a weak moan. I don't stop. She tastes like heaven. I feast in her juices, devouring her. I rub her clit, suck and nip her labia.

She tears at my hair, hoarse cries coming from her throat. She's incredible, the way she gives herself to me, so willing to receive all the pleasure I need to pour on her. Her untrained body is infinitely responsive. I penetrate her with two fingers, find her G-spot on her inner wall, and work it until the tissue hardens and wrinkles.

"Jackson. *Jackson*. Please. I can't take any more." Her knees cinch around my head.

I penetrate her with both tongue and fingers then return to sucking her clit, pumping three fingers in and out of her until she comes for the third time tonight, her channel squeezing and releasing as she lets out a long, keening cry.

I wish it was enough. I know I've already exhausted my little human. Precious, beautiful female.

I climb up to sit on the bed and pull her across my lap. Her scent punches me into animal mode again. I spank her pretty ass, fast and hard. "Jesus, kitten. The scent of your arousal makes me crazy. I can always smell when you're turned on. I knew it that first day in the elevator after I touched you."

She whimpers, and I register than I'm hurting her but can't seem to stop. It feels so damn good to smack her juicy ass, and the little cries she grunts she makes only feed my frenzy. My wolf starts to howl.

I spank her until her ass turns red.

"I'm sorry!" she cries, and I work my hand under her hips, twiddle her little clit again. I keep slapping, loving the way her cheeks flatten and spring back under my hand.

"I don't need you sorry. I only need your surrender. This is the only way I keep my wolf from marking you."

She wriggles over my hand, her cunt leaking juices down my fingers.

"Do you like that, baby?"

"*No...yes...ohhh,*" she pants. "Too much. Too much, Jackson. I can't take any more."

I push her off my lap, but there's no stopping me. "Inside you," I growl. I lift her to her hands and knees then force her upper body down, so her face presses into the covers. Somehow, miraculously, I remember to don another condom. I snap it on and push into her wet heat. My fangs punch out longer; a snarl rips from my throat.

Don't mark. Just. Fuck.

Mate, the wolf roars.

Just. Fuck.

My balls slap against her, cock sliding in and out of her tight channel. She takes all of me in this position, takes me deep. My thighs shake, balls draw up tight.

She moans and wails, her cries both pitiful and wanton at once. Her pussy is still wet and willing. Generous in how hard a fucking it takes.

Just fuck just fuck just fuck. Don't. Bite.

I come again with a roar. Kylie's screams join my snarl, and she orgasms, milking my cock with her tight muscles, drawing even more cum out of me. I shudder, chills and heat running through me like I have a fever.

Kylie lets out a sob as I slip out of her. I dispose of the condom and catch a whiff of salt. *No.* A tear slides down her nose.

The scent immediately takes my wolf down. He whimpers and retreats. The lust-induced haze over my brain dissolves. *Oh fates—my female. Have I hurt her?*

"Baby, baby, baby," I croon, quickly disposing of the condom. I scoop her into my arms, cradle her against my chest. I settle back on the bed. "Are you hurt?"

"Not hurt...just wrung out." She tucks her head under my chin, her limp body molding to mine.

"Tell me you're okay," I plead.

She kisses my neck. "Yes. I'm okay. I love you."

I go still, and she stiffens, seeming to realize what slipped out. "I mean—"

"Shh. Don't you dare take it back," I warn. I cradle her face in my palm and turn it to look into her warm brown eyes.

"I love you." I don't say *I love you, too*, because I don't want it to sound less serious than her admission. I utter it like a vow. I don't know how the fuck I'm going to make things work with a human, especially if every full moon is like this, but I sure as hell have to try. I'm not giving her up for anything.

And that means I need to eliminate all the threats to my female.

"Kylie, I need to know what happened at the Louvre."

She blinks in surprise and tries to pull away. I literally can see her emotional retreat before my eyes.

"Don't run," I command. "Look at me. I need to know."

"Why?"

"You've been in hiding since then. And now you've been outed. Are you in danger?"

She shakes her head. "Not for the next seven to ten years."

"Tell me."

"It was my father's partner in the heist. A double-cross. My father planned to return the painting to its rightful owners—relatives of the Jewish family it was stolen from during the war. As soon as they had the painting, he stabbed my dad and took the canvas. He didn't know I'd come along. Never knew there was a witness. I stayed in hiding as a precaution. I figured if he knew where to find me, he'd want me dead. But, strangely enough, he became the victim of quite a few cyber attacks over the last few years, including one that stole enough evidence to send the FBI after him." My brave little warrior smiles up at me. "So, I'm safe for now. Until he gets out of jail and comes looking for me."

I growl. *Not good enough.* I vow to eliminate that threat completely. But at least I know, for now, she's safe from that direction.

Kylie lifts her chin. "What about you? Anyone want you dead?"

I rub my forehead. "Maybe. If I returned home, I'd probably be challenged."

"Why?"

My head suddenly aches. I lean my forehead against hers. "You don't want to know, baby."

"I told you mine. You tell me yours." Her voice is firm, the challenge clear in her eyes. My female is alpha all the way.

"I killed my stepfather." The only person I've ever told before is Sam, although Garrett might know if he's done any research into my history.

To her credit, Kylie doesn't flinch, doesn't show any shock. She touches my face. "What happened?"

"He was the pack leader. Alpha. A first class asshole. Beat my mom regularly. Not like a spanking, the way wolves establish dominance. With his fists."

Kylie pales but remains quiet.

"He put my mom in the hospital once. Shifters heal fast, so you have to know how bad it was." The memories raced back to him. Seeing his mother bloodied and battered on that hospital bed. *I'm not going back, Jackson*, she told him. *You don't go back, either.*

"She didn't heal. I can only guess she didn't want to. Or that he'd battered her mind so badly, too, that the ability to heal shut off." I was only fourteen. Old enough to want to fight my stepfather, but too small to stop him. "She died three days later. I watched her just slip away. And I..." My throat works. I don't want to tell her this part.

She strokes my arm, listening. Waiting.

"I killed him."

"How?"

"Don't ask me that, baby. I don't want you to think of me—"

"You can tell me," she murmurs. "It won't change how I feel about you."

Like hell it won't.

"I ran home from the hospital. My fangs were probably down like they were tonight. I'd only just started shifting and had little control of the animal inside. He heard me snarling and came outside the house. Stood there like a son of a bitch with his hands on his hips. *What?* he sneered. *Your mama send you after me, boy? Is she still pretending not to heal?*

"It's hard to kill a shifter. A bullet to the head usually does it. Or severing the head. There was an ax sitting there on the chopping block. I picked it up and came at him. I said something like, *She's dead, you miserable piece of shit* and then

I swung. I figured he'd stop me. Maybe kill me, too. I'd tried to fight him before and always ended up bloody.

"But he just stood there as I came at him. Probably the shock of hearing he'd really killed her. He shifted after the blow, but it was too late. He died just a few seconds later."

Her breath hitches, but she keeps her face smooth. "Wow. That's...intense. I'm sorry, Jackson. I'm sorry you had to go through that." She blinks her big doe-eyes up at me, and they swim with sympathy.

Not horror.

Relief pours through me. Lightens the heaviness in my chest I've carried every day since my mother's death. Sharing my terrible secret with Kylie eases the burden of it.

"So then what happened? You left? Do you have a buried identity like me? Are you wanted for murder somewhere?"

"Yeah, I left. I didn't lose my identity. No one ever came after me. No police reports were filed, but I'm from the backwoods of North Carolina, where the entire town was made up of shifters, sheriff included. Shifter business is generally kept to shifters."

"And you haven't been back?"

I shake my head. "Never. I left a much younger stepbrother behind. I hate myself for that. But the whole town was made up of my stepfather's extended family. He would've been well taken care of. I knew that much."

"You took Sam in to make up for it."

My eyebrows shoot up at her guess. "Yeah, I suppose so."

She tucks her head under my chin and hums softly. I can't believe I'm snuggling. With a human. And nothing has ever felt so right in my life.

I stroke her hair. "I won't let anything happen to you, kitten." Even if it means protecting her from myself.

9

Kylie

Jackson wakes me in the morning by pulling a T-shirt over my head and picking me up into his arms. "Come on, sweet girl. I'm taking you back to my house." He carries me out of the cabin to his car. "There's not enough good food for you here. Besides, I want Sam nearby so he can protect you if anything happens."

I make a contented purring sound in my throat. I love being carried like I weigh nothing, gently deposited in the car seat. Jackson even buckles my seatbelt for me. When did the big bad wolf turn so damn sweet?

He climbs behind the wheel and drives down the mountain, shooting concerned glances my way every now and then. "How do you feel this morning?"

I stretch, still hatching from sleep. "Good. You?"

He drops a hand to my thigh and drags it up to my bare pussy, lightly brushing his fingers over my sensitive flesh. "How about this sweet pussy? Too sore?"

I flush a bit at having my pussy be the topic of conversation before eight a.m. "A little sore," I admit. "But I'm not complaining. That was the hottest sex of my life last night."

Jackson makes a choked sound, and pride battles with disbelief on his face. "You were a virgin two days ago."

"So? It still was hot."

"It was fucking *nuclear*. Baby, I want you to know, I've never had sex like that with any female before—human or wolf."

I smile at the serious tone he adopted.

He shoves the hem of my T-shirt—his, really, but the one I'm wearing—up to my waist, exposing my bare pussy. "Spread those creamy thighs, baby. I need to see your pink heart."

My breath stutters, but I part my legs. He cups my mons. "You remember who this belongs to?"

I flush.

"It's mine. And if I was too rough with it, you'd be within your rights to pout a little, kitten. Make me kiss it better when I get home tonight."

The thought has my nipples tightening, pussy clenching. The image of us as some kind of 1950s married couple floats through my mind. I'm the sex-kitten wife, waiting for him to come home from a hard day at work. Offer him a drink and loosen his tie before I pout and make him lick my pussy as compensation for pounding me too hard the night before.

Okay, I'm getting way too excited. And there's work to be done. Serious work.

He pulls into his garage and insists on carrying me inside. "Your ankle is sore, and you're not wearing panties."

I laugh. "So those are the two criteria for getting carried?"

"That's right. Now, watch the sass or I'll have to see to that pretty little ass of yours before I go. Is it sore, too?"

I reach back and run my hand over my bare cheeks. "No." I can't decide if I'm glad or disappointed. He settles me on the couch. "Listen, I didn't tell you something that happened yesterday. I got a call from the blackmailer—with the robotic voice. They identified themselves as Catgirl. Said they installed corruption code to wipe out all of SeCure's backup data. Told me to transfer five hundred million dollar by midnight tonight if I want it back."

I sit up straight. "Tell me you have the information backed up somewhere else." Of course he does. He's Jackson King, genius of cyber security.

"I do. Triple saved. Not even my infosec team knows how." He flicks his brows, and I understand he believes this threat came from the inside.

"So what did you tell them?"

"I told them to go fuck themselves."

I laugh. "I believe I used those exact words, too."

His eyes crinkle, and he kisses the top of my head. "I have it handled. I just wanted you to know. No contact with me. Stay off your phone, or they'll trace you here."

I roll my eyes. "Yeah, yeah, yeah. Preaching to the choir, big guy. I wrote the manual on going dark."

He gives a reluctant nod. "Okay. Make sure you eat and get more rest."

It's too good to be true. I like it way too much. The practical little voice in the back of my head tells me not to get used to this. Not to trust. He's already made it plain he can't be with a human. And I can't stay in hiding in the mansion of a member of the Forbes Fortune 500 CEOs.

I need to put my head on straight, fix this situation, and get lost. It doesn't matter how good the sex was. How much I want to be claimed and marked and kept by Jackson King. It can't happen.

Won't happen.

I grab some toast and coffee and start to work. I start by opening Mémé's favorite Parisian antique message board. Mémé and I have prearranged to message each other there if we are ever separated or need to get in touch. We made the arrangement years ago, and I forgot it until last night. I hope her memory serves her better. I search out her alias and click to private message her. Even though it's a private message, I keep my note cryptic.

Looking for you. Can we meet?

I hope she remembers.

From there, I click open the DefCon boards. The place where hackers meet. The place I let slip, years ago, that I'd hacked into SeCure. Someone there had set me up. And now that I realize that, something in the malware has jogged my memory. If I can find the conversation I'm remembering, I might have my hacker.

~.~

Ginrummy

Something is wrong. He should be hearing more about the blackmail threat. They should all be scrambling to try to decode my corruption. He knows SeCure doesn't have additional backup. He's in charge of this shit.

And the FBI clowns should be all over it, too.

Which means Jackson King didn't tell anyone about the call. Why in the fuck not?

Perhaps out of nostalgia, he opens the DefCon boards. It would be interesting to see if they were talking about the

SeCure hack. Some idiot is probably bragging in there that it was him.

He finds a direct message in his DefCon inbox. From Catgirl.

His pulse stutters as he opens it.

Ginrummy,

I need to talk to you. In person. Meet me at the Park 'n Save at the Tucson airport at one p.m.. The shade structure on *Row 7.*

~Catgirl

His heart pounds triple time. He knows, without a shadow of a doubt, going to that meeting would be a huge mistake. He should let the FBI know he's had a tip she'll be there. But what if she presents the FBI with the dirt on him? Better to tell Mr. X.

But that thought just doesn't sit right with him. He now has no doubt they will kill Kylie like they did her grandmother. And, while he should be glad he's working with an organization willing to tie up loose ends, he can't stomach it.

Catgirl means something to him. Even if she doesn't reciprocate. Even if what she means is mostly in his head. He's not willing to let go of that fantasy.

What does she want to say to him? Why does she want to meet? The fascination with her every move, every thought hooks him like a barb, reels him in. How does that brilliant mind work? Is she planning a counter-blackmail?

She asked to meet at the Tucson airport. Does that mean she's headed out of town? If she is, he'll let her go. Let her disappear into hiding again, bearing the suspicion for his crime. Perhaps she just wants to let him know she knows.

Or maybe she wants to kill him.

No. he doesn't think Catgirl's a murderer. She has principles. Very high moral standards. He remembers long discussions they had about right and wrong, which he later realized must have been colored by her parents' vigilante thieving.

So, what does she want with him?

Damn. The temptation to meet with her overrides reason. The need to know, to see the beautiful hacker one last time infiltrates his being, sucking him down the rabbit hole of bad decisions.

He has a gun. He'll bring it to the meeting, in case she tries anything. And he won't notify anyone—not the FBI or Mr. X just yet.

Better to figure out her game first, then make a decision about how to react.

~.~

Jackson

Work is still a public relations nightmare. I'm on teleconference with the board most of the day, and many of them are calling for my resignation. Our stock price is down, and there are threats of lawsuits.

All I can think is *fuck them all.*

I can't even make myself give a shit about SeCure's stock price or what I'd do if the board fires me. My mind is only focused on one thing. Figuring out who framed Kylie.

Apart from me, I try to remember who from SeCure knew Catgirl hacked us eight years ago. *Luis.* A few members of the infosec team at the time. Who were they? Stu?

No, he didn't work here then. Why did he pop into my head, though?

I remember Kylie's interview. How eager he was to get her hired. At the time. I'd thought it had to do with her beauty, the Batgirl tits.

But what if Stu was the one who orchestrated her hire? He'd be capable of writing the code that infected our system —he's a damn good programmer and probably another hacker-turned-infosec professional.

A prickle runs up the back of my neck, and I stand. I need to have a word with him.

As if I've conjured him with my thoughts, I catch sight of his slouchy figure out my window, walking to his car. The prickly feeling hasn't gone away, so I head for the door and take the stairs down to the parking lot at shifter speed. His car pulls out the gates. I jog to my Range Rover and climb in. It's all I can do not to screech the tires following him, but good sense wins out, and I keep a distance. He drives for a long time. This isn't a quick lunch date. It's a forty-five minute drive to the south side of downtown.

Though I have nothing to go on, my gut tells me to keep following.

He pulls into the Park 'n Save at the Tucson airport and parks near a shade structure. Rolls down his window like he's about to make a drug deal. My instincts flare into high alert. This is not normal. Whatever he's doing is totally suspect.

I hang back by a few cars, park a distance from him, and stay in my car. He also stays in his car. A growl rumbles in my throat as my wolf prepares for danger.

I stop cold, though, when a familiar motorcycle zooms in front of me and pulls up alongside his car, the long-legged brunette looking way too good on Sam's motorcycle. *What in the fuck is Kylie doing here?*

Pain pushes through my heart like a nail in a coffin. Punctures straight through to the other side and leaves me wheezing for breath.

Betrayed.

She's been working with Stu all along? A great roaring starts up in my ears, deafens me. My body goes numb, freezing cold as it all clicks into place. She and Stu are working together on this. I was so stupid to believe all her lies. A known thief, a known hacker, I actually *saw* her install the malware into my system, and I didn't realize I was being played? She took me by the balls.

What in the hell is wrong with me? I was thinking with my dick, not my brain, that's what. I let a pair of sexy legs and Batgirl tits lead me around by the nose. What a fucking idiot.

I watch, like a dead man, as she pulls off her helmet and dismounts from the bike. She leans back against it, folding her arms across the same breasts I worshipped only last night.

I can't tell what they're saying. Even if my wolf hearing could detect their voices through the window, the rushing in my ears keeps me from being able to concentrate.

I turn weak, like she's wrapped me up in silver chains—a werewolf's kryptonite. Power simply drains from the soles of my feet, leaks beneath the car like blood.

The betrayal coats my mouth, puts a red filter over my vision. Darkness falls across everything—the peachy future with Kylie I'd been trying way too hard to figure out. It blackens the time we spent together, muddies my trust in my own instincts.

Like I'm that teen again, covered in my stepfather's blood, I go numb. Just shut off.

~.~

Kylie

"You going to shoot me with that thing?" I ask, peering in at Stu through his open car window.

He has a gun in his pocket pointed at me. He's pale, sweat beading his forehead. "What do you want, Catgirl?"

"My grandmother. Where is she?"

Something that resembles sympathy flickers over his face. "Right. They took your grandmother. I'm sorry, I don't know." He rubs his forehead with the hand not holding the gun. "I had no idea they would do something like that."

A sick twist wrenches my stomach. "Who is *they*?"

He shrugs like we're out to coffee discussing code or what we think about the boss. "Guy calls himself Mr. X. That's all I know."

My hands turn clammy, and I sway on my feet. "You just took down the country's top credit card security company working for a man named Mr. X? Have you met this guy?"

A flash of misgiving passes over Stu's face before he hides it. "We've been in communication for over a year. He's placed a good faith down payment in my offshore account."

"Offshore account, hm?"

"It's hack proof, Catgirl."

I'll see about that. I cut him with my most scornful glance. "You must be pretty proud of yourself, framing me to make yourself rich."

Again, a flicker of regret seems to pass over his face. "Get out of town, Catgirl. You can still leave. They'll never find you. You're as hack proof as they come. That's one of the reasons I picked you. You won't be any worse off than you were before. Hiding and assuming new identities is what you do best."

I must be crazy because I actually see his logic. "I need to know where my grandmother is."

"I'm sorry. I really don't know, but...I wouldn't wait around." Again, he looks almost sorry for me. "Get out of town, while you can."

I eye his gun. It was crazy of me to come here unarmed, but I just had to look him in the face and hear him say for himself what he's done. He's telling me my grandmother is dead. My hands start shaking—whether from rage or shock, I'm not sure. Either way, there's nothing I can do now. Not when Stu has a gun and I'm completely unarmed. Besides, physical violence has never been my way. I've always been the cyber attack sort. If he thinks his money will sit quietly in his offshore account, he's fucking delusional.

I nod, once. "Okay."

Relief flickers over his face. "Okay? You'll leave town?"

I shrug. "What choice do I have?"

"Good." He rolls up his window, and I watch as he puts the car in gear and coasts away. I want to throw Sam's helmet through his back window, chase after the car and pull him out of it, stand on his throat until he tells me where to find Mémé, but I'm helpless. Just like when I watched my father murdered and couldn't do a thing to save him. Didn't do a thing to save him.

I've always wondered if things would be different if I'd gone after his partner that night instead of hiding like a terrified child. He'd already stabbed my father, but what if I'd found a way to kill him? Would that have been the honorable thing to do? Instead of hiding and going after him the sneaky way? The shameful way?

Now, I'm doing the same thing. Letting Stu drive away after basically admitting Mémé's been killed.

The sound of a car door slamming nearby makes me jerk my head up. My throat closes when I see the figure storming toward me, dark and furious.

Jackson.

His huge hand shoots out and grips me by the throat.

"Jackson," I choke, real fear shooting through me. His eyes are ice-blue, inhuman.

As if he catches the fear, something flickers in his expression. The fury slips away, replaced by something far more raw and broken.

"So." He brings his face right up to mine. "You've been working with Stu all along. Played me for a fool, didn't you?"

"No," I gasp. "You have it wrong. I came—"

"Shut up." He gives me a little shake. With my weight suspended by the column of my neck, he pulls me to my tiptoes. "All I have to do is squeeze to crush your throat." There's a sharp menace to his voice I've never heard before. It terrifies me. "Or snap to break your neck." I remember this is the man who lost control of his wolf and killed his stepfather with an ax. Who hunts and runs wild on the mountain. He's no stranger to violence. "Which would you prefer?"

"No." It's hard to speak around the fingers partially cutting off my air, around the crushing panic, because strangulation feels a lot like claustrophobia.

Tears spike, drip out the corners of my eyes.

His nostrils flare, and he releases me abruptly, a look of horror on his face. He shoves his fingers through his hair.

"Get out of here. Get out of my sight before I harm you. You aren't safe with me."

"I'm not working with Stu," I rasp, my throat sore from his fingers.

He lunges for me again, covering my mouth with his hand. "No more lies from that pretty little mouth. No more. Just. *Leave.*

He takes my helmet from my hands and puts it over my head, buckles it even. He tugs the chinstrap forward and stamps his lips over mine.

I moan into his mouth, hope flaring that he is still with me, that he will listen, but he makes a broken sound and, when he pulls away, he doesn't even look at me.

A goodbye kiss.

Fuck.

That's what it was. It guts me.

He stalks away without another word.

I open my mouth to call after him, to explain, but tears choke my voice, followed closely by anger designed to protect against the kind of injury I sustained.

Heartbreak.

He should have let me explain. Why would he give me the benefit of the doubt all along and then choose *now* to believe I'm against him? Now, when I'm already hopelessly in love with him? Now, when I can no sooner walk away from him than I can from Mémé?

Tears streaking my cheeks, I throw a leg over Sam's motorcycle and take off. I have nowhere to go, no leads to follow. Stu was right. I should get out of town while I still can.

Why, then, would I rather cut off my own arm?

~.~

Jackson

Driving back to the office, it takes me a long time to realize my phone is ringing. I check the screen.

Garrett.

Because the guy doesn't call me often, and that means it's wolf business, I take the call. "King speaking."

"It's Garrett. Listen, do you know anything about a female called Kylie?"

The distortion in my vision and the roaring in my ears fall away, my attention sharpening to a razor point.

"What about her?" I snap.

"You *do* know her?"

I wait, my fingers fisting around the steering wheel, ready to rip it off.

"An elderly cat shifter showed up here this morning suffering from four bullet wounds, including one to the head that should've killed her. She couldn't shift for a day, but she finally limped into my place, disoriented and badly dehydrated.

"Cat shifter?" I repeated, my brain skipping in twenty directions.

"Yeah. Jacqueline Dumont. You know her?"

"What does she have to do with Kylie?" I demand through gritted teeth, impatience tearing at me, even though I already know the answer.

"Says she's her grandmother. Thinks Kylie works for you and is in trouble. Is this the woman who's been all over the news for hacking your place?"

"Fuck. Yes. Where is she now—the old woman?"

"My place."

"I'll be right there."

"She's under my protection," Garrett warns.

"I'm not going to hurt her," I practically yell into the phone before tossing it onto the seat.

Downtown is just a few exits away. I follow roads that should be familiar as if I'm driving in a new city. My mind turns over the new information. Kylie really has a grandmother. Who was shot multiple times. If she wasn't a shifter, she certainly would have died.

And ho-boy—Kylie's grandmother is a cat shifter? Is Kylie? She can't be. Her fear when I partially shifted was genuine. But how would she have a shifter for a grandmother and know nothing about werewolves?

Another thought creeps in, full of heat and tingles. Kylie has shifter blood. No wonder my wolf wanted to mate her. And it means she probably would have survived it.

But that is water under the bridge. Kylie just met with Stu, proving she was in cahoots with him the whole time.

Except, now that this new information has knocked me out of my stupor, doubt creeps in. Could there be another explanation for her meeting with Stu?

I pull up in front of Garrett's apartment and get out, walking swiftly in and onto the elevator. I stop on Garrett's floor and get off. The scent of shifters—both wolf and, yes, the distinctly feline smell as well, hits me.

I knock on the door and one of Garrett's housemates answers it and steps deferentially aside to let me in. The old woman is on the sofa, pale and weak. She's dressed in one of the wolf's T-shirts—far too big for her.

She sits up when I come in, eyes glowing gold. "Where is she?" She speaks with a thick French accent.

My eyes narrow. It's not my habit to answer anyone's demands, especially someone I've just met.

"Jackson, meet Jacqueline," Garrett says, appearing from the kitchen.

"I smell her on you. Where is Minette?" Jacqueline demands.

"I don't know anyone named Minette."

She makes an impatient slash of her hand and attempts to stand, but it's obviously too much for her. She sags back against the sofa. "My granddaughter, Kylie. They say she works for you. She's in trouble."

I pull a chair from the kitchen table and place it beside the sofa, settling into it. "Kylie is in trouble, yes. She stole hundreds of millions of dollars from my customers."

"Pfft." She waves her hand dismissively. "No, she didn't. These men did." She points at a place on the side of her head where she must have been shot. The hair is growing back, and the skin closing, but she's extremely lucky she didn't die.

The wall I spent the last forty minutes erecting shudders, as if moved by an earthquake.

This is the moment. I either go on believing in Kylie and her story as I have from the beginning, or I stick with my newer, excruciating understanding that she betrayed me.

If Kylie was in cahoots with Stu, there wouldn't be an old Frenchwoman lying on a couch with bullet wounds, would there? An old woman who greatly resembles my little hacker. The high cheekbones are unmistakable, along with something about her mouth.

Which means...*I've made a terrible mistake.*

For the second time in an hour, my heart stutters. Stops. Starts again to a new beat.

Fates. I sent Kylie away to face her enemies on her own.

It's unforgivable. I swallow hard. "Tell me what happened to you."

She blinks at me with her big golden eyes, as if judging whether I'm worthy of her story. I must pass her test because she says, "Men came to our house. They were different nationalities. One Irish, one American. Two Germans, from the sound of their accents."

I lean forward.

"I was returning from the grocery store. Minette's car was there, but no lights were on. They surprised me—were waiting in the house. Drugged me before I could shift and fight."

What a surprise it would've been for the men if the old lady had transformed into a giant cat and attacked them. Too bad she hadn't had the chance.

"How did you escape?"

The woman groans, and her expressive hand flutters toward her face. "They kept me drugged. I was never able to fight because every time I woke, they stuck another needle in my neck." She rubs a place below her left ear. "Next thing I knew, they'd taken me out in the desert and filled me with bullet holes. They must have thought I was dead when they left me. Thank the fates they were too lazy to bury me." With noticeable effort, she swings her legs to the floor to face me sitting up. "Now, I have told you my story. You tell me where to find my Minette."

She exhibits the same steely determination I've witnessed in Kylie, and my chest aches.

I scrub a hand over my face. "I just sent her away. I believed she had betrayed me."

Jacqueline's eyes move over my face, and she must see my misery because something akin to understanding flickers in her eyes. "You care for my Minette?"

I nod. How could I make such a mistake? The wolf knew, all along. I should have trusted my instincts. To distract myself from the searing pain that sliced me open from neck to groin, I ask, "What kind of cat are you?"

"Panther."

"Kylie doesn't know?"

"*Non*. My Minette never manifested. Her mother died when she was still a girl, and she was apart from me during puberty. Her father knew to contact me if she showed signs of shifting, but she never did. I reunited with her after her father's murder, but she hasn't needed me. Not until now." She peers up at me, and I'm not sure if she means because of the men who framed her or because of me.

"Is she half or quarter?"

"Half. Her mother was truly the cat burglar."

My skin prickles. *Half shifter.* No wonder my wolf wants her.

Mate.

I didn't mean to speak it out loud, but I must have because Jacqueline's eyes glow with curiosity. "She knows about you?"

"Yes. She saw my teeth when the wolf wished to mark her."

The old woman shifts and, even with her obvious frailty, her movements evoke the grace of a cat. "Did you mark her, wolf?"

I immediately feel like a young teenager getting the third degree at his girlfriend's parents' door. Shame tinges my reply. "No. But I frightened her."

Jacqueline's eyes glint in that unearthly manner cats have. I can't read her reaction.

I slide to the edge of my seat. "Jacqueline, come to my mansion. I will protect you, and we can find Kylie together."

"*Non.*" She doesn't even hesitate. "I will not be your bait for my granddaughter. I am safe here. If Kylie wishes to see you, she will make contact. In the meantime, Garrett will protect me."

The band around my throat tightens. It's like the woman already knows I don't deserve to see Kylie again. I fucked up —put her in danger, failed to trust the female who had placed herself in my hands so many times.

I let out a low curse—not at Jacqueline, but at myself. I write my cell on my business card and hand it to her before I stand. "Please contact me if you hear from her. Tell her I'm sorry, and that I made a mistake. I'll do anything I can to help her. That's a vow."

I go through the motions of shaking Garrett and his pack member's hands on the way out, but my movements are jerky. Mechanical. I'm already a thousand miles away, searching for my mate. Figuring out how I'm ever going to make this up to her.

~.~

Kylie

I ditch Sam's motorcycle downtown and check into the No-Tell Motel on Miracle Mile, a place where you can pay for a room with cash and rent by the hour. Porn is showing on the television in the room. Nice. Very nice atmosphere. I switch it off and pull out my laptop.

I'm dying to lose myself in code. No, I'm dying in general. I haven't felt this lost, this destroyed since my father's death. Back then, Mémé was the only thing that kept me going. If I don't have her now...

No. I can't think that. My gut says she's still alive, and I have to trust she is. She's tough, even for an old woman.

So my new plan is to find Mémé and leave town. But the emptiness of that plan, even being reunited with Mémé, leaves me thinner than a ghost. Leaving Jackson believing the worst of me is unthinkable. One part of me hates him for not trusting in me—after what we did last night, he thinks I played him?

But maybe that's why it cut him so deep. He isn't someone who gives his trust easily or to very many. Last night, he shared his deepest tragedy with me. Seeing me with Stu must've felt like the worst betrayal to him. But understanding doesn't lessen the sharp cut of his mistrust. He flayed me in a million pieces back at the airport.

Still, I need to make things right. I won't let him believe I destroyed his entire life's work. That I stole from him.

And even if I didn't care about Jackson and SeCure, I need to make those fuckers pay for involving me in their greedy plan. Stu, included.

I get to work following the money trail. The FBI should eventually be able to follow it, too, but by the time they do, the money will be long diverted.

I have to hack into five different banks, which takes me the rest of the afternoon, but I pick up the trail.

Bingo.

I let out a wicked witch chuckle as I send the money back to the first place from which it was diverted and reverse every transaction. Most of those accounts will be frozen or on hold. Issued new numbers. But the point is, the money will be tied up while the banks try to figure out where it's supposed to go.

Take that, Mr. X. Take that, Stu. Framing Catgirl was your biggest mistake.

The light has dimmed, and I take a break and check the antique board for a message from Mémé. With a surge of joy, I see a message in my inbox.

Minette, I am with friends. Call them at 520-235-5055.

My heart pounds. I don't dare use my phone, but I

immediately hook up an Internet voice line and dial the number. A male voice answers. "Hello."

For a moment, I freeze, not sure who I'm talking to or whether it's safe.

"Hello?"

"May I speak to Jacqueline?"

"Ah. She's been waiting for your call." He says nothing more, but Mémé's voice comes on. "Minette! *Dieu merci.* Is it safe to talk?"

"Yes. Where are you?"

"I am with the Tucson wolf pack. Downtown."

For a moment, I simply replay her words as my brain struggles to catch up. "Did you say wolf pack?"

"*Oui.* I'm sorry, I never told you, Minette. I am a shifter—a cat. Your mother, too."

I've had too many surprises today to take it all in. My hand drops limp at my side. "Wh-what?"

"Where are you, Minette?"

Minette. The French word for *puss.* She's always called me little cat because...*she's a cat.* My mind topples ass over tea kettle down a slope of dawning. "My mom?" I croak.

"Yes, your *maman*, too. This is why this wolf is attracted to you. Where are you, my sweet?"

"Not far from downtown. Are you hurt? What happened?"

"I was hurt, but I will be better soon."

My engines finally start firing. "We need to leave town right away." I stand and pick up my leather backpack purse.

"Are you sure?" There's something coaxing in Mémé's voice, but I can't decipher it. "Your wolf was just here. He said he's sorry and wants to help."

The tightness in my chest gives way to relief, followed quickly by anger. A wedge of stubbornness rises in me. He doesn't get to flip-flop so quickly. I flip him a mental bird. He's not my knight in shining armor. I'm the one saving his ass. I'm going to stick to my plan of reversing the money trail and refunding the millions in transactions and getting the hell out of Dodge.

If Jackson wants to beg for my forgiveness when that's all complete, I might consider it. We'll see.

"Give me the address where to find you, Mémé."

She must hand the phone back to its owner because the young man returns and rattles off the address of one of the few Tucson high-rise apartments downtown. He clears his throat. "Your grandmother needs some fresh clothes when you come, too."

I hate the icy spines that needle up my arms at hearing that. "I'll get her some clothes," I promise.

I consider my options. I'm without a vehicle, since I already ditched Sam's motorcycle. I could wait for a cab. I could hack Uber and set up with a credit card with one of my new ID names. But, for some reason, I want to do this without breaking the law. I don't know, maybe I need to prove I'm not the criminal the entire world thinks I am.

My house is a few miles away. Mémé's clothes are right inside. The FBI will be watching. What about the supposed Mr. X? Probably.

Damn. I have a bag packed on my bed already. It'd be so great to run in and grab it and some things for Mémé. Maybe what I need is a diversion.

I call for a cab and wait for it to arrive. Then I call in a violent robbery in progress at the house across the street from mine.

I lose the cab a block away from my place and head through the back alley, sticking to the shadows in the cover of night. Sirens screech in from several directions at my neighbor's house. I creep up my back steps and use the key hidden in the mouth of a ceramic frog in the garden.

Inside, the house feels wrong. People have been inside. I don't know how I can tell, but I know it without a doubt. But that's no surprise. Surely the police have already searched the place. I move through the dark without turning on any lights. I grab my suitcase and move to my grandmother's room. I hear the gun cock just before a hand claps over my mouth and hard metal prods the back of my head.

~.~

Jackson

I've never felt so impotent in my life. I fucked up with Kylie, my company's in the gutter, and I'm pacing my office after midnight, unable to come up with a strategy to fix things.

I told Special Agent Douglas about my suspicions of Stu, although I didn't want to tell him about the meeting with Kylie. I couldn't very well tell him about Kylie's grandmother, either. Somehow I doubt, "I saw the old lady, but it turns out she's a shifter so the bullets didn't hurt her a bit," would fly.

My cell phone rings.

Garrett.

I take the call, biting out, "This is King."

"Jacqueline expected her granddaughter to pick her up here hours ago. The old cat thinks something happened."

Ice washes over me, and I curse loud enough to shake the windows.

"I know, bro."

"Where was she coming from? What was the plan?" I demand.

"She didn't say where she was. I've tried the number she called from, but it just rings and disconnects. She said she was on her way over and asked for the address. I told her to bring some clothes for Jaqueline because hers were ruined with blood. That was around seven p.m."

I partially transform, my wolf wanting out to kill. I fight to bring my human side back, but my voice comes out pure growl. "I'm going to sniff around her house. Keep in touch." I hang up without waiting for his response.

I curse my office building for being so far from Kylie's house. I want to shift immediately and run there, but I dare not waste precious time. I drive, hands nearly tearing the steering wheel in pieces. Two feds are sitting across the street in a van, staking out the house. I knock on the door of the van as I go by and walk up to the front door. I catch a variety of scents, human males. Nothing fresh. I walk around the house, wishing to fates I could shift, but I don't dare. It's okay. My human nose still works better than most other humans' olfactory senses. I catch a whiff of Kylie at the back door. Her *fresh scent.* I try the handle and find it open.

Her scent is easy to follow—into a bedroom, but what terrifies me is the aroma of a human male. Not Stu—some other man. And gunpowder.

Fuck.

Kylie ran into trouble. *Damn her.* Why in the hell had she risked coming back here? She should know better.

I slam back out the door, sniffing the breeze, trying to find out where he's taken her. It wasn't out the front door—I would've smelled it there. Besides, the feds would've seen. I catch a trace of both their scents in the alleyway and then it disappears. There must have been a car waiting.

Christ on a stick, this couldn't be worse. I pick up my phone, then dial Garrett, communicating with him what I've found.

Jesus fuck. If anything happens to her, I am going to tear the throat out of every man I even *suspect* of knowing about it.

For the hundredth time, I curse myself for mistrusting her. For sending her into danger on her own.

Kylie. My kitten. Out there on her own in mortal danger.

I lift my mouth to the moon, barely holding back a howl of rage and anguish.

~.~

Kylie

I'm in the trunk of a car, my hands duct taped behind my back, another strip covering my mouth. I'm choking to death on my own spit. My breath sucks in and out with frantic, tearing attempts, but my nostrils seal closed, keeping me from succeeding.

Stars dance before my eyes. The trunk spins.

Don't make me grope you again.

I must've passed out, because I hear Jackson speaking to me. I conjure the feel of his hands pressing firmly against my sternum.

My breath eases off its frantic, suffocating pace.

I imagine Jackson lying behind me in the trunk, his huge arms banded around me, palms pinning the center of my chest.

I'm triggering your calm reflex.

I let the relief flow over me the way it had in the elevator. The sense of security being near Jackson brought me. The sense of belonging, of home.

Of course, I know that is best forgotten, but if deluding myself in this moment with the memory of Jackson King helps, I'm doing it.

The car pulls onto gravel and then slows to a stop. I tense, preparing to fight. My foot shoots out the minute the trunk opens, but the asshole dodges out of the way and punches me in the face. Pain explodes in my cheek, shatters the little concentration I'd gathered.

I wilt, sickness rising in my belly, desperation bleeding in.

The guy hauls me out. We're at some kind of warehouse. He drags me inside where several other men are gathered, including Stu who sits bent over a computer set up on a card table. "Look who showed up at her house," my captor drawls.

I glare at Stu, who has the nerve to look sickened by my appearance.

"The first fucking thing that's gone right all day," a guy answers in a crisp British accent. "Sit her down here." He kicks out the chair beside Stu. "Someone reversed the money trail on the hijacked cards. I've got Stu working on it, but how much you want to bet this little hack had something to do with it?"

I want to say *damn straight*, but I'm not suicidal.

I'm thrown down in chair, and I look over Stu's shoulder at his screen. He splits a glance between me and the screen. Desperation is present in his face. And fear.

Looks like Stu bit off way more than he can chew. I should be gloating, but I'm not happy for his misery. Having the one villain who's half an ally to me be in trouble with the rest of them doesn't help me much.

"How about we cut off her fingers? Permanently stop her from hacking?" This comes from the peanut gallery, one of four men leaning against crates, smoking cigars and talking.

"Shut up. You cut off her fingers, she can't fix this." British Accent walks over to me.

"Too bad we already killed the old lady. She would've been good leverage, now," another from the peanut gallery declares.

I attempt to look casual despite the terrible throbbing in my cheek where the guy punched me. Like it's my first day on the job, not like I've just been kidnapped and threatened. I cross one leg over the other and lean close to Stu. "So, what's going on?"

British Accent grabs a handful of hair and yanks my head back so hard my teeth rattle. "Did you reverse the money trail?"

I give him my most mulish look. "Why would I help SeCure? Jackson King thinks I'm responsible for all this."

He slaps me, reigniting the wicked pain of my bruise. "Get him back into the system," he commands.

I wiggle the fingers taped behind my back. "I'll need my fingers free," I sing out.

"No fingers. Talk him through it."

Damn.

I ignore British Accent and direct my attention to Stu. "Okay, where are you?"

He's attempting a straightforward hack into SeCure, which we both know isn't going to work. It occurs to me he might not be trying that hard. Maybe he's seen the writing on the wall. They're probably going to get rid of him as soon as he finishes the deal.

British Accent yanks my hair again. "Help him."

I allow my anger to show. "Okay asshole. Do you know anything about hacking? No one ever knows the way in. It's about experimentation. You just keep trying things until you make some headway. If I'm going to help Stu, I need my own computer and my fingers. Me looking over his shoulder just slows us both down."

British Accent—I'll call him BA, looks at Stu, who shrugs. "She's right."

It's too much to hope they'll give me my computer, but he does slide the tape off my wrists and shove another laptop in my face. Despite the fact that I'm still wearing the mini skirt from days before, I prop one ankle on my knee to make a desk and flip open the laptop.

I've been in Jackson's system all week through his computer, but I left an open door for myself, which is how I transferred the funds back today. I don't go in through the door, now. I go at the firewall, same as Stu.

"Is she doing it?" BA demands.

Stu looks over my shoulder. "Yeah."

I ignore them all, my fingers flying over the keys as I set up automatic password reveal programs.

As soon as they look away, I start a hack into Verizon, which was how I made my phone call to Mémé before. Stu looks over, and I flick to the open window behind it, keeping my fingers moving. I hold my breath.

He looks a moment too long, and I know he's seen me. I wait for the hammer to come down.

Nothing happens.

"You know, with Kylie working on this, you don't even need me. I'll just slow her down." Stu closes his laptop and stands up.

The sound of a gun cocking makes both of us freeze. BA

—who, by now, I believe must be Mr. X—holds the muzzle of a pistol to the side of Stu's head. "Are you sure you want me to believe we don't need you?" His icy tone sends shivers up my spine.

I think it made Stu nearly pee his pants because he lets out a weird squeak, sits down and opens his laptop. Still, I gotta hand it to him because he really brings it back. "You're threatening me? You have nothing without me. Zero."

"You just told me all I need is her."

"And who's going to know if she's hacking SeCure or into your mother's IRA?"

Mr. X palms the pistol and smacks Stu on the side of the head with it, hard enough to make him fall to the floor with a groan.

I wince, mostly at the sound of metal on bone, but also at the pathetic crumpled heap that Stu became.

Reminder to self—I am on my own, here. Nothing new, though.

I switch screens again, enter the number I'd memorized for Mémé, and send a text message.

Need help. In warehouse, 10-15 minute drive from my house. Red Toyota Corolla parked in front. Lic. DCR 583.

I close it out and flick back to the main screen.

Mémé would get help to me. I'd been stupid to go back to the house, but I might still survive this. Especially since now they need me alive.

All I have to do is stall for time...

~.~

Jackson

I wear a hole in the floor pacing at Garrett's apartment.

Sam is there, too. It's two in the morning, but no one's asleep. Jacqueline appears paler and more worn than this afternoon, her fear over Kylie aging her another ten years. I'd comfort her, but I'm ready to tear the building down.

The ding of Garrett's phone makes everyone look. He reads the text aloud. Instantly, all his men stand, a unified force. It's the first time I've had a warm feeling about a pack in years, maybe ever. But this solidarity, this support, is something I've cut myself off from.

I don't fool myself into thinking they're doing it for me. It's clear they all love the old lady. Plus, they're natural bred heroes. Garrett has an army of young, fierce twenty-somethings. Warriors, ready to defend their pack.

"That can't mean too many places. There are warehouses on South Kino, and some south of downtown, on the other side of the train tracks." He pulls a map up on his phone and holds it flat for everyone to see. "We'll divide up, take drive-throughs. If you spot something, you call in. No one goes in on their own, understood?" Garrett barks the orders, and, for once, the alpha in me doesn't even bristle. His head is way more level than mine right now. I'm grateful for his leadership.

"Jackson and Sam, take these square blocks east of Kino."

I nod and head out the door, not even waiting for him to finish divvying up the areas.

Kylie needs help, and I'm sure as hell going to find her. We drive to the warehouse district and drive slowly up and down the streets and alleyways, looking for the Corolla. Thirty minutes slip by. Forty-five. The knot in my stomach is so tight, it's twisted up to my throat.

My phone rings.

"We found it. 738 North Toole."

I don't bother answering Garrett, just step on the gas, peeling around the alley corner with a spray of gravel. I'm there in two point five minutes. I cut the engine before I reach the building and pull into the shadows. A motorcycle with one of Garrett's soldiers already stands there. Three more pull in behind me, all equally silent and cautious. Smart boys, Garrett's men.

We pull off our clothing and shift.

~.~

Kylie

I hear something outside, but no one else seems to notice. I hope it's the cavalry but don't dare let myself believe. Metal scrapes near the door, and all five men reach for their weapons.

"Shh—what was that?" Mr. X hisses.

I surge to my feet. "Hey, I gotta pee," I announce in a loud voice. "Where's the bathroom?"

"Sit the fuck down."

I walk forward. Maybe I took stupid pills, I don't know. Maybe I was just so sure help was coming. I underestimated how trigger-happy and dangerous these men were.

Guy points his pistol at my chest. Stu—like a crazy man —jumps in front of me and takes the bullet just as the blast rings in my ears. I watch him fall, see the life slip from his eyes.

Damn. Stu just died for me.

Chaos erupts everywhere as the metal garage door shoves open and a pack of giant wolves flood in.

Guns fire. Bullets fly. Above the terrible ringing in my

ears, I hear the whine of wolves being struck and the scream of men attacked by the beasts' snapping jaws.

Though there are many silver wolves, there's no mistaking mine. Huge. Majestic. Ferocious. He sees me at the same time, and it costs him a moment of distraction. One of the assholes aims and fires.

"No!" I scream and dive in front of him. Pain sears through me, through the front, out the back. White hot flames of heat. I try to keep running toward Jackson, but my body crumples into a heap. Satisfaction rises up and licks my face. For once I didn't stand there and watch someone I loved die. Stu saved me. And, now, I've saved Jackson.

And yes, I love Jackson. I know it with absolute clarity. He is my safety. My home. He is my past and my future. My now.

Jackson leaps over me in a fifteen foot graceful arc, and a gurgling sound fills my ears. I don't look, because I know he's just taken my shooter's throat out.

Then he's here, beside me. He stands over me, protecting my fallen body with his own. Licking my face, whining.

A terribly prickling comes over my entire body. Flashes of heat strike me like lightening. My vision narrows to a tunnel, yet seems to sharpen. Sounds grow louder, smells stronger. My vision flashes to black at the same time my cells seem to split apart. I am nothingness and everything at once.

Holy afterlife, Batman. I just died.

It doesn't seem fair. I've only just found Jackson. Allowed myself to admit my love for him. Believed we could be together.

My vision clears and, with it, all my pain returns with

brutal intensity. I try to groan, but the only sound that comes from my mouth is a low growl.

Growl?

Jackson shimmers and shifts, his human face looming before mine. He blinks back tears, but he doesn't look sad. His face is full of wonder. "That's it, kitten. You shifted. You showed me your panther self."

Panther self?

I look down at giant black paws. *Holy shift, Catgirl.*

Jackson strokes my muzzle. Smooths my fur. "You're going to be okay, baby. Shifters can heal from bullet wounds." He manages a watery smile. "Thank the fates. You shifted. You did it, baby."

A beautiful rumbling sound comes from my chest. Purring. It increases the bite of the bullet wound, yet I instinctively know that's good. It's healing me.

Jackson continues to stroke my face and ears, staring down at me with fierce attentiveness.

Sirens sound nearby.

A wolf barks, sharp and loud. It sounds like an order.

Jackson scoops me into his arms and runs outside. I stare over his shoulder at Stu's lifeless body. At a man who righted the scales of justice in the end. Became a hero in death, instead of a criminal. Something about his act righted more than this fucked up situation. It feels like redemption for my father's death, too. Like the universe owed me. No, like the universe is showing me proof that there's still good. That I can trust more than just family.

Hell, all around are people—shifters—who showed up to help me. Shifters who don't even know me.

Sam is by the Range Rover, yanking on a pair of jeans when we get there. He throws the door to the back seat open for his pack brother, and Jackson climbs in, still holding me.

Sam jumps in the driver's seat and starts the vehicle, driving off without turning on the lights. The sirens grow louder.

I lay my heavy head in Jackson's lap and close my eyes, the pain too much. He continues to stroke my fur and murmur softly and I believe—no, I know, without a shadow of a doubt—that finally, for once in my life, everything is going to turn out right.

~.~

Jackson

The first rays of light come up over the mountains as Sam pulls into my garage.

On my orders, he stopped to pick up Jacqueline. I knew how worried her grandmother had been, and vice versa. I want Kylie to have all the support she needs, especially considering it's her first shift. While the shift was necessary for her survival, she may not know how to shift back when the time comes.

I carry her in. Sam tries to carry Jacqueline, but the old cat insists on walking on her own, leaning heavily on Sam. We install them both in the upstairs guest bedroom. Jacqueline shifts and curls her body up beside Kylie's, lending her purring vibrations for her granddaughter's healing.

I sit beside the bed, my heart rammed up behind my chin, my fingers moving over Kylie's sleek black fur.

She's fucking magnificent. A huge black panther with golden eyes. Truly awe-inducing. It's the first time in my life anything's made sense. Of course my wolf chose this incredible female. She's everything I could ever hope for in a mate—strong, brilliant, beautiful. And a shifter.

Morning comes on like a freight train, my phone ringing

off the hook with calls. I leave the room so I won't disturb Kylie, then give orders and make statements on calls with Luis, Sarah in PR, and the CFO at SeCure. The money has been restored—all of it. I tell Luis to have SeCure take credit for the reversal because I know, without a glimmer of a doubt, who is responsible. My star employee, Kylie McDaniel.

When I come back into the room, Kylie's breathing flows even and relaxed, her wounds already closed.

"Looks like all the money is back where it belongs. You did that, didn't you, beautiful?" I murmur, rubbing her cheek. She pushes into my hand.

"Can you change back, kitten? Bring Kylie back?"

The great cat's eyes widen. As I feared, she doesn't know how.

"When Sam tried to lose himself on a California mountainside, I stood on his throat and demanded he transform. The animal can take over, if you go too long without the human side. You forget who you are."

Jacqueline shifts and re-dresses. She murmurs to Kylie in French. I catch words I understand here and there. "Find" and "quiet" and "remember." I don't know if it's different for cats, so I'm glad Jacqueline is there to help.

Kylie moves restlessly. Her eyes open and close, paws flex, showing enormous, sharp claws. She rolls over and stands up on the bed. Rolls back down to her side.

Jacqueline speaks again, a constant stream of coaching.

Kylie claws the bed, shredding the sheets and blankets.

"Come back to me, kitten. I want to kiss you," I murmur.

She turns her golden eyes on me, and our gazes lock. Neither of us seem to breathe. Finally, the air around her shimmers.

"That's it, baby," I encourage, but the shimmer fades.

"You were onto it there. Try again. I need to kiss that pretty mouth of yours."

The air shimmers again, and Kylie appears, pale, but even more beautiful than I remember.

"Baby." I lunge to wrap a blanket around her and pull her up into my arms.

"Where's the kiss you promised?" she croaks.

"Get her some water," I bark at Sam, who's leaning in the doorway. He immediately disappears.

"Well?" she demands.

I don't hold back. I claim her mouth with every bit of ferocity inside me. The need to possess, claim, mark, mate her flood from me in a torrent. The need to *punish* her for taking a bullet meant for me. The need to show her my love, my affection, my promise to be there for her next time. Not to let her down the way I did this time. I part her lips with my tongue, twine around hers. I slant my mouth over hers, demanding more, taking it all. I drink her in. I devour her.

"I'm so damn sorry," I croak when we finally part, both gasping for air. "I will never let you walk away from me again. I'll never leave you. That's a goddamn promise."

She smiles weakly, and I'm reminded of the fragile state of her health. A stab of guilt for kissing her so hard pricks me.

Sam returns with the water, and I snatch it from him to hand to my mate. "Jeez, man. Is this how it's going to be for the whole pregnancy?"

Everyone in the room freezes as I flip his words over in my head.

Pregnancy?

Jesus. *Yes.* Kylie's scent has changed. Victory pummels me like a meteor. My wolf does a double backflip and moonwalks in a circle around Kylie while fist pumping. *She's carrying my pup.* My *pup.*

Jacqueline covers her mouth. "*Mon Dieu,*" she breathes then launches herself at us, clucking rapidly in French.

Kylie's bewilderment blooms into moist eyes.

I clutch her against my body, my wolf fiercely protective even with no present threat. "That's how you shifted, kitten. My cub's DNA tipped the scale."

She laughs through her tears. "I'm pregnant? How do you know? Are you sure?"

Jacqueline, Sam, and I all nod. "Your scent has changed, baby. You're pregnant." Tears prick my eyes.

Jacqueline and Sam have the grace to slip out of the room, closing the door behind them.

"Kitten, I knew you were my mate from the moment you walked into that elevator. I need you. You're the only person I've trusted, the only thing I've believed in. Ever. I can play games with you right now, pretend I'm offering you a choice to be my mate or not, but the fact is, you're mine. You run, I'll follow. You hide, I'll find you. So, please, make it easy on both of us, and tell me that you'll stay."

Kylie purses her lips and whistles. "That might be the worst proposal I've ever heard."

I can't fight the smile tugging my mouth. "Is that a yes?"

She gives me a long look—long enough I stop breathing, have to force myself not to fidget. "I'm still mad at you for not believing in me."

I cradle her cheek. "I know. I fucked up. But I promise I will spend the rest of my life making it up to you. You and your grandmother will rule my fucking life."

Her eyes mist again, and she leans her forehead against mine. "I thought you were the one who liked to rule."

"Mmm hmm. Yes. Always. Can you live with it?"

"Yes." She didn't hesitate this time, and I nearly fall down with relief. "There's just one small problem."

My shoulders tense. "What is that?"

"I'm wanted by the FBI."

"I'm fixing that," I promise. "Garrett stayed to stage the bodies at the warehouse so it appears Stu and his cohorts killed each other. You will be given all the credit for the recovery of the money. Don't think of it again." I can't stop my hands from roaming over her soft skin, sliding up inside her T-shirt to cup her breasts. "The only thing you need to worry about is growing our baby."

She tips back her head, offering me her mouth again, and I claim it, scarcely believing she's truly mine.

"When are you going to mark me?" Her voice sounds husky, not afraid.

"Just as soon as you're recovered, baby. Right after I turn that pretty ass red for taking the bullet meant for me."

She wiggles her ass in my lap. "You know you'll always be my hero." She touches my face. "I just couldn't watch helplessly while another person I love got killed."

My heart ricochets around my chest. "You love me?"

She laughs the husky laugh that drives me wild. "I love you, wolf. I've told you that, before."

"I don't mind hearing it again."

"I love you, I love you, I—"

I shut her up with a kiss, smothering her mouth with mine, stroking her lips, joining our tongues. "I love you, kitten. You're home now."

She let her head fall back and closed her eyes. "Yes," she sighed. "You are my home."

EPILOGUE

One month later

Kylie

"Pull that skirt up, baby. Let me see what's waiting for me when we get home." My mate hasn't grown any less bossy since marking me. Our drive home from work together has become just one of the many pleasures of working for Jackson King. Shared lunch breaks are another one. And getting to help him with his new code.

He stares over at me like a starving man. Like he hadn't already fucked me over his desk after using a ruler on my ass during lunch. Like he doesn't have full access to me every night at home.

"*Now*, kitten. Every second you make me wait will earn you a stroke with my belt."

I already reached for the hem of my tight fitted skirt, but I stop now, flashing a naughty grin. "Is that so?"

Now that I've switched on my shifter DNA, my body heals almost instantaneously, which means Jackson can employ any form of punishment he desires and the pain is only fleeting. It's a bit sad, really. Because now I can never get enough.

Jackson grasps the fabric and rucks my skirt up to my waist, tearing the fabric with the force of it. He slaps my thighs apart. "Show me what's mine." His voice is thick. I love hearing him like this, halfway gone with desire for me. Now that he knows I'm a shifter, he's not afraid to be rough with me.

Last full moon, he installed me in his cabin again and claimed me in every position, angle, and orifice ever invented. I'd thought he'd been insatiable last time, when he'd been trying not to mark me, but it turns out mating him doesn't ensure my safety when the moon is full.

Not that I'd ever complain.

I reach down and stroke the notch between my legs. "You looking at this?" I purr.

He bites out a curse. "Off," he growls. "Panties down or I tear them off."

I make a show of shimmying out of my panties and dangle them in front of his face while he drives.

He snatches them, brings them to his nose, and inhales deeply before shoving them into his breast pocket. He's in a suit today, which had me wet all day. I love when he wears his CEO garb almost as much as I love the tight T-shirts and jeans.

"*This*, baby." He reaches across the car and wedges his hand between my legs. "Open those thighs wider for me. I need to see my pussy."

I attempt to obey, but it couldn't be seen anyway because his fingers are tap-tap-tapping, spanking my clit and my feminine folds, making me squirm as heat floods between my legs.

Jackson's rumbling growl fills the Range Rover. He pushes one finger inside me.

"Jackson," I gasp. "Not while you're d-driving."

He tsks and slides the beautiful, intruding digit in and out, sending spirals of heat and pleasure careening through my body. "Who gives the orders around here, kitten?"

I moan as he works the finger even deeper. I don't know how he's managing to drive straight. I'm blind with desire, my world tilting and rocking, sliding to one side then righting itself and sliding to the other. "Y-you do."

"That's right, baby."

I grind my clit against the heel of his hand, taking his finger deeper.

"Who owns your every orgasm?"

I lift my pelvis to meet his thrusts, gritting my teeth. "You do! P-please, Jackson."

He growls. "Beg for it, kitten."

I'm not too proud. "Please, please, please, Jackson!"

He leans forward to change the angle and inserts a second finger.

I lift my hips from the seat cushion, swallowing a scream just before I come.

"That's right baby. Come all over my fingers. You'll be squeezing my cock when you come again as soon as I get you home. *After* your whipping."

My thighs tremble as I fall back, limp and shaky from the release.

Jackson pulls into his driveway—*our* driveway, as he keeps reminding me. I still can't believe how fully enmeshed our lives are now. We get out of the vehicle, and I adjust my skirt. Jackson circles around the car and shoves me up against it. He captures my face with one hand and holds it prisoner for a hot, rough kiss.

"I know that pussy is still squeezing for me." How he knows this, I have no idea, but he's right. The hand holding my face drops to cup my nape. "So we're going to go inside and kiss Mémé and eat dinner. But, when I give you the signal, you will scurry upstairs and take off everything but those sexy high heels. And I want you waiting for me with your ass in the air and your face in the blankets. Understand?"

The squeezing between my legs becomes more distracting.

"Yes, sir."

He smiles and traces the pad of his thumb over my lower lip. "Good girl. Let's go."

Inside, the house smells of Mémé's heavenly cooking.

"Ah, you're home." Mémé beams. She's wearing the goofy apron Sam bought her that has the French food pyramid on it—French bread, cheese, and quiche.

Jackson kisses her on the cheek. "What smells so good, Mémé?"

"Steak for the wolves. Salmon for the cats. Rice and salad and fresh bread for all of us."

Sam comes in the back door carrying a platter piled high with steaks from the grill. "Your meat, mademoiselle." He gives Mémé a bow and a wink.

She blushes like a schoolgirl. She and Sam get along famously. At first, Sam had suggested he move out, but Mémé and I wouldn't hear of it, and Jackson backed us up.

"You are my pack," he insisted. "The three of you. I need you all at my house where I can protect you. And, Sam, I need you around to protect my females when I'm away."

"Bring it to the living room," Mémé directs Sam now, and shoos us in after him. I try to sit in my chair, but Jackson pulls me onto his lap, instead. He still hasn't grown tired of feeding me. Something about a wolf's privilege.

As I watch my small family gather around the table, my heart swells so large, I'm sure it will burst. As strange and unlikely a pack as we are, with them, I experience a profound sense of belonging. *This* is the normal I've been searching for all these years.

I'm finally with my own kind, loved beyond measure.

Home.

***

Thank you for reading Alpha's Temptation! If you enjoyed it, we would so appreciate your review—they make a huge difference for indie authors.

Jump into the next Bad Boy Alpha book, Alpha's Danger. (Turn the page for a preview).

WANT MORE? CHECK OUT ALPHA'S DANGER

Alpha's Danger - Prologue

Amber

Note to self: Crazy people subject to visions should stay away from crowded airports.

I roll my suitcase up to the sink in the bathroom and gaze at my face in the mirror as I wash my hands. My migraine has turned me into a monster, eyes bloodshot and sunken, as if they're receding into my skull to get away from it all. I dry my hands with a paper towel and pat the damp paper against my cheeks, suppressing a groan.

What was I thinking, flying here? Nothing triggers my hallucinations like being around too many people. A guy in a business suit bumped into me and his memory flashed in my head: him in bed with a woman. He's cheating on his wife.

I don't know how I know, but I do. And I wish I didn't.

Maybe I'll just hide in the bathroom until they call for my flight. Yeah, that's a plan. Crazy Amber, hiding in bathrooms because she has visions wherever she goes. I went to law school for this?

My phone beeps. 10:42 a.m.. Fifteen minutes until boarding time, and five hours before my interview. I dig for aspirin, wincing at the rattle of pills in the bottle.

Note to self: buy pain meds in gel caps.

"Excuse me." A warm voice sounds behind me, and an old woman touches my back as she reaches past me for a paper towel.

I mean to duck away without eye contact, but the woman has me trapped between the sinks and the paper towels, unable to escape. I glance up with my polite smile pasted in place.

The woman has long white hair but a surprisingly youthful face, and wide blue eyes. "How long have you practiced the intuitive arts?"

I look behind myself, even though I knew no one else is there. But the woman couldn't be talking to me, could she? "Excuse me?"

She still touches me, her fingers lightly resting on my sleeve now. "The intuitive arts? How long have you been practicing?"

A chill runs through me. "I'm sorry, I don't know what you're talking about."

The woman's face clouds. "Oh." Her expression clears. "Well, you're supposed to, honey, and you're going to keep having headaches until you do."

My vision blurs with the fast-motion movie reel pictures I'd been trying to suppress. Nausea blasts through me. I see a huge, muscle-bound man standing on a beach, brow wrinkled, fists clenched. Then a wolf in a cage, snarling.

I force the breath out of my lungs and draw in fresh oxygen, shaking my head as if that might clear the stupid visions. When my focus returns to the bathroom, I blink. The woman's gone.

Grabbing my suitcase handle, I wheel it out of the bathroom, scanning for the white-haired woman when the clock catches my eye. 10:42 a.m. That has to be wrong.

I check my phone just as the two changes to three. Almost no time passed in the bathroom, but there's no sign of the woman.

How did she just vanish into thin air?

Three Years Later

Alpha's Danger - Chapter One

Amber

I step into the elevator, propping the door open with my foot to hold it for the group approaching.

"Thanks." A deep voice resonates in the small space. A large hand tattooed with a the phases of the moon wraps around the door followed by a blue-eyed giant of a man. Underneath his faded t-shirt and tattoos, he's got muscles like Conan the Barbarian. He could probably eat me for lunch and still be hungry.

Two younger men, just as hulking in size, flank him. Shaved heads, a mess of piercings, and more tattooes. I have to stop myself from recoiling.

What are the Hell's Angels doing in my apartment building?

Don't show fear. The first thing I learned in foster care. *Study the threat.* Again, foster care, though the lesson carried over to the courtroom nicely.

I draw myself up to my full five foot, three inch height.

No matter that I barely come up to the shortest guy's shoulder. I'm a badass, too. Maybe I don't have giant ear gauges or an eyebrow piercing--ouch, talk about suffering for fashion- - but I'm wearing pointy pumps. They're pinching the hell outta my feet, but with a three inch spike heel, they'll double as a weapon.

"Visiting someone in the building?" my voice has a dubious lilt. I'm not actually a snooty bitch, but when my safety is compromised, the claws come out.

The first guy gazes down at me and the corner of his mouth twitches. "No."

At least this guy looks somewhat normal, except for his huge size. Scratch Conan the Barbarian. This guy is all Thor, right down to his square jawed good looks.

The three men file onto the elevator, choking the small space. There's so much testosterone in here, it's a wonder I can breathe.

I lean against the wall, hope these guys aren't up to no good. I don't want to judge, but I wouldn't have survived childhood if I ignored a threat. And these guys look rough. Their presence makes my skin prickle. Not the stomach-roiling of a full blown vision, but a slight buzzing that can only mean one thing.

Danger.

I stare at Thor's barrel chest, the raised contour of muscle standing out under his t-shirt, and curse my nipples for beading up at such an obvious display of masculine power. What in the hell is wrong with me? I rarely get turned on by men and my hormones choose this moment to rev into gear? Choose this motorcycle-driving He-man? He's probably a criminal. I cock a hip and wait for him to explain why The Three Thugs are here.

He says nothing, but one of the younger guys smirks at me.

My hand flutters to my neck, ready to knead away the tension at the base of my skull. I cover the defensive gesture by checking to make sure my updo is secure before pushing the button for the fourth floor. "Which floor?" I ask in my best "I could kick your ass in court" tone.

"Same as yours," Thor drawls.

Is that a come on? Or a threat? Are they following me? No, that's silly. They could've just grabbed me in the parking lot if they wanted. I heard their motorcycles roll up, though I never imagined the riders were coming in here.

Thor looks at me, though I refuse to meet his eyes. I hold my briefcase in front of me like a shield until the elevator stops and the doors slide open to my floor.

Please don't let them be after me. Paranoia, my old friend. I'm being judgy here, but the whole reason I'd moved into an apartment building instead of buying a house was to feel safe.

You'll never be safe.

Cell phone out at the ready, I wait for the motorcycle gang to get out first. Let's see if they actually have someplace to go. The men saunter off, heading past the door to my apartment and--*oh crap*--they stop at the very next door.

No. *Way.* It couldn't be. "Y-you're my neighbors?" I've lived here a few weeks, but haven't met anyone, yet. The new high rise is right downtown, and the rent is pretty high, even for my salary. Not be rude, but these guys in their ripped up t-shirts and jeans don't look like they can afford the place. Unless they are drug dealers. Which would be just my luck.

"Is there a problem?" Thor asks.

"Ah...no. Of course not." *Not until you throw a disgustingly loud party complete with biker babes and too much booze.*

Frankly, I can't believe they haven't already. These guys look like trouble with a capital *T*.

I slide my key into the lock, glancing back to make sure they're really going into their apartment. Thug Number Two--the smirking one-- lunges at me, snarling like a ferocious dog.

I scream and drop my briefcase, cringing against the door.

Thug Number Three laughs.

Thor grabs the scruff of the barking man's shirt and yanks him back. "Knock it off," he says. "Get inside. You don't need to scare her." His eyes land on me again. "She's doing a good enough job of that herself."

The two young men stroll inside, still chuckling. I grab my briefcase. Tendrils of my hair break free from my hair clip, and I swipe at them to hide my flushed cheeks. Damn punks. My hand shakes and I hate that most of all. I didn't survive my disjointed childhood just to cower in doorways.

My head feels a little tight, herald of an oncoming vision. I haven't had one in a while, so this one should be a doozy.

Great.

Heart hammering against my ribs, I enter my apartment and start to shut my door. A steel-toed boot jams inside the doorway, stopping me. My eyes fly up to Thor's face, landing on the startling blue eyes. The corners crinkled and he gives me a predatory half-smile.

I shiver.

"I'm Garrett." He extends his large hand through the gap in the door.

I stare at it for a full two seconds before good manners win out over fear. I transfer the phone to my left hand to take his palm. The heat from his hand envelopes mine, a shock of connection running up my arm. A strange sense of knowing runs through me--like this guy and I are old friends, and I've just forgotten.

I shake off *deja vu.* Gotta keep Crazy Amber at bay.

"Sorry Trey scared you. I'll make sure it doesn't happen again." His voice is deep and velvet-smooth, matching his rugged good looks. It sends heat curling in my low belly. He appears to be not much older than my twenty-six years. Too old to be dressing and acting like a punk. Although he does it *so well.* Faded t-shirt stretched across giant pecs, tattoos peeking at me from his sleeves and collar. Tousled, just out of bed hair, and midday scruff. Mmmm.

Note to self: tattooed bad boys make my ovaries sit up and beg.

I shove my awakening lust back down. This is no time to be turned on. This guy looks dangerous.

"Are--" I clear my throat, trying to sound conversational instead of paranoid. "Are all three of you staying there?"

"Yeah. So you'll be safe with us around." He flashes a full smile that takes my breath away. He has deep dimples and remarkably full lips for such a manly man. Chris Hemsworth has nothing on this guy.

Safe. Yeah, right. "Fantastic. I feel better already. Would you mind removing your foot from my door?" I'm going for cool, calm and collected, but it comes out sounding a little tart.

He gives me a lazy smirk that unfortunately ignites a slow burn between my thighs. "You never told me your name."

"I know." I look pointedly down at his foot.

He tsks, folds his arms and leans against my doorframe. "Look, princess--"

"Don't call me *princess.*"

He raises a brow. "Then what do I call you?"

"Ms. Drake. Amber Drake."

"You a teacher or something?"

"Lawyer. And you're close to a harassment charge." He's not actually. They haven't done anything wrong. I don't usually throw my lawyer weight around, but I want to get inside my apartment before I have a vision. Don't need my hot new neighbor knowing I'm crazy.

"We didn't mean to scare you."

"You don't scare me," I say quickly.

"Then what was with you clutching your pearls? You acted like your panties were twisted in a knot."

Oh lordy. He's talking about my panties. "I'm not wearing pearls," I say in my most lawyerly tone.

"What about panties?"

The sensitive bits covered by said garment contract at the mention. "No comment." I yank the door, but it doesn't budge. He raises his hands in surrender.

"Figure of speech. You'd be clutching them if you had them. The pearls."

The image of me clutching my panties instead, as he rips them off me with those strong, white teeth makes my breath hitch. To hide my mounting lust, I go back to scowling, giving up on tugging the door.

"Listen," he says. "My guys are cool. They may look rough, but they're motherfucking Boy Scouts."

I wince at the ill-placed curse word. "Well, Mr...Garrett, maybe you should get back to helping old ladies cross the street." I shoo him but he doesn't budge.

"I'd rather help you across the hall to my apartment." He leans closer and heat rushes over me. It's been a long time since I've been hit on by someone this hot. Maybe ever. The lack of subtlety has me rolling my eyes but I have to admit, there's something to his cocky directness. No. I am not tempted in the least.

Note to self: find nice, normal, non-scary guy and flirt with him. Never, *ever* entertain the thought of going over to my scary hot neighbor's place wearing nothing but tiny panties and pearls. And maybe a pair of heels.

Oh God.

"Seriously," Garrett's voice drops an octave, the low rumble thrilling me. "Come on over, have a beer. Get to know us."

Can Lawyer Amber turn into Amber the Biker Chick? For a split second, I see myself out of my chic business suit and in tight jeans and a tube top. Hair down around my shoulders, cheeks sun kissed and tilted into the wind. I cling to Garrett, leaning into the curve of the road as we ride.

I blink. Did I just have a vision? My head pulses a little in answer, but there's no pain.

"So what will it be, princess?" Garrett's still looking at me, blue eyes friendly. A girl could get lost in that cerulean sea.

Not. Safe.

"No, thank you."

"Okay. Your loss." He withdraws his boot.

My tight hold on the door makes it slam in both our faces. I yelp like an idiot. *Lordy.* I draw in a long, shaky breath. Something has let loose in my belly and somersaults around like a balloon releasing its air.

Locking the deadbolt, I press my ear to the wood and listen. Three seconds pass before I hear footsteps walk away. I sag against the doorway, put a hand to my head. The slight throb is gone.

Note to self: call building management tomorrow and

find out just exactly who those guys are and whether there are any complaints against them.

For all I know, my apartment might have come available because no one wants to live next to those guys. I sure as hell don't.

At least, that's what I'm telling myself.

"I don't even have pearls," I mutter, toeing off my pumps and setting my briefcase on the table as I speed dial my best friend.

"Hey, girl," she answers. I might be boring and normal (or at least I try to be), but my bestie is cool. Her mom was a hippie, though, which is how she ended up with an outrageous name.

"Hey, Foxfire. How's it going?"

"Trying to keep busy...you know, to keep my mind off it." Foxfire caught her boyfriend cheating the weekend before and kicked him out. About time, but break ups suck, so I've appointed myself her number one cheerleader and activities coordinator until the risk of her caving and asking him back is over.

"Do you want to come to my place? We could watch Netflix and chill." I'm ready for a bit of mind numbing television tonight. Nothing like silly reality shows to keep my crazy visions at bay. If only it helped my headaches.

"No thanks," Foxfire sighs.

I sense a sad spiral coming on, and scramble. "Hey, you know what we should do?"

"What?"

"Go out dancing tomorrow night. The Morphs are playing at Club Eclipse."

"I don't know. I don't really feel like it."

"Are you kidding me? They're your favorite. You're always telling me how good they are in concert." Most days,

I avoid clubs, bars and any other loud spaces like my sanity depends on it. Which, given my tendency to have visions, it just might. *Foxfire, you better appreciate this.* I take a deep breath and lie my face off. "Now I really want to go."

"You? You hate going out. Usually I'm the one dragging you."

"Uh, yeah, and now I miss it. I know you don't feel like it--that's not the point. The point is to force yourself to get out and be social." I use the argument she's used on me many a time. "I bet a million guys hit on you."

Foxfire snorts. "I doubt it. But I'd love a Cosmo."

"Me too." It's my turn to sigh.

"So what's with you? You've been working so much lately."

"Yeah, the center's been busy."

"Lots of kids coming through the system?" Foxfire says with gentle sympathy.

"A few."

"Well, I know you're helping them. You almost give lawyers a good name."

"I don't know about that. But helping these kids is necessary. Jesus, so many of them have the most fucked up lives. They deserve at least one person representing them in the system who cares." I grab a sponge from the sink and wipe down the counter, even though it's already clean. "So...I just met the guys who live next door."

"Oh yeah?" Foxfire says in a suggestive tone.

"No, not like that. Scary-looking guys." I recall Garrett's blue eyes and dimpled smile. Maybe he's not that scary. But he definitely left me feeling flustered and off-kilter. "I don't know. I couldn't tell if they were intimidating me or flirting."

"You sound interested."

"No, definitely not." *Total lie.* My hand tingles where

Garrett grabbed it. A man like him would big enough to climb like a jungle gym. Would he let me ride on top? Oh jeez. *Head out of the gutter, Amber!*

I don't want him in my bed. Even though he's probably really good. But good in bed doesn't mean he'll be a good neighbor. Unbidden, the image of me joining one of their all-nighters in my panties and pearls pops in my brain.

Stop it.

"Are they hot?" Leave it to Foxfire to read between the lines.

Even though I'm alone in my apartment, my cheeks grow warm. I let out a strangled chuckle. "Um...yeah. One of them was--is--whatever. But not my type. Definitely not my type."

~.~

Garrett

I lift my palm to my face and inhale the scent still lingering from the pretty blonde human. She wore the hell out of that short fitted skirt and jacket, and as much as she wanted to project prim and proper, I smelled her interest. She was aroused. *By me.* And when we touched hands, I'd felt the shock of something.

My fingers still tingle from our connection.

I smelled a little fear on her, but mostly the notes were warm and sultry, vanilla, orange and spice. My wolf didn't want to scare her--which is a first. He usually likes throwing his weight around, and feels only impatience for human women. Why would I be interested in a human? And she definitely is all human--I went in close to be sure.

I have no idea why she made my dick so hard. Sassy

little thing, pulling her uptown girl act while her knees shook with fear. I wanted to push her up against the elevator wall, wrap those knocking knees around my waist and plow the sauciness right out of her. I bet she's never had a proper orgasm. I just might have to show her what it's like to come all over my cock, my name falling from those berry lips like a prayer.

I rearrange my swelling cock in my jeans before plunking down on the leather sofa. Trey and Jared have already opened bottles of beer and stand out on the balcony, talking loudly. Probably not the best for new neighbor relations.

Maybe I'm getting too old to live with my pack brothers. My mom's been telling me for years I needed to take a mate, act like an adult, and make the Tucson pack into something more than an MC club of mostly male shifters. We live loose and free, but the fraternity feel makes most wolves wanting to start a family move away to my father's pack in Phoenix, or out of state.

My phone rings and I check the screen. "Hey, sis," I answer the call.

"Hi, Garrett," she sounds breathless. "Guess where I'm going for spring break?"

"Um...San Diego?"

"Nope."

"Big Sur?"

"Nope, not California."

"Where, kiddo?"

"San Carlos!"

"No." I make my voice deep and forbidding. San Carlos is a Mexican beach town several hours south of Tucson, but according to the news, is having trouble with drug cartels.

"Garrett, I'm not asking." At twenty-one, my sister,

Sedona--named for the beautiful red-rocked Arizona town where my parents conceived her--is still the coddled baby of the family. She wants full autonomy when she demands it, and full support--financial and otherwise--the rest of the time.

I was ten when Sedona, an "oopsie-baby" was born, so she's more like a daughter than a sister. "Oh, you'd better be asking or we have a big problem." I sharpen my tone. My folks only allowed Sedona to go to University of Arizona because I live close enough to watch over her. I might be an easy-going guy, but I'm still an alpha. My wolf doesn't tolerate tests of my authority.

"Okay, I'm sorry, I was asking," she capitulates, changing from stubborn to pleading. "Garrett, I *have* to go. All my friends are going. Listen--we're not going to drive through Nogales--we found out there's a safer route. And we'll be in a big group. Besides, I'm not human, remember? Drug gangs can't harm me."

"A bullet to the head would harm anyone."

"I'm not going to get a bullet to the head. I won't be buying drugs, obviously, and I won't be around places where stuff like that goes down. You're being way too overprotective. I'm an adult, in case you've forgotten."

"Don't get sassy."

"Pleeease, Garrett? Pretty please? I *have* to go!"

"Tell me who's going."

A pro at wrapping people around her little finger, Sedona picks up on my crumbling resistance. She plows eagerly into her description of the group. Four boys, five girls, of which two are couples. All human, besides her.

If they were wolves, I'd put my foot down about the mixed genders--not that I'm old-fashioned. With humans, though, no male would be capable of overpowering my sister in any scenario. Still, a spring break beach trip sounds like it would consist of too much drinking and partying, which always results in poor decision-making.

A whoop from the balcony makes me glare at my roommates.

"I want to meet these kids," I tell my sis.

"Garrett, *please*! You will totally embarrass me. That's not fair."

"Then my answer is no."

She huffs into the phone. "Fine. We'll stop by on our way out of town to say goodbye."

Very clever. I'd be the biggest jerk on Earth to pull the plug on her trip at the last minute. My dad would do it, but not me. Which is the main reason Sedona picked a college in my town, versus going to Arizona State.

"Okay. When are you leaving?"

"Tomorrow."

"You're calling to ask permission the night before your trip?" I growl into the phone.

"Well, I was trying to avoid the asking permission thing," she says in a small voice.

"You're lucky you reconsidered." I force my hand to relax. I don't want to break another cellphone.

"So I can go?"

"You will not allow anyone to drive drunk at any time."

"Right."

"And you will never drink more than two drinks in one night."

"Aw, come on, Garrett, you know I can drink more than that."

"I don't care. I'm giving you my stipulations. If you want to go, you'd better agree to them."

"Okay, okay, I agree. What else?"

"I want a check-in text every day."

"Got it."

I sigh. "Did you get Mexican insurance for the car?"

"Yep. We're all set. I'll see you in the morning. Love you, big bro. You're the best!"

I shake my head, but smile as I hang up. Whoever mates my sister has my pity. It's impossible to deny her anything.

"Hey, boss, you headed to the club tonight?" Trey ambles in from the balcony.

"Not tonight," I examine my phone for cracks. Sedona brings out the protective side of me unlike any other. At least, until I met little Miss Prim 'n Proper next door. For some reason, my wolf has already decided she'd under my protection, whether she likes it or not.

"'Cause I was thinking about inviting our new neighbor out. See if she has a wild side."

"No," I growl. My phone crunches in my grip. Rage flares up out of nowhere, surprising the hell outta me. "Leave her alone." Trey's eyes drop to the floor. Beyond him, Jared freezes.

"Just stay away from our neighbor." My wolf is close, making my voice husky.

"Yes, Alpha," Both wolves bow their heads.

Instead of an explanation, a growl rises in my throat. I'm alpha. I don't have to explain. "And no more drinking on the balcony," I add with a glare. When I open my hand, pieces of my cell phone drop to the couch.

My anger fades as they slink away, but the feeling of satisfaction remains. My wolf is happy we protected Amber. But why? What does one little human matter to me?

~

Alpha Danger, Book 2

"You broke the rules, little human. I own you now."

I am an alpha wolf, one of the youngest in the States. I can pick any she-wolf in the pack for a mate. So why am I sniffing around the sexy human attorney next door? The minute I catch Amber's sweet scent, my wolf wants to claim her.

Hanging around is a bad idea, but I don't play by the rules. Amber acts all prim and proper, but she has a secret, too. She may not want her psychic abilities, but they're a gift.

I should let her go, but the way she fights me only makes me want her more. When she learns what I am, there's no escape for her. She's in my world. Whether she likes it or not. I need her to use her gifts to help recover my missing sister--and I won't take no for an answer.

I own her now.

READ ALL THE BAD BOY ALPHA BOOKS)

Bad Boy Alphas Series

Alpha's Temptation
Alpha's Danger
Alpha's Prize
Alpha's Challenge
Alpha's Obsession
Alpha's Desire
Alpha's War
Alpha's Mission
Alpha's Bane
Alpha's Secret
Alpha's Prey
Alpha's Blood
Alpha's Sun

ABOUT RENEE ROSE

USA TODAY BESTSELLING AUTHOR RENEE ROSE loves a dominant, dirty-talking alpha hero! She's sold over a half million copies of steamy romance with varying levels of kink. Her books have been featured in USA Today's *Happily Ever After* and *Popsugar*. Named Eroticon USA's Next Top Erotic Author in 2013, she has also won *Spunky and Sassy's* Favorite Sci-Fi and Anthology author, *The Romance Reviews* Best Historical Romance, and *Spanking Romance Reviews'* Best Sci-fi, Paranormal, Historical, Erotic, Ageplay and favorite couple and author. She's hit the *USA Today* list five times with various anthologies.

Please follow her on:

Bookbub | Goodreads | Instagram

Renee loves to connect with readers!

www.reneeroseromance.com

reneeroseauthor@gmail.com

Click here to sign up for Renee Rose's newsletter and receive a free copy of *Theirs to Protect, Owned by the Marine, Theirs to Punish, The Alpha's Punishment, Disobedience at the Dressmaker's* and *Her Billionaire Boss*. In addition to the free stories, you will also get special pricing, exclusive previews and news of new releases.

WANT FREE RENEE ROSE BOOKS?

Go to http://owned.gr8.com to sign up for Renee Rose's newsletter and receive a free copy of *Theirs to Protect, Owned by the Marine, Theirs to Punish, The Alpha's Punishment, Disobedience at the Dressmaker's* and *Her Billionaire Boss*. In addition to the free stories, you will also get special pricing, exclusive previews and news of new releases.

EXCERPT: THE ALPHA'S PROMISE BY RENEE ROSE

Be sure to check out the Alpha Doms series by Renee Rose

The Alpha's Promise

A Bad Boy Shifter Romance (Alpha Doms Book 3)

By Renee Rose

Chapter One

Melissa headed up the sidewalk to the rundown rental house where she and her loser, soon to be ex-boyfriend had lived for the past eight months. She couldn't wait to be done with the place. Her heels clicked on the concrete, pencil skirt too constraining in the early June heat after a long day showing houses.

She braced herself for the annoying clutter of half-filled moving boxes. At least it meant that in less than a month Jeremy would be out of her life, forever.

The relationship never should've happened in the first place. She'd mistaken bonding in a crisis situation—Jeremy had saved her life after he and his buddy had kidnapped her last year—for true love. Maybe she'd just wanted what her sister had with her new husband.

In another of her classic bad judgement moves, she'd forgiven him for the kidnapping, been grateful for his change of heart. Moved in with the guy who'd put her life in danger. That f-ed up statement pretty much summed everything up. She was too loyal, too trusting. Thought that the attraction would last. It hadn't. Four months later she'd been totally over him, but it had taken her four more to figure out how to get out of their lease, even after they'd broken up. Her stuff was already packed into boxes. By this time next month she'd be free of Jeremy and this dump.

She unlocked the door and pushed it open, then stopped dead with a gasp.

The place had been wrecked. Destroyed.

Boxes had been opened and emptied—stuff was strewn everywhere. The pottery dishes she'd bought from her artist friend in college lay in a broken heap, paintings had been torn from the walls and smashed.

A sob rose in her throat. She turned in a slow circle, her heart thumping hard in her chest. When she saw the maroon spray-painted words scrawled across the back wall, she screamed.

Pay up by Friday or you both die.

A sheet of ice flashed through her. She literally couldn't move, couldn't breathe. Her body trembled all over. Her hand closed around her cell phone, but something stopped her from calling 911.

This wasn't just a break-in. It was personal. And it had something to do with Jeremy. Had something happened at the dispensary? He was always afraid they'd be robbed at gunpoint—it had happened at other dispensaries because they took in a large amount of cash.

Oh, God. She should've known. She should've run fast and hard from Jeremy the moment they were free of the kidnapping trauma.

He had a knack for landing in trouble. He associated with the wrong sorts of people. He liked to party and used drugs. He might even deal harder stuff out the back door of the dispensary—she didn't know, she'd been turning a blind eye to all that.

Would calling the cops ensure someone's death? She gulped. Hers?

With trembling fingers, she dialed her twin sister instead. Ashley and Ben had gone to the Canary Islands for their honeymoon. She shouldn't bother them, but... she really didn't know what else to do.

"Hey, Mel," her sister's voice called gaily through the earpiece.

"I'm sorry to bother you."

Her sister instantly picked up on the pinched, wobbly quality of her voice. "What is it, Mel? What happened?" Ashley asked sharply.

"I-I'm not sure. I just came home and the place has been wrecked. And there's a spray-painted message on the wall." She told her sister what it said, without having to voice her suspicions about it being some trouble of Jeremy's. Ben and Ashley already had the lowest opinion of him.

"I'm going to check upstairs, do you mind staying on the phone with me?"

"Of course I don't mind, but do you think you should call the police?"

She walked up the stairs, holding the phone tight against her ear, as if it somehow made her sister closer.

Ben's sharp tones had started at the mention of police, and she listened to her sister explain to him what had happened.

The intruders had trashed the bedroom upstairs, too. Her dresser drawers had been dumped onto the floor, hamper unloaded. It looked like they'd even torn the carpet up from the floor. What had they been looking for? Money?

"Mel? Ben's going to call someone he knows in Colorado Springs, so just sit tight, okay?"

"Okay." She was more relieved than she cared to admit to hear that Ben knew what to do.

"I'll call you right back," Ashley promised.

She hung up and stared at the mess, tears burning her eyes. What should she do? She wished she could pack up all her stuff and get out that second, but she didn't know where to go. Where could she rent a place on such short notice? And she didn't want to rent, dammit, she'd been so excited to buy her own place.

Ben Stone, her twin sister's wealthy new husband, had offered to help her with a down payment so she could buy a house of her own.

The sound of a car door slamming made her look out the window. Jeremy had better have a solution for—

But it wasn't Jeremy.

Three lethal-looking guys got out of a dark blue Range Rover and strode purposefully to the front door. They didn't bother knocking and she stupidly hadn't locked it.

Holy hell. They were here, *in the house.* They were going to kill her.

Heart jammed up high in her throat, she dived for the closet, squirrelling back behind the clothes.

Please don't let them search the house.

Her phone lit up, the first note of the ring sending her

into a wild swiping frenzy to shut it off. It went silent. She held her breath, listening to hear if the men downstairs had noticed, but only heard the sound of their voices calling to each other. Were they moving in to wait for her and Jeremy?

Her hands shook so hard, she could hardly read the phone, but saw it had been Ashley calling.

She texted her back.

They're in the house.

Cody Steele washed the plaster off his trowel and wiped everything clean. Almost finished—just a couple of quick coats of paint over this repaired hole in the wall and the house would be ready to go on the market. Buying historic buildings and homes, fixing them up and selling for a tidy profit had put his restless, hands-on personality to good use. CJ Steele properties had become well known in Colorado Springs for their real estate successes and his company provided jobs for most of the wolves in his pack.

Not bad, considering his dad had thrown him out of the pack at sixteen, saying he'd never amount to anything. It was a source of pride that he'd started and made his business successful completely on his own, starting a pack in a city where they'd previously been loose members of the Denver pack.

His cell phone buzzed and he pulled it out of his pocket and frowned. Ben Stone, the alpha from Denver. What in the hell did he want?

He answered it. "Cody speaking."

"Cody? Ben Stone, from Denver."

"I know who you are."

"I need a favor from you—a big one." There was a curt sense of urgency in the guy's voice.

He ground his molars. Pretty presumptuous for a guy who hadn't offered him or his pack even a hello since he took over as alpha nine months ago. "I don't recall owing you one."

Stone didn't hesitate. "I'll be the one owing. My sister-in-law lives in Colorado Springs and she's run into trouble. I'm out of the country or I'd come down myself to handle things."

"What kind of trouble?"

"Her place got broken into. There's a threatening message spray-painted on the wall. Probably her loser ex-boyfriend got himself into some trouble, but she's not involved. I need you to keep her safe."

Fuck.

This was the last thing he wanted to get involved in. But having Ben Stone in his debt would only be a good thing for his pack. Ben had all kinds of resources, money being at the top of the list. He also had a large pack with members of every skill set, and being friendly with them would mean he'd never have to turn to his father's pack for help. And he'd rather die than do that.

"Steele?"

He blew out his breath. "Yeah, okay. What's the address?"

"I'll text it to you. You'll go right now?"

"I'll go. What's her name?"

"Melissa. Steele—alpha's promise you'll give her pack protection."

Shit. What in the hell was he getting himself into? Stone wanted him to vow his own life to protect her. Well, that's what wolves did.

"Yeah," he grunted. "Alpha's promise."

"Thank you."

He closed his eyes and rubbed a hand across his face. He'd live to regret this.

Because his pickup was full of painting supplies, he left it in front of the house and jogged the few blocks to his own place, where he hopped on his motorcycle and checked the address Ben had texted.

His wolf instincts kicked into gear before he got there, putting him on high alert. He cut the engine and coasted silently up to a small two-story house. A dark blue Range Rover was parked in front, behind a white Toyota pickup. Tingles of warning raced across his skin.

The front door stood open and male voices barked inside. He skirted the building to peer through a window. Three guys sat on the couch. They all sported guns and one wore a fancy suit.

A chill made the hairs on the back of his neck bristle. Looked like Junior Rabago, a drug dealer out of Denver. He moved heavier drugs like cocaine and heroin through one of the local marijuana dispensaries. If Ben's sister-in-law was tied to him, this was bigger trouble than he'd imagined.

Fuckity fuck fuck. He should not have offered an alpha's promise to Ben for this. Now protection had just turned into a rescue. And he didn't even have a gun on him.

Ben had said his sister-in-law was here now. Had they killed her already? Or had she managed to escape in time? He scented the air. He didn't smell blood. Only the fresh scent of humans—mostly male, maybe one female. No wolves. He looked up the building. A window stood open on the second floor.

Was he nuts for thinking about climbing up there? Probably. But he couldn't see what other choice he had. It was that or camp out here to wait for the guys to leave and they didn't look likely to leave any time soon. He gripped the rain spout, hoping it was strong enough to hold his weight. It creaked, the metal scraping the side of the brick building when he swung onto it, but it didn't pull away from the building. He scaled it to the roof, then crept to the area above the open window and lowered his body down over the side, his toes landing on the sill.

The screen came out easily and he tossed it down to the grass below. He crept into what appeared to be a bedroom, which had been completely trashed. The human female scent was stronger here—an alluring smell, despite the fact that it didn't come from a she-wolf.

His instincts blared. Someone was in the room. He trained his sensitive ears and heard breathing. A rapid heartbeat. It came from the closet. Melissa? No—the scent was decidedly human.

He walked over and eased the door open, trying not to make any noise to alert the guys downstairs. Female clothing packed the closet—dresses and suits hung from hangers, filling the entire space. He didn't see the woman, but the staccato beat of her heart and the metallic scent of fear drew his attention to the back corner.

With a swift movement, he yanked the clothing to the side and reached out to snatch her, clamping one hand over her mouth to keep her silent. He hadn't planned for her knee connecting with his groin.

He doubled over, only barely preventing a groan from leaving his mouth.

The young woman tried to shove past him, but he grabbed her from behind, wrapping one arm around her waist, covering her mouth with the other hand. The contact sent a jolt of something unfamiliar through him. Like a warning, only more pleasant. The hairs stood up on the back of his neck. "Melissa?"

Maybe it wasn't her. The human struggled with more force than he'd expect out of a woman, her body lithe and strong beneath the soft exterior. Wrestling her aroused his inner beast, his cock thickening as if this were some wild mating dance, instead of a life or death situation.

"Ben Stone sent me," he growled low in her ear, in case she was the female he was supposed to save. Her scent filled his nostrils, exciting his body, despite the situation. Despite the fact that wolves aren't attracted to humans.

She went still.

Okaaay. Ben Stone's sister-in-law was human. Which meant Stone's wife must be, too. He hadn't heard that, although Stone's pack would probably not be in a hurry to spread that information.

She twisted to look back at him, eyes wide with fear. Her beauty struck him like another jab to the balls. Her eyes were wide and blue, thick glossy hair hung in long reddish-brown waves. He'd never seen such a beautiful human in his life. He eased the hand from her mouth to reveal lush lips, trembling with fear.

"I'm the rescue wagon," he said sardonically. It sounded more bitter than he felt, only because his attraction to her had taken him by surprise and he didn't like surprises.

Her lips parted but she didn't speak.

He didn't have a weapon and those guys down there had guns. Which meant fighting their way out was a no-go, especially since she was a weak human. "We'll have to go out the window. I'll jump down and catch you when you follow."

Her big blue eyes bugged out. "We can't. This is a second story," she whispered.

He turned her around to face him. "Do you know what I am?"

Please say she at least knew that her brother-in-law was a shifter.

She gave him an up-and-down sweep, gaze traveling over the paint-splattered clothes, the tattoos on his arms, his unshaven face. He realized his appearance was in sharp contrast to hers—she wore a tight pencil skirt and silk blouse, like some kind of young professional. Her lip curled with condescension.

It was a look he was well familiar with, the scorn for an uneducated manual laborer who looked more like a criminal than Colorado Springs' top real estate investor. For some reason, it bothered him this time, when usually he didn't give two fucks what people thought of him or his tough-guy appearance.

She swallowed, then licked her lips. "Wolf?"

He nodded, taking her hand and tugging her toward the window. "That's right, princess. Your wolf in shining armor. You jump, I'll catch."

Doubt scrambled her features. She glanced over her shoulder at the door, perhaps wondering if there was another way out. Her skin appeared ashen, but she nodded.

He jumped out the window, landing in a crouch on the grass below. When he turned to look for her, though, she stood frozen, looking down.

Shit. *Come on.* He wanted to yell up, but of course couldn't risk making a sound. A sense of urgency washed over him, his instincts roaring danger, his need to protect a pack mate—even a new foster mate like her—kicking into high gear.

He gestured urgently.

Still, she remained, looking again to the door, then down at him.

Hell, if one of the assholes from downstairs walked in there, he'd have no way to protect her now—he wouldn't be able to climb back up quickly enough. And he'd made a sacred oath to keep her safe.

Her head whipped back from looking over the door, eyes looking wild. Someone must be approaching. She squatted on the window's edge.

He made a frantic motion for her to jump. She twisted toward the door again and gave a scream, then launched herself into the air.

A male shout cracked the air as she plummeted toward him, but he didn't dare take his eyes from her falling body to see who had arrived. She dropped into his arms and he staggered at the impact, but then took off running, as fast as he could.

More shouting.

He made it to his bike and dropped her on the back of it, wishing he had a helmet for her fragile human skull. She looked horrified, her pencil skirt forced all the way up so she could straddle the seat, revealing creamy white thighs and pink lace panties.

Too bad, princess.

He hit the ignition button and the motorcycle spluttered. Dammit.

Two men ran out of the front door, waving guns.

The bike roared to life. He hit the gas and the back wheel skidded out behind them as they charged away.

The Alpha's Promise by Renee Rose

A DOMINANT ALPHA. A TEMPTING HUMAN. AN IMPOSSIBLE ATTRACTION.

After one loser boyfriend too many, Melissa Bell swore she was done with bad boys, but when her ex puts her life in danger it is a buff, tattooed, dirty-talking alpha shifter who shows up to save her. More disturbing still, her rescuer makes it clear that he regards Melissa's safety as his personal responsibly, and defying his instructions soon earns her a painful, embarrassing spanking. Though the punishment is humiliating enough on its own, however, it is her body's reaction to the tough, handsome wolf's stern dominance that truly leaves her blushing.

It doesn't take long for Cody to find himself wishing he'd never made an alpha's promise to protect Melissa, yet for some reason he can barely control himself around her. His inner wolf craves the beautiful human in spite of her snobbish attitude and constant sass, and when she is writhing over his knee with her bright red, well-spanked bare bottom on display it is all he can do not to mark her and mate her right then and there.

Each moment he spends with the alluring, feisty girl only increases his hunger for her, but Cody promised himself long ago that he would never take a human as his mate. Will his pride push Melissa away forever, just when he realizes he can't live without her?

Publisher's Note: The Alpha's Promise is a stand-alone book set in the same world as The Alpha's Hunger. It includes spankings and sexual scenes. If such material offends you, please don't buy this book.

OTHER TITLES BY RENEE ROSE

Vegas Underground Mafia Romance

King of Diamonds

Mafia Daddy

Jack of Spades

Ace of Hearts

Joker's Wild

His Queen of Clubs

Dead Man's Hand (coming soon)

More Mafia Romance

The Russian

The Don's Daughter

Mob Mistress

The Bossman

Contemporary

Black Light: Celebrity Roulette

Fire Daddy

Black Light: Roulette Redux

Her Royal Master

The Russian

Black Light: Valentine Roulette

Theirs to Protect

Scoring with Santa

Owned by the Marine

Theirs to Punish

Punishing Portia

The Professor's Girl

Safe in his Arms

Saved

The Elusive "O"

Paranormal

Bad Boy Alphas Series

Alpha's Temptation

Alpha's Danger

Alpha's Prize

Alpha's Challenge

Alpha's Obsession

Alpha's Desire

Alpha's War

Alpha's Mission

Alpha's Bane

Alpha's Secret

Alpha's Prey

Alpha's Blood

Alpha's Sun

Alpha Doms Series

The Alpha's Hunger

The Alpha's Promise

The Alpha's Punishment

Other Paranormals

His Captive Mortal

Deathless Love

Deathless Discipline

The Winter Storm: An Ever After Chronicle

Sci-Fi

Zandian Masters Series

His Human Slave

His Human Prisoner

Training His Human

His Human Rebel

His Human Vessel

His Mate and Master

Zandian Pet

Their Zandian Mate

His Human Possession

Zandian Brides (Reverse Harem)

Night of the Zandians

Bought by the Zandians

Mastered by the Zandians

Zandian Lights

Kept by the Zandian

The Hand of Vengeance

Her Alien Masters

Regency

The Darlington Incident

Humbled

The Reddington Scandal

The Westerfield Affair

Pleasing the Colonel

Western

His Little Lapis

The Devil of Whiskey Row

The Outlaw's Bride

Medieval

Mercenary

Medieval Discipline

Lords and Ladies

The Knight's Prisoner

Betrothed

Held for Ransom

The Knight's Seduction

The Conquered Brides (5 book box set)

Renaissance

Renaissance Discipline

Ageplay

Stepbrother's Rules

Her Hollywood Daddy

His Little Lapis

Black Light: Valentine's Roulette (Broken)

BDSM under the name Darling Adams

Medical Play

Yes, Doctor

Master/Slave

Punishing Portia

ABOUT LEE SAVINO

Lee Savino is a USA today bestselling author, mom and choco-holic.

Warning: Do not read her Berserker series, or you will be addicted to the huge, dominant warriors who will stop at nothing to claim their mates.

I repeat: Do. Not. Read. The Berserker Saga. Particularly not the thrilling excerpt below.

Download a free book from www.leesavino.com (don't read that, either. Too much hot sexy lovin').

EXCERPT: SOLD TO THE BERSERKERS BY LEE SAVINO

Sold to the Berserkers

A ménage shifter romance

By Lee Savino

CHAPTER ONE

The day my stepfather sold me to the Berserkers, I woke at dawn with him leering over me. "Get up." He made to kick me and I scrambled out of my sleep stupor to my feet.

"I need your help with a delivery."

I nodded and glanced at my sleeping mother and siblings. I didn't trust my stepfather around my three younger sisters, but if I was gone with him all day, they'd be safe. I'd taken to carrying a dirk myself. I did not dare kill him; we needed him for food and shelter, but if he attacked me again, I would fight.

My mother's second husband hated me, ever since the last time he'd tried to take me and I had fought back. My mother was gone to market, and when he tried to grab me, something in me snapped. I would not let him touch me again. I fought, kicking and scratching, and finally grabbing an iron pot and scalding him with heated water.

He bellowed and looked as if he wanted to hurt me, but kept his distance. When my mother returned he pretended like nothing was wrong, but his eyes followed me with hatred and cunning.

Out loud he called me ugly and mocking the scar that marred my neck since a wild dog attacked me when I was young. I ignored this and kept my distance. I'd heard the taunts about my hideous face since the wounds had healed into scars, a mass of silver tissue at my neck.

That morning, I wrapped a scarf over my hair and scarred neck and followed my stepfather, carrying his wares down the old road. At first I thought we were headed to the great market, but when we reached the fork in the road and he went an unfamiliar way, I hesitated. Something wasn't right.

"This way, cur." He'd taken to calling me "dog". He'd taunted me, saying the only sounds I could make were grunts like a beast, so I might as well be one. He was right. The attack had taken my voice by damaging my throat.

If I followed him into the forest and he tried to kill me, I wouldn't even be able to cry out.

"There's a rich man who asked for his wares delivered to his door." He marched on without a backward glance and I followed.

I had lived all my life in the kingdom of Alba, but when my father died and my mother remarried, we moved to my stepfather's village in the highlands, at the foot of the great, forbidding mountains. There were stories of evil that lived in the dark crevices of the heights, but I'd never believed them.

I knew enough monsters living in plain sight.

The longer we walked, the lower the sun sank in the sky, the more I knew my stepfather was trying to trick me, that there was no rich man waiting for these wares.

When the path curved, and my stepfather stepped out from behind a boulder to surprise me, I was half ready, but before I could reach for my dirk he struck me so hard I fell.

I woke tied to a tree.

The light was lower, heralding dusk. I struggled silently, frantic gasps escaping from my scarred throat. My stepfather stepped into view and I felt a second of relief at a familiar face, before remembering the evil this man had wrought on my body. Whatever he was planning, it would bode ill for me, and my younger sisters. If I didn't survive, they would eventually share the same fate as mine.

"You're awake," he said. "Just in time for the sale."

I strained but my bonds held fast. As my stepfather approached, I realized that the scarf that I wrapped around my neck to hide my scars had fallen, exposing them. Out of habit, I twitched my head to the side, tucking my bad side towards my shoulder.

My stepfather smirked.

"So ugly," he sneered. "I could never find a husband for you, but I found someone to take you. A group of warriors passing through who saw you, and want to slake their lust on your body. Who knows, if you please them, they may let you live. But I doubt you'll survive these men. They're foreigners, mercenaries, come to fight for the king. Berserkers. If you're lucky your death will be swift when they tear you apart."

I'd heard the tales of berserker warriors, fearsome warriors of old. Ageless, timeless, they'd sailed over the seas to the land, plundering, killing, taking slaves, they fought for our kings, and their own. Nothing could stand in their path when they went into a killing rage.

I fought to keep my fear off my face. Berserker's were a myth, so my stepfather had probably sold me to a band of passing soldiers who would take their pleasure from my flesh before leaving me for dead, or selling me on.

"I could've sold you long ago, if I stripped you bare and put a bag over you head to hide those scars."

His hands pawed at me, and I shied away from his disgusting breath. He slapped me, then tore at my braid, letting my hair spill over my face and shoulders.

Bound as I was, I still could glare at him. I could do nothing to stop the sale, but I hoped my fierce expression told him I'd fight to the death if he tried to force himself on me.

His hand started to wander down towards my breast when a shadow moved on the edge of the clearing. It caught my eye and I startled. My stepfather stepped back as the warriors poured from the trees.

My first thought was that they were not men, but beasts. They prowled forward, dark shapes almost one with the shadows. A few wore animal pelts and held back, lurking on the edge of the woods. Two came forward, wearing the garb of warriors, bristling with weapons. One had dark hair, and the other long, dirty blond with a beard to match.

Their eyes glowed with a terrifying light.

As they approached, the smell of raw meat and blood wafted over us, and my stomach twisted. I was glad my stepfather hadn't fed me all day, or I would've emptied my guts on the ground.

My stepfather's face and tone took on the wheedling expression I'd seen when he was selling in the market.

"Good evening, sirs," he cringed before the largest, the

blond with hair streaming down his chest.

They were perfectly silent, but the blond approached, fixing me with strange golden eyes.

Their faces were fair enough, but their hulking forms and the quick, light way they moved made me catch my breath. I had never seen such massive men. Beside them, my stepfather looked like an ugly dwarf.

"This is the one you wanted," my stepfather continued. "She's healthy and strong. She will be a good slave for you."

My body would've shaken with terror, if I were not bound so tightly.

A dark haired warrior stepped up beside the blond and the two exchanged a look.

"You asked for the one with scars." My stepfather took my hair and jerked my head back, exposing the horrible, silvery mass. I shut my eyes, tears squeezing out at the sudden pain and humiliation.

The next thing I knew, my stepfather's grip loosened. A grunt, and I opened my eyes to see the dark haired warrior standing at my side. My stepfather sprawled on the ground as if he'd been pushed.

The blond leader prodded a boot into my stepfather's side.

"Get up," the blond said, in a voice that was more a growl than a human sound. It curdled my blood. My stepfather scrambled to his feet.

The black haired man cut away the last of my bonds, and I sagged forward. I would've fallen but he caught me easily and set me on my feet, keeping his arms around me. I was not the smallest woman, but he was a giant. Muscles bulged in his arms and chest, but he held me carefully. I stared at him, taking in his raven dark hair and strange gold eyes.

He tucked me closer to his muscled body.

Meanwhile, my stepfather whined. "I just wanted to show you the scars—"

Again that frightening growl from the blond. "You don't touch what is ours."

"I don't want to touch her." My stepfather spat.

Despite myself, I cowered against the man who held me. A stranger I had never met, he was still a safer haven than my stepfather.

"I only wish to make sure you are satisfied, milords. Do you want to sample her?" my stepfather asked in an evil tone. He wanted to see me torn apart.

A growl rumbled under my ear and I lifted my head. Who were these men, these great warriors who had bought and paid for me? The arms around my body were strong and solid, inescapable, but the gold eyes looking down at me were kind. The warrior ran his thumb across the pad of my lips, and his fingers were gentle for such a large, violent looking warrior. Under the scent of blood, he smelled of snow and sharp cold, a clean scent.

He pressed his face against my head, breathing in a deep breath.

The blond was looking at us.

"It's her," the black haired man growled, his voice so guttural. "This is the one."

One of his hands came to cover the side of my face and throat, holding my face to his chest in a protective gesture.

I closed my eyes, relaxing in the solid warmth of the warrior's body.

A clink of gold, and the deed was done. I'd been sold.

~

When Brenna's father sells her to a band of passing warriors, her only thought is to survive. She doesn't expect to be claimed by the two fearsome warriors who lead the Berserker clan. Kept in captivity, she is coddled and cared for, treated more like a savior than a slave. Can captivity lead to love? And when she discovers the truth behind the myth of the fearsome warriors, can she accept her place as the Berserkers' true mate?

Author's Note: *Sold to the Berserkers is a standalone, short, MFM ménage romance starring two huge, dominant warriors who make it all about the woman. Read the whole best-selling Berserker saga to see what readers are raving about...*

~

THE BERSERKER SAGA

Sold to the Berserkers

Mated to the Berserkers

Bred by the Berserkers (FREE novella only available at www.leesavino.com)

Taken by the Berserkers

Given to the Berserkers

Claimed by the Berserkers

Rescued by the Berserker - *free on all sites, including Wattpad*

Captured by the Berserkers

Kidnapped by the Berserkers

Bonded to the Berserkers-coming late summer 2017

ALSO BY LEE SAVINO

Exiled To the Prison Planet

Draekon Mate

Draekon Fire

Draekon Heart

Draekon Abduction

Draekon Destiny

Draekon Fever

Draekon Rogue

CPSIA information can be obtained
at www.ICGtesting.com
Printed in the USA
BVHW031637150221
600166BV00001B/80